THE
MATING CHALLENGE

Book 5 in the Werewolves of Montana series

BONNIE VANAK

THE MATING CHALLENGE

Copyright © 2015 Bonnie Vanak
All rights reserved.

ISBN: 978-1-941130-24-7

This book is a work of fiction. Names, characters, places, brands, media, and incidents are either the product of the author's imagination or are used fictitiously. With the exception of recognized historical figures, the characters in this novel are fictional. Any resemblance to actual persons, living or dead, is purely coincidental and not intended by the author.

Published in the United States of America.

For our beloved Dolce.

You were the best. Miss you.

See you on the other side, li'l buddy.

Prologue

The Mitchell Ranch, northern Montana

"You're an animal, Mitchell. Beast. Not a wolf. You're a savage."

Click.

Aiden Mitchell dragged in a deep breath and hung up the phone. Nothing like being insulted by the woman he'd intended to make his forever mate. But he was accustomed to her sharp edges. Liked them, in fact.

Nikita's mood had grown worse as the Mating Challenge drew closer. He supposed it was the stress.

It was almost time for him to finally get mated, and claim the female he'd chased after for five long years.

Nikita Blakemore. Alpha leader of the Blakemore pack and owner of the Blakemore Ranch. Sweet and fiery Lupine, one of the toughest wolves he'd ever known.

Almost as tough as himself.

Inside his office at the pack's lodge, Aiden Mitchell propped a booted foot upon his desk as he regarded the birdhouse before him. Painted powder blue, it had little hearts and flowers decorating it. He'd spent hours thumbing through catalogues to find the perfect birdhouse as a mating gift.

Nikita would adore it. She had an array of bird feeders in her back yard, and mentioned wistfully wanting to have hummingbirds nest and feed there.

Soon as he won the Mating Challenge and Nikita, he'd build her a nice nest, too. A big one, with a king-sized bed for all the hours he planned to make long, slow love to her.

Or hard and fast love.

Or upside down.

Hell, he could find several ways to sexually bond with her. And bite her on the neck, giving her his mating mark to seal their union and prove she was his. His blood ran hot and thick as he envisioned Niki naked beneath him, her sweet blue eyes dazed with pleasure as he nudged open her plump thighs and pushed himself deep inside her body...

He just had to remember that could never, ever do something stupid as falling in love with her. No, not him. Long ago, he'd made a promise to his old man. The bastard.

You're a godsdamn fool if you fall in love, Aiden. You're incompetent enough as it is and you'll make a lousy alpha leader. Don't be an ass, too. Love is a bitch that will rip your heart apart and an alpha must never let that happen.

Alastair, his father, had fallen in love with his mate, and when she died, everything went to hell. Aiden vowed he'd never do the same. No woman, not even his future mate, would rule his heart.

He just needed to get the Mating Challenge over with, and beat the hell out of his opponents. And then he'd deed Niki's ranch back to her, as promised, for he held the mortgage on the considerable spread.

He'd bought the note to force her into a Mating Challenge, for the proud leader of the Blakemore pack had refused to take a mate.

Aiden sat up, took a length of red satin ribbon, tied a bow around the birdhouse. It looked lopsided, but good enough.

A brisk knock came at his door. He glanced up. "Yeah?"

Kyle Morgan entered, his jeans dusty. One of the two best hunters in the Mitchell pack, Kyle was a good cowhand as well. The ranch ran like a well-oiled machine, thanks to Kyle.

Aiden's gaze sharpened. Wide shouldered and leanly-muscled, Kyle looked like just another tall, muscular cowboy, except for the distinctive Z slashing his left cheek.

"Did you finish building the new corrals?" he asked. They'd need them for Niki's horses when she came here to live at the ranch with her pack.

"Assigned that to Garth and Jake. I had to round up some stray cattle." Kyle pushed back his Stetson. "I know you're leaving for Nikita's soon, so I stopped by to wish you luck. Not that you'll need it."

"Thanks." Aiden pushed away from his desk and looked at Kyle. "I need to see Sam. Where is she?"

"She and Darius went riding. When I saw them, they were going to take a shower."

As Aiden started for the door, Kyle added. "Together."

Terrific. He shook his head. "Going to be a long shower."

"Uh huh." Kyle shuffled his feet. Aiden glanced at him. The half Lupine, half Satyr shifter was taciturn, but never this quiet.

"What's up?"

Kyle finally dragged his gaze up to meet his. "Arianna's pregnant."

Joy and envy rushed through him. Aiden swallowed back the envy and engulfed the shifter in a giant hug. "Congratulations. About damn time."

A dull flush tinged his cheeks. "Yeah, we tried. Hard. She's about three months."

Three months? Aiden stared, waiting for the explanation.

"We wanted to wait to tell you until we were sure she was far enough along. In case she lost the baby."

Still, he waited.

"Ah, we didn't want to make a big announcement. Because of your…ah…status."

His status. His unmated status. Aiden massaged the tensed muscles of his neck. "I'm the one who urged you two to get pregnant. Congratulations, Kyle. Soon as I return, I'll throw a party for you and Ari."

He headed for Darius' suite of rooms on the third floor. When Darius and Sam completed their bonding in the mating rite, Aiden had given them an entire section of rooms in the lodge for privacy. His best friend and beta deserved it. Deserved to be happy, after spending ten years believing that his mate was dead.

In the hallway, he went to knock and hesitated. Privacy. He needed to give them space. But he needed Sam. He'd grown to love the half-Lupine, half-Elf like a sister, and trusted her judgment.

Nikita would also need a female friend when she

came here to live at the Mitchell Ranch. Sam was a good choice.

Aiden paced in the hallway, hoping they would finish. Soon.

"Careful."

"I'm always careful around you, sweetheart," Darius murmured.

Standing beneath the gentle spray of water in the shower, she watched her mate. His brow furrowed in concentration, he gently scraped the razor over her soapy skin. When Sam insisted on showering, he'd insisted on joining her, and helping her shave.

Shaving her legs had never been so much fun.

Sam shuddered with pleasure as he finished, set down the razor and then slid his fingers down her ribs to the curve of one hip, and then cupped her thatch. "Shall I shave this?"

"Leave it. It'll take too much time."

He trailed his tongue across her breasts, down her belly. Leaning back against the marble wall, she moaned as he parted her legs and began to tongue her. Slow, succulent licks just the way she liked, each flick of his tongue stroking her sex with expert caresses. Darius' strong hands squeezed her bottom as he buried his face between her legs. Sam gripped his hair as the orgasm slowly built and then she squeezed her inner muscles, feeling herself shatter. She screamed.

Darius lifted his head and gave her a wicked grin, water beading on his face. "Like that?"

"What do you think, wolf?" she whispered as he stood and placed his hands on her hips. She glanced down at his erect shaft straining toward her. "Of course I liked it. But I think I'll like what you're going to do next much better. Get inside me. Now."

She opened her legs wide as he settled between them, and then he lifted her by her ass with one hand, using his other hand to guide his thick penis to her soaked core. Darius grunted and thrust hard.

"Open your eyes."

He always wanted her eyes open when they made love because he craved the connection and bond between them. He wanted her to see him, know it was him. Darius licked her ear and then buried his face into her neck, right at the pattern of intricate runes where he'd marked her during the mating rite.

They strained together, wet flesh slapping together. She felt her inner muscles squeeze tight, signaling another orgasm. "Hurry," she begged. "I'm so close."

With another powerful shove, he shouted, "Now!" She let herself fall, climaxing so hard she saw stars as he grunted and shuddered against her, the hot wash of his seed shooting deep into her core.

Panting, he rested his head on her shoulder as she stroked his wet hair. After a few minutes, he released her. She loved this Lupine and couldn't imagine her life without him. With him her heart was full.

And then she thought of Aiden and felt a small pang, because their alpha remained single, and without his true mate.

Darius shut off the shower as she climbed out. He gently toweled her dry, taking extra care between her legs, wicked mischief glinted in his blue eyes as he knelt at her feet and rubbed the towel between her swollen folds.

Then he pressed his mouth against her belly, resting his cheek against it.

Sam touched his head, feeling a sudden sense of loss. "I'm going to miss you so much."

He looked up at her, gaze solemn. "Me too. But Aiden needs me."

"Then tell him to hurry up and defeat all the challengers, mate Nikita and bring her back." Sam slid her arms around her mate's neck as he stood and gathered her close. "Because I need my man back here, in my arms, where he belongs."

Darius kissed her, a kiss of possession and claiming, his tongue sweeping inside her mouth. She kissed him back with equal ferocity.

They finished drying off and dressed quickly. Darius opened the door leading to the hallway.

Only to see Aiden, pacing madly. Darius' smile died on his lips. "What's wrong?"

Their alpha's expression remained blank. "I need to talk with Sam. Alone."

A scowl tightened Darius' face. Still possessive, he didn't like other males alone with her, but this was their alpha. Sam put a gentle hand on his tensed arm. "Honey, why don't you go downstairs and make me breakfast? I'm starved. Eggs with some of those delicious strawberries we ate last night, sprouts, and peppers."

The scowl vanished, replaced with tender amusement. No matter how hard she tried, she couldn't suppress her Elven half's need for greens.

"Sprouts? You'll never stop being partly a

vegetarian, will you?" But he gave her a swift kiss on the lips, a meaningful look at their leader, and headed for the stairs.

Sam held the door wide open. "Come in, Aiden."

She sat on the green and white striped sofa and patted the space next to her. Aiden had bought the furniture for them as a mating gift. The big alpha sank onto the couch. Black-bearded, his shoulder-length raven hair tousled as if he'd run a hand through it, the alpha stood over six feet tall. He could strong-arm everyone in the pack, but ruled through respect, not intimidation. This morning he wore a red and black plaid shirt rolled up at the sleeves to display his thickly muscled forearms. Faded jeans encased his long legs and he'd stuffed his feet into worn Western boots. But instead of the leather belt with the monogrammed brass buckle, Aiden wore a gold buckle etched with the symbol of a wolf howling at the moon.

His symbol.

She nodded at the belt. "Making a statement when you enter the challenge?"

Aiden glanced downward. "All the competitors are required to display their pack symbols."

Interesting. She knew little about formal Lupine rituals. "What is the competition's symbols?"

"Probably an omega cowering and showing his belly."

Sam laughed and Aiden cracked a brief smile, which faded fast.

She touched his arm. The alpha had never been this hesitant. Always direct and tough, but fair, he didn't waste time or words. "Aiden, what's wrong? Why do you need to talk to me?"

"I need your help." He ran a hand through his hair. "This challenge, I need you there."

Stunned, she leaned forward. "Darius told me the rules state no females are present except those who live with the alpha female hosting the challenge."

"Yeah, well, the rules say one female from each challenger's pack can be present, but she has to remain with the females. I want you."

She had a bad feeling about this. "Why me?"

He rubbed a hand over his bearded chin. "I hate asking you. It's going to be brutal. Rough. A Mating Challenge is not pretty. And Darius won't want you present. Aw hell. I don't know if you can handle it."

"Really?" she asked dryly. "I've survived being bitten by snakes, having my mate go feral on me, getting lightning bolts tossed at me by my stepbrother, and nearly lashed to death by mutant tree branches. You don't think I could handle it?"

"I don't want you to get hurt…"

"Darius won't let me get hurt. Neither will you. Tell me why you need me."

Aiden's dark gaze filled with torment. "I need your calming influence on the males if they go into a frenzy, surrounded by the females."

"And?"

"And I need you there to talk to Nikita. So she can see a gentle female influence and know we're not all…beasts in this pack."

Sam's heart squeezed tight. She went on her knees before Aiden and gathered his hands into hers. "You're not a beast, Aiden. You're our alpha. You do what you must to keep us together and thriving."

"She thinks I'm a savage." Aiden looked away and

she saw his jaw tighten. "She just called me one before she hung up on me."

Suspicion filled Sam. "Did you say anything to anger her?"

A frown dented his forehead. "Nothing I can recall. I only asked her what kind of sheets she liked."

"Liked for what?"

"When she sleeps naked in our bed."

Sam bit back a smile. "You're such a romantic."

He stared at her, his frown deepening. "I don't want her uncomfortable. I want everything to be just right for her to come live here. But she acted as if I'm a total and complete ass."

Sam rubbed her cheek against his work-toughened hands. Males. So clueless. She loved them, anyway. "In time, Nikita will come to realize what you are is pure alpha, a strong leader who will give his life for his people. She may not realize it now, Aiden, but she needs you. Just as we need you."

Sam rested her head on his lap and felt him stroke her hair. She relished the contact, the strong but gentle touch of her alpha. There was nothing sexual about it. It was the touch all Lupines craved, and her Lupine half needed it as much as her elven half needed sprouts and greens.

"Thank you," he said quietly.

"Darius and I would do anything for you. We want you to be happy. If it means we fight alongside you, we will." She raised her head, letting him see the tears in her eyes. "You saved my life, Aiden. If not for you channeling your powers into me when I fought James, I would have died. And Darius would have died with me. He'd vowed that if I went, he'd go too."

This big, tough alpha who had nearly sacrificed his life held her heart as much as her mate did. They needed him. Most of all, they needed him happy and whole. And Aiden would not be both until he claimed his mate, the Lupine he'd wanted for all these years.

Gently, he reached down and wiped a tear away from her brimming eyes. "Don't cry, Sam."

As she stood, he did as well and hugged her tight. "Now get your cute little butt downstairs and have breakfast. Darius is making you a meal fit for your elf self."

"My elf self." She smiled and wiped her eyes, loving that nickname.

He kissed her cheek. "Everything will work out fine."

But as he left, she saw it in his eyes.

He wasn't certain it would.

And there were bigger problems at hand, ones he wasn't sharing with her or his beta. Big ones that could affect the entire pack.

Sam felt confident Aiden would win the Mating Challenge.

She only wished she felt as confident he could deal with the mysterious situation with the Blakemore pack. All the males seemed to have vanished, and there were rumors they had died.

Aiden needed to win the challenge, and bring Nikita and her pack here to the ranch.

Because she feared the longer they remained at Blakemore ranch, the greater the chances none of the males would be returning home.

Except in a coffin.

CHAPTER 1

The two nude alpha werewolves fought to be the most dominant, the one to mate and breed with the female leader of the Blakemore pack.

Sounds of flesh smacking hard flesh echoed through the ballroom of the Blakemore Ranch as Richard Armador and Aiden Mitchell battled on the elegant parquet floor. Overhead two lead crystal chandeliers spilled golden light upon the sparring males.

As dictated by law, the men had removed their clothing to fight naked, to show they had no concealed weapons. The female alpha had the right to see the merchandise, so to speak. See exactly how much power and strength she'd be taking into her bed.

Perched on a gilded throne, Nia Blakemore watched the men fight. In this arena of blood and violence, hardened Lupine alpha warriors battled to lay claim to the female alpha's lands, her pack, and her body. She felt like a tightly coiled spring, ready to snap with tension.

Alpha males from eight packs had been formally invited. Now the strongest two males remained. Of course one was Aiden. The fiend had been chasing her for years, warning her he'd eventually catch her and make her his.

He'd bought the mortgage on her ranch to force her into declaring this challenge. Bastard. If she hadn't hosted the challenge, he could have foreclosed on her property.

And yet, as arrogant as Mitchell was, he still turned her on. Especially now.

Nia's heart raced as the two men fought. She was their prize, and the males fought in the most primitive of ancient Lupine rites. Then the guilt set in. Neither realized her big secret.

They thought she was Nikita, the rightful alpha of the Blakemore pack. The males who wanted her didn't know she was Nia, the younger twin, the one who'd assumed her sister's identity from infancy.

Her admiring gaze swept over Aiden as the alphas drew close to the throne and Aiden punched his rival. Sweat dampened his thick black hair, slicked his hard body and droplets clung to the dark hairs of his chest. His skin was golden and tanned, gleaming beneath the light of the twin crystal chandeliers. As fine as smooth, chiseled marble, his powerful body flexed as he danced around his opponent. The taut globes of his ass came into view as he spun around, using his long legs to kick Richard and throw him off balance.

The males were driven by the instinctive need to mate and breed. It was basic biology, the dominating male werewolf's drive to spread his seed and sire offspring to rule after him. In this rugged region of Montana, male werewolves outnumbered females. The Blakemore pack with its abundance of unmated and fertile females was a prize for these two virile males to claim.

But first, she had to make sure the boys played by the rules.

Nia's sharpened gaze swept the assembled werewolves. A scowling Lupine in a green silk shirt leaned against a faded tapestry. Her eyes narrowed. Definitely hiding something behind his back.

Nia removed the honed dagger hanging from the diamond-studded belt on her white velvet robes. The fight took the males closer to the crowd hovering by the west wall. Aiden punched Richard hard, sending the alpha male crashing down. As the leader of the Mitchell pack leaned over his opponent, Silk Shirt detached from the wall and raised his hand.

Light caressed the gleaming steel blade he held over Aiden.

She stood and flung her dagger. It sailed through the air and sank deep into Silk Shirt's wrist, pinning him to the wall. He screamed and dropped the switchblade.

She'd taught herself that move years ago, perfecting it to protect the pack females from lusty males.

Richard stood, wiping blood streaming into his eyes. He growled at the offender, snapped his fingers. Two males rushed forward to obey.

"Bring him outside and guard him. He'll be dealt with later," he ordered. "He knew the rules. No weapons. No assistance from pack."

Silk Shirt whimpered as Richard's men pulled the dagger from his wrist and lifted him under the arms.

"Wait," Aiden ordered.

He took Nia's blade. The dagger arced, slicing the air and then the male's throat. As the werewolf burbled his last gasp, Aiden used the dying man's shirt to wipe the blade clean.

No mercy on those ruthless features as Aiden twirled the blade.

"Dealt with," he said.

Inside, Nia shivered at his ruthlessness, though she agreed with the action. Werewolves battling for power in this brutal challenge searched for any display of weakness. Aiden couldn't ignore such a blatant insult by Richard's pack. Nia returned to the throne and smoothed out her expression to show no trace of emotion. Nothing to incite the 200 plus assembled males from both packs to disregard the rules and engage in an all-out war they couldn't afford.

The Blakemore pack could barely defend themselves, a fact Nia had desperately hidden. They needed strong males to help protect their territory. And they were all going hungry, for the ranch had lost too much income in the past year. Even game in their forest was scarce.

The fighting males thought they would win the Blakemore alpha female as a mate, the entire Blakemore pack to call their own, and the Blakemore Ranch as a nice bonus.

They didn't realize she wasn't an alpha female, there were only females left in the Blakemore pack, and the ranch was stricken with disease that killed all males of shapeshifting age.

Nia drew in a trembling breath, hoping the fight would end soon. The longer all these males remained on her land, the more nervous she became. *Hurry up and finish. Then, please, go home and stay safe. This place is cursed.*

Roxanne Valmont, the Blakemore pack beta, retrieved the dagger as Richard's men rushed the dead werewolf outside. Aiden nodded to Nia, touching his forehead in a gesture of respect, then resumed the battle with Richard.

Nia didn't know how the hell they'd resolve this mess. After she and her twin were born 25 years ago, their father had insisted there was only one living girl born to the Blakemore alpha pair. Nikita had been hidden, for it was prophesied in their family that the eldest girl twin born on the seventh day of the seventh month belonged to the Silver Wizard. He would come for her after she lived 25 years, and take her to his home in Tir Na-nog, the afterworld, to become his bride. And she would die, for no mortal being survived in the afterworld.

The twins had traded places to let Nikita out once in a while, but only their aunt Mandy, close friend Roxanne and a few elder females in the pack realized they were twins.

It was an effective ruse they'd managed to pull off up until now.

Nia gripped the armrests as Aiden moved on the floor, his actions smooth and flowing as he ducked Richard's punch. Richard was smooth arrogance, a blond charmer who came from wealth and privilege. Adding his lands to theirs would make his domain even more powerful.

Sex with him would be bland and dutiful. Safe.

Not so with dark-haired Aiden, with his wide shoulders and heavily-muscled body. Raw and untamed, he fought as if the idea of bedding her drove him to a mating frenzy. Sweat dripped down his temples as he slammed Richard against the wall.

A very female part of her appreciated the flex of

powerful biceps, the thick muscles dividing his back. Not an ounce of fat on him, not on the ripped abdomen, the narrow hips or his strong limbs.

Her gaze darted down to the thick thatch of black hair at his groin. At rest, his penis was impressive. Big, like Aiden himself. The thought of taking all that male hardness into her untried body, feeling him move over her as they consummated their union...

The flush of arousal filled her as she watched the powerful werewolf fight. She'd fantasized about the male in the dark night, wondering what he'd be like as a lover.

Aiden fought for her sister's hand, not hers. He fought to mate with the alpha of the Blakemore pack and technically, her older twin was the alpha.

I am pretending to be someone I am not. A leader, an alpha like he is. My whole life has been based upon a lie to keep Niki hidden.

But after masquerading as her twin for all these years, she wished someone could see her for herself. Love her as an individual, not as the Lupine they knew as Nikita Blakemore.

The grunts and groans of the two sparring males echoed through the ballroom. Her peripheral vision caught sight of her aunt Mandy entering the ballroom. Nia's heart pounded hard with every click of Mandy's boot heels across the parquet floor.

Upon reaching the throne, Mandy whispered into her ear. Nia stiffened.

"Now?" Nia asked.

Mandy nodded at the fighting men. "Now, before the fight is finished and one of them wins."

She released a sharp breath and followed her aunt

out of the ballroom, away from the crescendo of male grunts and the crack of a fist slamming into muscle. Razor sharp fear surged. She wasn't certain how much longer she and her twin could carry on this ruse.

Things had dragged on far too long. And soon, she would have to pay the price.

Naked, sweat dripping down his temple, Aiden Mitchell watched in incredulous disbelief. She was leaving? He was getting his ass kicked, doing some fine ass kicking of his own, and the female leader of the Blakemore pack walked out, her heels clicking sharply on the floor.

As if all this blood and violence bored her.

Well, when all this fighting was over, he'd punish her for the insult. Again and again. Give her five orgasms worth of punishment so she'd never turn from him again. Keep her occupied in bed and Nikita wouldn't walk away.

His blood surged, testosterone racing through his system. He forced a calming breath. No good getting cranked up sexually when he needed his strength to win.

Taking advantage of Aiden's momentary stupor, Richard sprang to his feet and swung hard. His bruised fist connected with Aiden's chin, sending him staggering backwards.

Recovering, he tackled his opponent. Playtime was over. Richard fought because he wanted Nikita's forest rich territory, and he thought she was cute.

The stakes were much higher for Aiden. He needed the unmated, fertile females in her pack to breed with his pack's strong, very lusty males. Every day brought them closer to the edge, bringing about more testosterone-driven fights to relieve their sexual frustration. They needed the soft, gentle influence of a woman, needed to breed and make the pack stronger.

He craved Nikita like a junkie needing a fix. He lusted to have her. Soon, she would be his exclusively.

He released the full fury of his 200 pounds of muscled strength, enough to let Richard know he meant business, but not enough to mortally wound.

With a low grunt, Richard collapsed on the floor. Panting, Aiden stood over him, fists bloodied and bruised.

Then he extended a hand to his rival. Bewilderment shone in Richard's swollen and bruised eyes.

"Nikita has left the room. I'm calling a formal time out until she returns."

He helped the other werewolf to his feet. Richard looked around. "We're wasting time."

"Rules are rules. We can't fight until she's present." Aiden rubbed his nape.

"Fine. Then I'm shifting."

Startled he watched the man stretch out his arms and shapeshift into a large gray timber wolf.

The hell with this. Aiden shifted into wolf too, more muscled and larger. He circled around his rival, watching him warily. Lupines healed faster in wolf form and Richard, the bastard, was taking unfair advantage of Nikita's absence.

Around them, the males in Aiden's pack shifted as well, not wanting to leave their alpha vulnerable. But Richard's pack did not, only looked nervously at their leader.

Pacing the ballroom floor, Aiden studied the Blakemore pack females. Only females. Were the few remaining males, out of deference to their female leader, discreetly out of sight? Were there *any* males on this ranch?

He didn't trust Roxanne's explanation. Too much testosterone already with the competition, she'd told him.

He wondered.

Aiden inhaled the delectable fragrance of soft skin and faint arousal. Some were in heat already, and the male Lupines, with their heightened sense of smell, knew it.

Shit. He trotted over to his pack, issued a warning growl as a few males began stalking over to the females. The males stopped, watching their alpha in perfect obedience.

On the sidelines, Darius, Aiden's beta, paced restlessly in wolf form. Sam, his mate, remained the only female in the room who was not part of the Blakemore pack. As the rules dictated, she stood in a neutral area with the Blakemore females.

Roxanne addressed the crowd. "Nikita has been delayed. She begs your patience while she attends to a matter of urgent pack business."

The males began moving around restlessly. One of Richard's Lupines sauntered over to Sam. He braced a hand against the wall and leaned close to her.

Savage fury arose in Aiden, but he tamped it down and glanced at Darius. Aiden gave a brief nod.

In wolf form, Darius trotted over to Sam and rubbed his muzzle against her leg. She stroked Darius' head almost absently. Then his second in command gave her hand a gentle nip, enough to mark the skin, but not tear it. She cried out, seemingly more surprised than pained.

With a low growl, Darius thrust his nose between her legs. Sam ran her fingers through his fur. Then she looked up at the male who had tried to make the moves on her.

"Go away," she stated clearly.

The male laughed. "He can't do anything to me. House rules. No males other than the alphas in the challenge are allowed to touch each other."

Sam flicked out a hand. Sharp claws tipped each fingertip. "But I can. Now go away before I turn your pretty face into road kill."

Aiden gave an approving nod to Sam as the male scrambled away. Darius shifted back. During the Challenge, he wasn't allowed to touch her in Skin form, only as Lupine. Then his beta turned, nodded at Aiden, and jogged back to join his pack.

Darius had Sam. Soon as Aiden won the Challenge, Nikita would be his, and his males would finally select mates.

Desire heated his blood as he envisioned the lovely Nikita female naked on all fours for the joining ceremony, her lush curves finally bared for him… For five years, he'd craved her. Other females had briefly sated his lust, but his passion for Nikita would not end. Until he claimed her in the flesh, Aiden would never be satisfied.

All the more reason for him to fight harder for her hand.

Tension knotted his spine as he prowled the ballroom. Where the hell was Nikita and why did his instincts warn trouble brewed ahead?

CHAPTER 2

Upstairs, Nia closed and locked the door to her private study. Nikita and Mandy stood near the French doors leading to the lodge's wrap-around balcony. Beyond the balcony, gray morning mist layered the meadows stretching out to the jagged, white-capped mountain peaks ringing the valley. The Blakemore ranch boasted thousands of acres of fertile wilderness.

And no longer a single adult male in the pack to tend them. All the men had died.

Nia picked up an apple from the wood bowl on the side table, her fingers stroking the glossy surface. Hunger rumbled in her stomach. The pack had grabbed a hasty meal before all the males arrived for the competition, but as usual, Nia was last and didn't even gulp down a single bite.

Mandy looked at Nia and sighed.

"No lunch, again? Are you ever going to take care of yourself?"

Nia set the apple down, her stomach too tense to tolerate food. "Food doesn't matter now. Tell me what's wrong."

"I can't take this anymore, Nia. They have to know the truth about us," her twin burst out.

"No!"

She went to her sister, and laced her fingers around her wrists. "Just a while longer, sweetie. You can fake it a while longer."

"And after? When Aiden wins? What then?" Nikita collapsed onto the sofa.

Her long gold hair, as silky and luxurious as Nia's, was swept up into a French braid. They had the same arresting blue eyes, plump figures and full breasts, and heart-shaped faces.

There, the differences ended. Nikita was gentle and sweet, with a disposition that soothed her pack when she left her hiding place to walk among them.

Nia could be an utter bitch to everyone, except for her twin. Everything she did, she did to keep her twin safe and hidden. Even after their beloved father died from the parvolupus disease and their two older brothers succumbed to it, she stayed strong. Five years after Pandora's Chest was opened, releasing the disease, she stayed strong.

Some days, she wished she had a little help. Gods, she was tired of being in charge and having everyone rely on her. Having a little help would be nice. But she had to keep it together, keep the pack surviving.

Keep her twin hidden and safe.

Mandy, their aunt, sat next to Nikita and stroked her hair. "It's okay, Niki. Everything's going to be okay."

But it wasn't. "What's going on, Mandy?"

Mandy pointed at the apple. "Eat, before you faint."

Another loud grumble from her empty stomach. The hell with it. Nia bit into the apple and perched on the edge of a nearby chair. She swallowed a few bites and studied her aunt.

"Now, tell me what was so important you had to drag me out of there, in the middle of the challenge. What is it? The weather? Any reports of the Banshee Winds?"

Anxiety churned in her stomach. The Banshee Winds were brutal, magick winds that destroyed their crops and killed Lupines. But the winds had not shown up in a long time, for they were brought about by young boys experiencing their first shift into wolf.

"No winds. We're safe for now. Good news. I know where Pandora's Chest is hidden."

The apple tumbled from her hands to the carpet. Nikita leapt up at the same time Nia did. "Are you sure?" Nia asked.

"I'm sure I know where the map is that shows where your father buried the chest, which is as good as finding the chest itself."

"Tell me," Nia demanded.

"I was patrolling near the pond and stumbled over the old well. And then I remember how your father filled in the well shortly after he got the chest. I'm sure he buried the map there. When we were growing up on the ranch, he used to bury his penny jars near the well. I needed to tell you this before the challenge ended and the winner formally took over the ranch."

"So close," Nia cried out. "All these years we've searched and—"

"It was right under our noses," Nikita finished.

The twins looked at each other and then hugged. Tears formed in Nikita's eyes and a lump clogged Nia's throat as her twin released her.

"The boys will be saved now," Nia whispered. "They'll be safe."

So much strain and heartache these past few months. Nia had done all she could to save the boys. She'd travel to hell if it meant the pack's remaining male children could be saved. She'd travel even further to save her twin.

Ten years ago, Niki ate poisonous berries, fell ill and was close to death. Desperate to save her, their father had procured Pandora's Chest from a wizard. The chest granted the dearest wishes of the person who opened it. Niki was saved, but the chest released a horrible plague they nicknamed parvolupus. It infected all adult male Lupines and killed them, including boys who reached puberty and experienced their first shift into wolf, while women remained immune and uninfected.

Soon, two more boys celebrated their 13th birthday and were doomed to the same fate. Aiden and the other males present today were safe for now, for the parvolupus targeted males who lived on the ranch for longer than two weeks.

Nikita had spent years studying the ancient Lupine texts and trying to find a cure, while Nia, Mandy, and Roxanne searched the grounds for the buried chest.

"You know what this means," Nikita said slowly. "Once we find the chest, it must be returned to the Silver Wizard in order to lift the curse and give us the cure for the parvolupus. He is the rightful guardian of Pandora's Chest. I am the one who should return it."

Nia's stomach clenched. "No."

"You can't protect me from him forever, little sister. Tristan will find me eventually. He is a powerful wizard and I'm certain he knows we have practiced deceit all these years." Nikita shivered and the blood drained from her face.

Fear ruled her twin's life. Fear of the dreaded Silver Wizard finding her and taking her away. It would not happen, Nia vowed. No matter what she had to do.

"How could he know? Dad's mystics warded our ranch years ago to reinforce the illusion that only the younger twin survived at birth," she pointed out.

"The magick has eroded by now, I'm sure," Nikita countered.

"We can't believe that. We have to keep positive or else he'll come here and take you away and you'll die. The prophecy..."

"It could be wrong." Nikita looked hopeful.

Nia gave a bitter laugh. "I'm not gambling with your life. When we find the chest, and we will find it, I'm giving it to him in exchange for a cure, but you are not part of the package. Mandy, return to the well. I'll join you and we'll start digging."

"Aren't you forgetting something?" Her twin pantomimed boxing. "Aiden is waiting for you."

Damn. "You'll have to wait until tonight, Mandy. Make sure no one else is around. We can't risk outsiders knowing what you're doing. Especially if it's Mitchell who wins. His men are smarter than Richard's Lupines."

"Aiden will win and claim his prize," Nikita told her. "You, disguised as me. You will share Aiden's bed. It's you he's wanted all these years."

The thought made her body tingle with anticipation. Nia shook her head. "I should tell him the truth about the chest, the disease and our men—"

"No!" Nikita shook her head. "And forget your

promise to Father on his deathbed? Never, ever tell outsiders of our secrets. You promised, Nia. You promised him in blood. You can't trust anyone."

Nia fell silent, knowing her twin was right. A deathbed promise was sacred, but one made in blood even more so.

Sometimes she wondered what her life would have been like had their father told the truth 25 years ago. She had been denied a life, even denied her name. Their father had gotten their names mixed up after they were born, announcing the surviving twin was named Nikita.

Nia glanced at her gentler, frailer twin and felt a stab of guilt. At least she hadn't been hidden away her entire life, her existence a deep secret.

"Fine. I won't tell Aiden. But we've dragged these males into a deathtrap if they decide to live here instead of the Mitchell Ranch. Our only hope is to get them out of here as quickly as possible. The longer they remain here, the more they risk exposure to the disease."

She gave her twin a pointed look. "And if Aiden wins and finds out I'm not the true alpha, there may be hell to pay. He might foreclose on the ranch. You sure you want me to take your place and carry this through?"

Blood drained from Nikita's face. "I can't do it, Nia. You have to mate with Aiden. You're the one he's determined to claim. How can I have sex with a male who makes me physically ill?"

Ever since her twin started experiencing vivid dreams of a mysterious lover a few weeks ago, Nikita got sick each time she came near Aiden Mitchell.

"The dreams are worse?"

Nikita nodded. "Even a sleeping potion can't help me. That man keeps appearing to me every night. He loves me so deeply and then he leaves, screaming, and I wake up crying."

Nia had begun to wonder if the dreams were memories from a past life, a love that ran so deep, it haunted her sister.

"Even if he didn't make me sick, I couldn't pretend to be you in bed, Nia. Aiden is too overwhelming. He called yesterday while you were sleeping. When he asked what kind of sheets I like to sleep on naked, I called him names and hung up on him. Just like you would."

Nia gurgled with laughter. She found the question sweet, and typically arrogant of Mitchell. She tilted her head. "We could still pull it off. Aiden may not win. Richard would be easier to fool."

"Aiden will win. You know it," her twin said softly. "And he is not so easily fooled."

Nikita pulled her over to the full-length mirror on the wall.

Two identical women with full, lush lips and high cheekbones stared back. The only discernible difference remained in their clear blue eyes. Nia's were filled with confidence and hope. Fear and doubt shadowed her twin's. Despite being the eldest, Nikita had always been more fragile.

It was easy enough in the past to deceive fellow Lupines, and Skins, the word Others used to describe humans. But fooling Aiden Mitchell in bed?

Niki was right.

Mandy joined them at the mirror. She gave a critical look at Nia and pointed. "Make sure you wear more cover-up. Your scar is showing."

Nia turned her head and saw with dismay her aunt

was right. She went to the desk and retrieved a bottle of makeup, returned to the mirror and put it on.

"Men are men. They desire a pretty, fertile mate to bed and breed, and her lands to join their own. They think more with their cocks than their brains," Mandy said.

But Nia didn't agree. She'd seen the sharpened awareness of Aiden Mitchell. Aiden was an alpha who handled duplicity by killing his betrayer.

Nia shivered. The male was powerful and virile and his searing sexuality and strength hinted of many long sessions in bed.

"Go back to the challenge. I'll return to my room." Nikita looked wistful. "I found a passage in the ancient texts last night that mentioned using hawthorne and mint mixed with other herbs to reinforce a Lupine's immune system. I want to study it."

"I still don't understand. If the parvolupus is a bacteria, then why can't it be killed with the right medicine? We have antibiotics for Lupines. You're the smart one, Niki. Explain it to me."

Nikita gazed into the distance. "Initially it spreads like a bacteria, similar to how tuberculous infects Skins. It's spread from person to another through the air. And then once it infects mature male Lupines, it targets the cells in their DNA that allow them turn into wolves at will. And then the parvolupus affects their immune system. With the women, we get infected, but our immune system is able to fight it off. We don't even get sick. The parvolupus in us is like latent TB. We never develop the disease."

Worry filled Nia. "If it's like latent TB, we're still infected and can be carriers and spread it to the Mitchell males. Can I infect Aiden if I sleep with him?"

"No. Just like latent TB can't be passed to another person."

"Great. Then all we have to worry about is trying to get all these men off our ranch before they get sick." Nia thought about the dozens of males milling about in the lodge and shuddered.

"If it were a normal disease, and didn't carry strains of magick, I could defeat it through antibiotics strong enough for Lupines, just like certain antibiotics can cure TB. But it keeps mutating. I thought when the last mature male Lupine died, the disease would die. But it remained active. Like mold spores."

"How can we fight a magick disease with science when it works more like a curse?" Nia felt hope slip through her fingers.

"That's why I'm studying the ancient texts. But it's slow work because the language is finicky." Nikita sighed. "I have to get back to work. I'm getting close. I'm experimenting with vials of Father's blood."

"Please be careful," Nia begged.

They hugged. A lump formed in Nia's throat. If something happened to Nikita, her world would shatter.

Her twin, the only one she truly loved since their mother died birthing them. Nia gave a jerky nod.

"I'll do it."

"It will be fine. There's nothing to fear. The mating ceremony will take place tomorrow, everything will be fine."

But Nia wondered. What would Aiden do if he found out he'd mated the younger sister and he did not have a legal claim on the pack?

CHAPTER 3

I can do this.

Sitting on the throne, Nia watched Aiden and Richard resume their fighting. Although Richard seemed to gain the upper hand, Aiden's fierce fighting warned he might be the victor.

Her mate.

Aiden was the only male who'd ever touched her. That time he'd first met her, he'd taken her hand and kissed it, his mouth warm and firm upon her knuckles. Werewolves thrived on touch, needed it. But outside of her twin's occasional hugs, Nia lived without that comfort.

Every time she'd encountered Aiden, she left sexually frustrated. She'd spent a long time in the shower with the showerhead, trying to ease her body's aches.

Now an image surfaced, Aiden naked in her bedroom. Nia's mouth went dry as the image sharpened. Aiden leaning over her, his thick cock posed at her wet entrance, his taut ass flexing as he thrust deep inside her.

Claiming her in the flesh.

I hope he doesn't win.

Richard, she could handle in bed. Richard was mild, a pleasant, trickling creek.

Aiden was a tidal wave. Rumors swirled in the compound about the alpha's fierce sexuality. He was strong, and passionate, with a dominant streak. Aiden could sweep her away on a crest of pure erotic pleasure. He'd give her no quarter, no mercy.

Panting, he shoved Richard to the floor. As the other alpha lay still, Aiden turned.

Nia's mouth watered as her gaze swept over the sweat-dampened dark curls matting his chest, the flat, rippled abdomen, his narrow hips and long limbs curved with hard muscle. Then her gaze flicked to the thick nest of dark hair at his groin.

Nia's female center dampened and clenched as she imagined him fully erect, probing at her virgin passage to mark her as his mate. She remained untouched. It had sweetened the prize for the two competing males, knowing the victor would be Nikita's first lover. When he ejaculated inside the Blakemore alpha leader, there would be no doubt about the parentage of a conceived heir.

But of course no one realized she wasn't the true alpha.

Aiden's smoldering gaze met hers, and his cock twitched, as if already claiming the prize. He locked his heated gaze to hers. Moisture gathered between her legs as she pressed them together, as if trying to keep him out of her body as well as her mind. Nia arranged her face in a smooth, bored expression to hide her arousal. But his nostrils flared and a small smile touched his full, sensual mouth.

He'd scented her.

She gripped the chair's armrests as Richard struggled to his feet. Aiden delivered a powerful punch to Richard's temple. The other male staggered and fell.

Richard did not get up.

Low growls of approval rang through the opulent ballroom. Aiden's large group of unmated males swept their hungry gazes over the appreciative females applauding his triumph. The scent of female arousal filled the ballroom, making the males restless and edgy with the furious need to mate and claim.

A full sixty seconds later, Richard still did not rise. Aiden growled, bunched his fists, and shifted into a wolf.

The muscular gray timber wolf loped over to his rival. And in a stunning display of pure alpha arrogance, Aiden lifted his leg and pissed on the man's unconscious body. Cheers rang through the ballroom.

Amused and alarmed, Nia gripped the armrests harder. Her desperate gaze raked the ballroom and landed on Roxanne, who raced to her side and thrust a cell phone at her. "Perimeter alert, in the southern woods by the pond," her beta whispered.

Nia took the phone and immediately raised it to her ear. "Report," she bit out.

Anxiety filled her as she listened. Nothing else mattered but pack safety, protecting the young and innocent.

Snapping off the connection, she left the throne, heading for the bedroom to change into her fighting clothes.

He was the winner.

Aiden's blood thickened in his veins. He itched to formalize this mating. Sign the contract, take Nikita upstairs, strip her naked and claim her so his men could select their own females. The rules on this match were ancient and rigid. Even the sexual position required had been dictated. The female must willingly lie beneath him in the traditional position, surrendering to his dominance.

If she managed to throw him off her body, he'd lose it all.

Aiden's body tightened at the thought of Nikita naked. He'd admired her from the moment they'd met when she'd hired him to fix the ranch's broken tractor. With her clear blue eyes, curved hips and waterfall of long, gold curls, Nikita was lovely.

But what drew him to her was her passionate, tough spirit. He needed an heir and Nikita would make a splendid mother, for he sensed she'd protect their children with the same zeal she showed to her pack. He wanted to make babies with her. Many babies. Many long hours in his bed, achieving the deed.

He smiled grimly. *Get ready, sweetheart.*

His smile dropped as her aide dashed forward, handed Nikita a cell phone. Worry lines dented her forehead as the Nikita took the call, and then left.

Aiden dressed quickly, his anger rising. Was the woman ever going to stick around? How many more times would she insult him? His wolf nudged him to chase. Chase her, toss her to the ground and mate. *You are alpha. You cannot tolerate this rudeness.*

He told his wolf to quiet. The man advised caution. The man knew he was on her territory and Nikita held all the power until they formally signed the blood oath. He must tread cautiously and make sure everything was done by the rules or he would lose her.

Later, he'd indulge his wolf when he chased Nikita around the bedroom and then caught her and showed her his dominant side.

As he stuffed his feet into his boots, Richard gained consciousness. His nostrils flared. For a moment, hatred and anger flared. Aiden watched as one of Richard's pack hurried over with a towel and the alpha leader dried himself off. Then Richard headed for the clothing one of his pack held out.

Nikita entered the room as Richard finished dressing. She'd exchanged the traditional formal robes of an unmated female pack leader for black leather pants, kick ass boots and a tight black T-shirt. Richard's gaze remained riveted to those generous breasts, but Aiden watched her expression.

Something was wrong.

Cell phone cradled to her ear, she held up a finger. Suppressing his annoyance, Aiden leaned against the wall, folding his arms. Richard hovered, wiping the blood from his face with a shirt sleeve.

"Increase the patrols. Order them to draw first blood if any are sighted."

She thumbed off the cell and turned, all smooth business. Approval shone in her gaze as she studied Richard's bloodied shirt, his shattered jaw, and the two swollen eyes.

Aiden stepped forward, shook Richard's hand amicably. The other alpha nodded in respect, and then glancing at Nikita, touched his forehead.

Dismay tightened her features as Richard and his

pack left the room. Nikita watched as the doors closed behind them. "I can't believe you won."

"Try not to sound so enthused."

"I'd try harder, but I'm not a terrific actress."

Aiden stepped close, enjoying her rich scent of spring flowers, vanilla innocence and musk. Taking a long curl in hand, he wrapped it around his finger, forcing her to step closer. Close enough for him to see the desire and alarm swirling in her eyes.

"I bet I can coax a little enthusiasm from you when we're alone."

She looked around the crowded room. "We're far from alone now, so you can stop thinking about sex."

"Sweetheart, when you're in the same room with me, all I can think about is sex."

He enjoyed the flush tinting her cheeks, knowing his words, and her own arousal, caused the coloring.

Hot, sweaty sex, those long legs wrapped about his hips as he pumped hard and fast into her soft, wet heat. Her scent wound around him, making his blood run thick and hot. He'd take her upstairs, make slow, gentle love to her the first time, then tutor her in passion and fuck her hard and fast. Keep her in bed until she conceived.

Aiden needed an heir.

But he needed Nikita more. Couldn't get the woman out of his system, hard as he'd tried. Aiden studied his future mate. He longed to nuzzle the sweet slope of her neck, trailing tiny, biting kisses down to her breasts. Mark her with each exquisite nip, culling little cries of pleasure from her plump, tender lips.

And then, the ultimate triumph, spread her legs open and taste her...

"I'm the winner, pixie. Get used to the idea."

"Pixie! I'm no fairy!"

"You keep dashing in and out of here like one. Can't fool me. But now you're staying put. I'm your mate. You can't deny me what I've wanted from you for all these years. Give in. It's time to make you mine."

"The full moon isn't due until tomorrow."

He stared at her mouth, making his intent clear. "I have no need to wait for a formal mating."

"Impatient much?"

"No, I've been quite patient," he murmured, tugging on another curl that had escaped the tight braid. "When I see something I want, I can be patient. Very patient."

Throat muscles worked convulsively as she swallowed, her gaze whipsawing around the room. The sour stench of fear mingled with her arousal. Was she afraid of him?

He followed her gaze and saw the worried expressions of her pack's females.

Something was wrong. Something not aimed at him or having sex.

Pushing aside his own raging need, he focused on the little worry line on her brow. He laced his long, calloused fingers around her fine-boned wrist. "Hold on."

She looked away. Dismay filled him. Damn, he did not want her afraid of him.

"What's going on? Talk to me."

"Nothing that I can't handle."

"Obviously it's something you can't handle. Something more than your people can handle." Aiden nodded to the worried pack members milling about the ballroom.

She nibbled her lower lip. He stared in fascination, tempted to trace its lush, plump curve with a finger. Aiden sensed an inner struggle.

"Pride won't get you anything but your people hurt. Or worse. If you need my help, say it."

"I have no right to request your help. You aren't beholden to this pact. The contract hasn't been signed yet." Those incredible blue eyes glanced up at him. "Or consummated."

"Then let's sign."

They moved to the inlaid table near the dais, upon which rested a white velum paper, a white feathered quill, a pot of ink, and a golden knife gleaming on a blue velvet pillow.

The ceremonial blade.

A formal, ancient tradition honored by all packs. Nikita obviously wanted to ensure this mating was legally binding.

He slashed his wrist, dipped the quill into the blood and signed the velum.

Face paling, but fully composed, Nikita took the knife, cut her finger, and did the same. Interesting. Females weren't required to sign in blood. The virginal blood spilled on the mating bed sufficed.

Aiden took her finger, kissed the cut she'd made. She trembled beneath the caress of his mouth. "As your tradition dictates, the mating ceremony takes place tomorrow beneath the first light of the moon. Now, tell me, where do you need us?"

Nikita glanced at Roxanne, who frowned at her. "We can handle this," the woman began.

Nikita seemed to struggle with a decision and turned to him, ignoring the aide and her shocked gasp.

"Beyond the fence, in the woods, a patrol sighted several gnomes moving into position."

"Most gnomes aren't dangerous."

"These are. They're dragon seekers."

Aiden went still, the sharp scent of fear in the ballroom seeping into his pores. He glanced around, then took her arm. "We need to talk in private. Your beta and mine, now, in your study."

Aiden nodded at a tall male in a black shirt. "And Garth."

She blinked. "Garth?"

"He's one of my best fighters. I want him to listen, offer advice."

The lavish study had an antique oak desk and a richly toned Oriental rug amid inlaid bookshelves. Nikita went to the windows and lifted the lace curtain, staring outside as he closed the double doors. Darius stood by his side, ready for action. Garth stood on Aiden's left. The Lupine with his dark gold hair and his broken nose looked intent.

And he kept looking at Roxanne, as if he liked what he saw. Aiden made a mental note to pair them together later.

Nikita flicked a hand at the chair behind the desk. "Have a seat."

By law, this was his room now. All these years she had struggled to hold her people together, had ruled over them and now she had to concede that power to a male. Aiden glanced at her firmly compressed mouth.

Nikita wasn't happy about it. He expected as much. It wasn't fair, but the laws of the Mating Challenge were clear—winner takes all. The contract had been signed, only the formal consummation remained.

Taking a seat behind the huge desk would assert his position of command.

Instead, he leaned against the door. Aiden didn't want to strong arm his mate. He wanted her cooperation. Honey worked better than force.

"Dragon seeking gnomes are cold-blooded. They haven't been sighted in this area in decades. Why are they sniffing around your land?"

Nikita let the curtain drop. "Maybe they heard how good my cooking is. I can whip up a mean snail soufflé."

A loud guffaw erupted from Darius, while Roxanne stopped her nervous pacing and offered a small smile. Aiden folded his arms across his chest.

"I don't doubt there are many things you do well. Talents I am certain I'll enjoy discovering." He let his gaze caress her body. "However, dragon seeking gnomes are more interested in treasure than food. The reason why they hunt dragons—"

"Tell me something I don't know, Mitchell."

The interruption was horribly rude, insulting a guest and the future alpha leader. Darius and Garth hissed disapproval while Roxanne gasped.

Lifting an eyebrow, he let silence descend. He locked gazes with Nikita in the first battle of wills between the two alpha leaders. Aiden refused to let his gaze drop. He could do this all day. Burn time while whatever the hell was out there drew closer.

And she realized it too, for she finally lowered her lashes.

He didn't smile or show triumph. Another male might, but Aiden knew how the sting of wounded pride hurt.

He wanted to tame her to his hand, not break her spirit.

"Gnomes attach themselves to powerful dragons to gain their treasure. The only thing drawing them from their underground caverns would be a promise of riches. Something far more valuable than a dragon's hoard of gold."

Roxanne bit her lip, casting a worried glance at Nikita, who'd gone very, very still.

Score.

Whatever it was, they kept it secret. Richard didn't know about it, nor did the other various packs scattered throughout the region. If any had, the pack alpha would've either taken the land away by declaring war, or simply have raped Nikita and claimed victory.

Fury filled him at the thought of that proud, stubborn spirit broken and violently abused. He dragged in a deep breath. Did she realize how damn vulnerable she was?

"Most gnomes are greedy, but cowardly," he reasoned aloud. "But if they sense there are riches close, they can be vicious and attack."

Guilty looks exchanged between Nikita and Roxanne. Bingo. *You win, Aiden.*

All his protective male instincts raged. Aiden fought the primal urge to lock her in the bedroom, toss away the key and fight this threat to her people until every single gnome lay bloodied and dead.

Claws emerged from his fingertips. He raked one across the gleaming wood door, scoring deep gouges. Darius' nostrils flared as he picked up his leader's scent of male aggression. A low growl rumbled from his chest. Garth's own claws descended as well.

Aiden glanced at Garth. "Ideas?"

"Cut them off from behind and circle around. As wolves we can take them down."

He liked Garth's confidence. Aiden gestured to the window. "Show us where they are, Niki." *We'll take care of it.* He amended the thought, knowing her stubborn pride. "We'll help you."

Nikita's eyes widened. "How many of you?"

"All of us."

Her jaw clenched hard enough to shatter rock. "You're under no obligation to help us. The contract isn't validated yet."

He gave a slow smile, filled with intent, and sheathed his claws. "It will be. Trust me, I have every intention of doing so. Many times over."

A delicate flush colored her cheeks, even as she withdrew the blade sheathed on her belt. "Let's get to it, then. Gather your strongest men and meet us at the barn."

Chapter 4

His strongest men numbered all 60 males who'd escorted their leader to the competition.

For once, Nia was glad for the overkill. They would need it.

The yellow sun hung overhead in a clear sky, though the temperatures remained brisk. A carpet of yellowed grass spread out before them in the gentle slope of the valley stretching before them. A cold wind nipped her cheeks.

Aiden and the males in his pack assembled before the red, empty barn. Every one of them stood over six feet, an army of muscled warriors ready for action.

They all screamed testosterone. Aiden detached himself from the group, and headed for her, his gait strong and confident. Stalking her like the predator he was.

How could she fool this powerful werewolf, who had desired her so much that he'd bought the note on her ranch and fought against strong alphas to have her?

Desired her, and the females in her pack. Not loved her.

She had to get them the hell off her land before the

disease struck all these healthy male Lupines. Fishing her favorite knife out of the scabbard strapped to her thigh, Nia gripped it, feeling the edges of the hilt. It felt like an old friend holding her hand.

Aiden scanned the grounds. "Where's the rest of your guards? The males?"

"My guards are out patrolling."

No lie, for the strongest of her guards were patrolling. He didn't need to know they were all females.

Guilt filled her. And now she had a pack of males on her land, land that could kill them. Damnit, why did Mitchell have to bring them all?

Nia swept the knife tip in a wide arc, pointing at all the men. "Overkill much? Trying to impress me, Mitchell?"

He frowned. "Why are you so edgy with me? You asked for my strongest men. All my men fit the bill. If they had been alpha and fought in the challenge, they might have beaten me."

"Too bad they didn't."

"I said, might have. I would have won, no matter what."

"You're pretty cocky and determined, huh Mitchell."

"When the prize is you, sweetheart, I can be very determined." Aiden studied her body, the heat of his gaze like a visual caress. "Have I ever told you how sexy you look in leather?"

She looked at his men, their loyalty to Aiden obvious. Next to her, Roxanne gave a real smile, adjusting the strap of her rifle on her shoulder and giving Garth a meaningful glance.

A glance promising hot sex. Nia knew the woman's

frustrations. And the depth of her loyalty. Celibate, until her leader had chosen a mate.

So long celibacy, nice to know you, Nia thought as she caught her beta making flirtatious eye contact with Garth.

She did not see one familiar face among the Mitchell males. Her niece's mate. "Where's Jackson?"

"I left him on the ranch to help run things while I'm gone." Aiden gave her a thoughtful look. "And I wasn't certain if you wanted him on your property for the challenge, seeing as you lost your niece to him. I know how much you love Lexie, and wanted her to stay with you."

Nia had formally adopted Lexie after her parents abandoned her for having a deformed foot. It had been a rough time for the entire pack, having lost their alpha to the disease. But having Lexie around, and trying to comfort the grieving, confused teen had assuaged Nia's own grief, and proved to be a welcome distraction.

"I love her, but I want her to be happy. Is Jackson making her happy, Mitchell?"

He nodded. "Very much so."

Nia sighed. "Then I can't ask for anything more. Let's go."

Aiden slowed his pace, keeping a possessive hand on the small of her back as they set out for the thick forest at the ranch's border.

"So you brought only the single males, except for Darius," she told him. "Are they here to support you or comfort you if you'd lost?"

"They want to select mates from the females in your pack."

"And what if you had lost?"

"They knew I would not." He smiled.

"You're that sure of yourself."

"I want you that much."

Such frank talk rattled her. She gave him a curious glance. "Desperate to settle down, Mitchell? What happened? Werewolf Mingle or another online dating site didn't work out?"

"I didn't want any other female," he said softly, his gaze giving her another one of those long, appreciative looks. "I want what is due to me, what you owe me, Nikita."

"I owe you nothing."

"Except your virginity." His dark gaze gleamed. "But I'm willing to wait until tomorrow night to claim my prize."

She bristled, her fingers curling tighter around the knife hilt. "I'm not a carnival toy you won by playing ring toss."

"I never said you were." He stopped and clasped her shoulders, his expression intent. "You're far too precious. But know this, Blakemore, when I see something I want, I stop at nothing to get it. From the moment I saw you riding Windstorm, your hair gleaming in the sun, laughing as you raced through the pasture, I wanted you."

She didn't have Windstorm anymore. She'd sold the mare to help pay for the ranch's bills. So much had changed since the day Aiden first saw her. Except his determination.

"I knew I'd do anything to have you."

A shiver coursed down her spine. The wolf was more ruthless than she'd ever expected. Nia stared at him.

He released her shoulders. "Please, put away the knife."

"I know how to use it."

"I'm sure you do." He gave a rueful glance downward. "On all the right parts."

Nia gave a grudging laugh and sheathed the blade. She really liked this male. Would hate for him to succumb to the fate of the ranch's other males. At that thought, she sobered. "After we're done here, send your men home."

"No. I want them to get to know your females better. My men have become a little, ah, testy. They need to settle down. They need a woman's touch around their homes."

"Barefoot and pregnant, waiting hand and foot on their men," she muttered, resenting the idea.

"Barefoot, yes." A crooked grin touched his full mouth. "Pregnant, eventually. But my men are accustomed to fending for themselves."

"Uh huh. Next thing you know, you'll be telling me they iron their own shirts and cook dinner."

"Of course. And bake cookies, too," he teased.

The ridiculous image of all those big, muscled males wearing aprons as they slid trays of cookies into the oven coaxed her to give the first real smile she'd felt in weeks.

Somehow this wolf always made her smile and she truly enjoyed verbally sparring with them. Her expression went cold. She must keep him at arm's length.

Had she a choice, she'd have remained single, chaste and alone. Freedom proved too valuable to her, and she enjoyed making her own decisions. Perhaps too much.

She'd been forced into this challenge because Aiden owned the note on her ranch. Nia had fought hard to maintain her ranch and her people in this untamed region of rugged country. But if her people were to survive once Niki found a cure for the disease, they needed mates. Strong males like the ones in the Mitchell pack. Emotion rose in her throat. Her own personal needs mattered little. The survival of the pack came first.

But Aiden didn't realize exactly what he was walking into at her ranch.

The alpha's dark gaze swept over the land, with its tangle of undergrowth and the overgrown pastures. Aiden had seen how her ranch had fallen into disrepair.

And he'd seen she had no mature males in her pack, a fact she'd hidden until now.

"What happened to all your men, Niki? Why did they die?"

She'd told him that many of the males left after her father and brothers died because they refused to be ruled by a female alpha. The explanation had suited him, until now.

"Die? Why do you ask?"

He stopped and gave her a level look, his black brows drawing together in a scowl. "If the males left because they refused to take orders from a woman, they'd have taken their families as well. Their mates. Lupines mate for life."

Her stomach churned and her palms grew sweaty. "Some of them do. And now you're questioning me on this?"

"I had my doubts before. Now that this is my pack as well, I want answers."

Resentment filled her. How easily he took charge. *And what about all my hard work? You would never see me as an equal, Mitchell. You're too alpha.*

"Can we deal with one question at a time, Mitchell? Like the question of how we're going to kill these gnomes?"

At his nod, she kept walking, but Nia knew he wouldn't let it slide. Aiden would needle her for hard answers she didn't want to give.

As they reached the forest's edge, Aiden halted. His nostrils flared and a muscle ticked beneath the crispness of beard stubble shadowing his jaw. His hand shot out, stayed her.

"That's no gnome."

Fear congealed on her tongue as she tested the air. "Worse. Skin."

Gunfire cracked in the distance. Aiden's jaw clenched. "Godsdamn it. Didn't you have a mystic ward the land against two-legged trespassers?"

Garth and Darius gave him an inscrutable look. Nia's jaw tensed. She heard Roxanne draw in a shaky breath. The most powerful mystic in their pack had died more than two years ago, leaving their borders vulnerable.

"Security Fail. New hashtag around these parts." Nia pushed at a stray lock of hair. "These intruders kill wolves. Nothing stops them. They're scared of only one thing."

Roxanne held up her rifle.

"And this." The knife slid into Nia's palm. She twirled it, staring into the woods that had been in her family for generations. "I prefer my combat up close and personal."

True enough. How many times had she gone on midnight raids to clear these woods of threats?

He seized her wrist. "Not that personal. Those are shotguns. They'll turn you into mincemeat before you can draw close."

Aiden glanced at Darius and Garth. "Take Roxanne and the men, follow the trail of humans and deal with them. I'll handle the gnomes. I want one for questioning, to find out why it's invading this territory."

Fear touched her. If the little pipsqueak blabbed to Aiden, their secret no longer remained safe.

She'd rather kill the gnomes herself.

"Nikita, stay behind me," he ordered.

Not giving him time to react, she tugged her arm free and raced into the forest, the sharp sound of his rich curses trailing behind her.

The gnomes were normally dull-witted, but sharp when it came to money. They scented the presence of Pandora's Chest and would do anything to have it. Trample over pack territory. If a rival pack or hell, any Other discovered the secret, they'd destroy her people in their madness for power.

This was the real deal, and Others killed for such power.

The real deal, that came at a terrible price.

Disease.

Death.

Fangs flashing and piercing, horrible screams, the empty look in the eyes of the males gasping their last breath as the parvolupus disease claimed them at last.

A tendril of scent, beer and sweaty Skin filled her senses. Nia hugged an oak tree and closed her eyes. Scent was her best ability, not sight.

A branch cracked to her left.

And then a hand closed over her shoulder, a warm, calloused palm slid over her mouth.

"Don't scream," a deep voice rumbled in her ear.

Nia clasped his wrist, her fingers barely meeting, and pushed away his hand from her mouth.

Fury raged in Aiden's dark eyes as he turned her around. He pinned her shoulders against the oak with his hands. "I told you to follow me. You didn't listen. Do you know how damn dangerous it is, tackling a pack of gnomes on your own? They can maim you before they kill you."

But his hands were gentle as he cupped her face. Aiden stroked his thumbs over her jaw. "You're never endangering yourself again. Deal? I'm not watching you risk getting crippled and scarred. I'll handle this."

Her lower lip trembled. Few in her pack other than her sister would notice if she returned with scars. They were all too busy trying to survive from one day to the next.

Nia managed to find her voice. "Don't be so arrogant, Mitchell. We'll handle this together. We can't risk keeping one alive. Have to kill them all. They're too slippery."

"Where are they?" His voice sounded so sexy and deep. She shuddered as he pressed tight against her.

"8 o'clock, about one hundred yards and closing in."

His erection pushed through his jeans against her belly.

"You sure you can fight them in your delicate condition?" she asked.

"Darling, I can fight in any condition." He blew a

warm breath into her ear. "But I'd rather make love to you so let's get this over with so we can look forward to consummating our union."

Aiden's tongue traced a line over the outer shell of her ear, and it felt like a lick of fire between her legs. Clenching her teeth, she brought up her knife as he moved out.

A bitter wind rustled through the trees, kicking up dead leaves and blowing them in puffed-cheek playfulness. Nia concentrated on the scents. Sour lemon fear and stale candle wax. Spongy rot mingling with metal and cordite.

A hunter with a gun, recently fired.

Aiden jerked his head to the left. She followed.

Beneath his shirt, his muscles flexed as he stalked through the trees, moving as silently as his wolf. He took the pathway flanking the ribbon of clear creek water that ran from the property's edge to the pond. When he reached a small clearing in the trees, he stopped and ducked behind the trunk of a tall oak tree. Nia joined him, biting back a hiss of real alarm. She pulled out her knife.

Twelve gnomes with little pointed caps and equally pointed teeth surrounded one scared Skin clutching a shotgun. The red of the gnomes' caps matched the human's hunting jacket.

A large wet patch stained the front of his jeans. Her nostrils flared at the scent of urine. Beside her, Aiden narrowed his eyes. His lips pulled back in a snarl, claws emerging from his fingers.

Nia wrapped her fingers around his thick wrist, shook her head.

Jaw clenched to granite, he scowled at her, but

sheathed his claws. Surprise filled her. The man was willing to follow her lead.

"The human can wait. Let him go," she whispered. "Have you ever killed a dragon seeking gnome?"

"Only a regular one."

"Easiest is to distract it by removing its hat. They're vulnerable with their heads exposed. Flick off the cap and then you attack. If you don't cut off their heads, they reanimate."

Twirling her blade, Nia stepped into the clearing. Seeing her, the hunter looked relieved, then he ran off.

Twelve red caps quivered, their owners' normally merry gray eyes filled with fury at being denied their toy. Their bright blue coats and dark green trousers were stained with dirt, and blood dripped from their neatly trimmed white beards. Gnomes gone wild. Nia lowered her blade, ready to attack.

The one closest to her held the tiny corpse of a sparrow, which it gnawed like a child sucking a Popsicle.

No one messes with my birds. She growled. Tensing her thigh muscles, Nia sprang forward, the blade pointed outward. The gnome glanced up, then dropped its meal with a snarl.

And then he raced away. She caught him. Flick. Her knife tip stabbed the gnome's hat, sent it spiraling into the air. Beneath the hat, the gnome had a bald head. The creature screamed, grasping for the cap. Nia kicked the gnome, sending it sprawling. It crawled away, fumbling with the tiny blade in its belt, but she pounced. Holding it between her thighs, she squeezed hard and then brought her blade down, slicing off its head. Bright greenish gray blood spurted over her leathers.

It wasn't as efficient as killing them in wolf form, but it sufficed.

A loud snarl sounded behind her. She turned, stunned at the sight of Aiden.

He'd shifted and tore at the creatures, snarling, jaws snapping. She'd warned him to cut off their heads, but the wolf was magnificent, a huge killing machine whose paws raked over the gnomes' heads, sending their caps sailing. And then Aiden snapped, his jaws tearing off the creatures' heads.

By the time she charged forward, ready to assist, he'd killed the remaining gnomes. He went and washed his muzzle in the cold stream.

Nia scanned the clearing. The ground was littered with gnome blood and gore, making it difficult to single out a scent. She circled the clearing's perimeter, searching for escapees.

Crunching leaves and breaking twigs drew away her attention. Aiden's males, accompanied by Darius, Garth, and Roxanne, raced into the clearing just as Aiden returned. The wolf loped up behind her, headbutted her thigh. Aiden lifted his dark eyes to her, the message in them clear. *Shift.*

Sorry, I can't. I haven't eaten raw meat in more than a month and I have a little trouble. But pride prevented her from telling Aiden this.

Aiden changed back to Skin and clothed himself by magick. "Niki, shift to wolf right now so we can patrol the rest of the area and flush out any stragglers. I don't want you fighting in Skin anymore. It's too inefficient and that damn knife can't protect you as much as your wolf can."

"No." She turned to Roxanne. "Report."

"Got the Skins." Roxanne gazed at Garth in obvious respect. "Garth gave them a lecture, and I didn't even have to show my gun. I believe he scared them off for good. We found the other hunter who fainted. Darius tied him to a tree."

Garth gave a modest shrug. "Treat Skins with the threat they fear the most. Not weapons, but lawsuits for trespassing."

Nia smiled, relief filling her. At least the Skin threat was gone for now.

"Any more evidence of stragglers? Or other intruders?" she asked Roxanne.

Her beta shook her head. "None. Our patrols have all checked in."

Good. Nothing to worry about.

Aiden laced his fingers around her wrist. "Nikita. I told you to shift."

"The gnomes are all dead, as you just heard. It's not necessary."

"Oh, but it is," he said softly. "Now that the threat is dispensed, it's time to address the issue of your disobedience."

Her mouth went dry. "I did nothing wrong."

"You disobeyed me. In front of my pack. I made my rules known to you when I signed up for the fight. Anyone, including my mate, who directly disobeys me, gets mounted by me to know their proper place." Aiden narrowed his gaze. "Shift into wolf. Right now."

CHAPTER 5

The males looked at her expectantly. Worry shaded Roxanne's eyes. The beta adjusted the gun on her shoulder.

Damnit. Nia bit her lower lip. Pack laws among Lupines were clear. If she refused to follow Aiden's directive, as alpha, he'd have just cause to inflict a more severe punishment.

How the hell could she shift into wolf? With the difficulty of finding game in her woods, and the lack of money to buy fresh meat, Nia hadn't eaten the raw meat all Lupines needed once a month to shapeshift. Any raw meat went to her twin to keep Nikita fortified.

As a result, Nia's own powers had waned.

Gathering her courage, she lifted her arms to allow the change to engulf her body.

Nothing. Damnit.

Okay, I can do this. Think wolf. She quieted her breathing and concentrated, centering all her magick to transform.

A tingle of pure power rushed down her spine and a tickle pulled at her belly. Suddenly she found herself in wolf skin.

Nia's senses sharpened. It had been too long since she'd embraced her wolf, and she missed this dreadfully. Around her, the trees became more pungent in scent, and her hearing picked up the scamper of small forest creatures scurrying far away from the threat. The crispness of leaves rustling in the wind, the thin stalks of grass in the pasture; everything had a richer scent. She heard the steady, rhythmic pumping of her future mate's heart, scented pine, forest and pure male.

Aiden shifted to wolf. The others shifted as well, forming a semi-circle around them.

Nia touched her nose to the ground. Quivering, she waited.

Aiden trotted over to her, sniffed her hindquarters. She felt the strength of his body as he mounted her from behind. It wasn't sexual. This was strictly pack, the alpha showing domination.

If she bent her legs, or worse, collapsed to the ground, Aiden's males would lose respect for her. She must hold her own, keep upright.

Ears pointed forward, not flattened, she bared her teeth in a clear threat to a gray wolf boldly locking his gaze on her as Aiden wrapped his paws around her midsection. Mitchell might be dominant, but a female alpha would not allow a lesser male to look her in the eye while her mate was delivering punishment.

The smaller male dropped his gaze. Finally Aiden dismounted, and then gave her a sharp, brief nip in her hindquarters, followed by a slow lick of his rough tongue.

The human female inside the wolf shivered at the promise of that tongue. That was clearly sexual, and intentional, marking his territory.

Nia waited for Aiden to shift back. He did so and conjured clothing and the others did the same. They waited on her. Nia summoned her powers and tried to change.

Could not.

Panic rose in her throat. She fought it, knowing if the animal took over, she'd never change back. *Think. Think!* Nia's mind raced as the others milled around, looking at her. The dark-haired Darius knitted his thick brows as he glanced at Aiden, who scowled.

"Nikita. Change back."

A direct order.

She could not shift back. Nia tensed, her muzzle lifted into the air.

Darius frowned, but Aiden crouched down, rubbed her thick fur. The gentle strokes of his fingers relaxed the tension knotting her muscles. Touch. So long since anyone had touched her like this. Craving more, she rubbed her muzzle against his hand when he stood.

And then found herself squatting on all fours, naked and human again. Someone snickered and she flushed. Aiden growled at the male.

"Go back to the lodge, all of you, except Roxanne and Garth. Now!"

As they scurried away, Aiden helped her to stand upright. She summoned her powers and conjured clothing.

Aiden gave her a long, thoughtful look. "Let's go interrogate the Skin."

Garth and Roxanne led them to the hunter, who struggled to free himself of his bonds. She nodded at Roxanne, who walked up to the Skin, and squeezed a muscle in his neck.

The hunter fainted. Good. Now Aiden couldn't question him.

"I told you we should question him." Aiden scowled.

She shrugged. "There's nothing he could tell us. And we need to cover this up. Do you want every Skin in Montana coming here to see if there are werewolves on the ranch?"

Nia turned to Roxanne. "Take him back the clearing, then call Carol and Susan and have them dump him beyond the boundary, leave him under a tree. Pour whisky on him. His friends will come searching for him, and when he starts babbling about nearly being eaten alive by garden gnomes, they'll think he's drunk."

Easily lifting the overweight human and hefting him over one shoulder, Roxanne started off. Aiden motioned for Garth to follow. The male's gaze scanned the area in a protective manner.

Already moving in. Roxanne had a future mate. Soon the other females would as well.

But what would happen to the males? They couldn't remain here long.

"Roxanne doesn't need an escort," she told Aiden.

"Garth is her escort now."

"You're arrogant, Mitchell. Let my beta do her work alone."

Aiden folded his arms. "No. It's too dangerous. Now, level with me and explain exactly why gnomes are on your land."

"Maybe they decided to become cowboys. This is a ranch."

"Don't toy with me," he said softly. "These gnomes have pointed teeth, red eyes and they'll gnaw your kneecaps until you fall, begging and screaming for death as they eat you alive. What is drawing them here?"

She looked away.

Two fingers on her chin forced her gaze back to meet his. "Nikita, what are you hiding?"

He'll know you're lying. So evade and dodge. "If something's hidden here, how would I know? It's a large spread. Do you expect me to count every single blade of grass? I'm not as anal retentive as you are, Mitchell."

A deep chuckle. "Minx. You're good at clever responses. Makes me wonder what other talents your tongue possesses."

She stuck it out at him.

"Don't stick your tongue out unless you're going to use it," he said softly, and then he lowered his head, and covered her mouth with his.

The caress of his firm mouth felt soft as the brush of velvet, the rough bristles of his beard tickling her chin and cheeks. His lips were warm and soft as velvet, too. She closed her eyes on a sigh, and felt him chuckle against her mouth.

A knowing chuckle, yet there was no smugness in it.

Aiden pulled her into his strong arms and slid one arm around her waist to draw her closer. He kissed the corner of her mouth, her cheek, her temple. The tiny kisses were soothing and not erotic, and yet made her dizzy with desire. She sighed with pleasure as he feathered tiny kisses down her throat, sliding his lips over the curve of her neck.

That's where he'd bite her and place his mating mark, claiming to the world she belonged to him. The bite would lessen her sexual appeal to single males.

His mouth grazed her throat, his warm breath feathering over her skin. Nia curved her arms around him, touching the strong muscles of his back, then sliding up to tunnel her fingers through the tangle of his dark, thick hair.

She clung to his broad shoulders as he tasted her, his scent of pine and male wrapping around her. A lick of scent pushed straight between her legs in a long, slow caress. Nia moaned beneath the tender assault on her mouth. Aiden kissed exactly like her dreams, claiming and stroking, with little, gentle nips along her lower lip, his tongue plunging and withdrawing. She forgot how to breathe, how to think, and lost herself in mindless oblivion.

When he drew back, desire darkened his gaze. She put hands to her burning cheeks. "Of all the damn males in the whole west, why did you have to cross my path, Mitchell?"

He thumbed her kiss-swollen mouth. "I warned you years ago, sweetheart, I would hunt you down and have you, no matter what it took. I vowed I would win you as my mate. And what I win, I keep and no one ever takes it from me."

Nia desperately wished she'd stayed away from this handsome, sexy Lupine who ravished her mouth, and laid claim to her body, but would never know her heart.

He gently stroked a finger over her cheek, where his beard had abraded her flesh. "I'll have to shave before we consummate our mating. You have such tender skin."

A roguish sparkle glinted his gaze. "Especially in the areas where I plan to kiss you very thoroughly."

A blush heated her cheeks. Nia pulled away from

him. "You won the challenge, but I'm still the leader of my people. You can't give them orders."

"Already have. These grounds are off limits except when one of your females is accompanied by a male."

"What?!"

"I'm ordering my men to patrol your ranch and keep a sharp eye out for more gnomes." He narrowed his eyes. "For the protection of the pack."

Damnit! How was Mandy supposed to search for the chest without someone seeing? Nia scowled. "I can protect my own people."

"Our people now. What I say is law, Nikita."

She really hated him using her sister's name and wished he would call her something else. The masquerade she'd pulled off all these years was wearing her out.

"The mating hasn't been consummated yet, wolf. You're a little ahead of yourself. You riding roughshod over me just to prove you're a big, tough alpha?"

"When it comes to your safety, I'll always ride roughshod over you. Deal with it."

He clasped her hand, and she walked with him, through the woods to the two ponds where she'd stocked carp to feed her pack. Despite the aeration filters she'd installed with the last of her money, the fish were dying and her people were hungry. Big game like deer and elk had not frequented these woods in months.

They headed up the paved pathway leading to the lodge and her cabin. Then suddenly he halted and turned to her, his jaw tensing beneath the black beard.

"What's going on, Niki? What aren't you telling me? You're being so secretive. I wish you'd open up to me."

She shrugged. "I'm always like this. Get used to disappointment."

Halfway up the path, they encountered Darius, Samantha, Garth and Roxanne. The foursome hovered over a figure lying on the ground. Nia's heart pounded faster.

Oh crap, this so was not a great way to end her afternoon.

She beat Aiden as they raced up the hill to the Lupines. Nia looked down and her stomach turned over.

Lying on the gravel was a medium-sized male Lupine wearing a red T-shirt and blue jeans. A silver button with an insignia of a wolf holding a spear was pinned to his shirt.

Nia recognized him as one of Richard's wolves.

"What happened?" Aiden demanded.

A guilty look from Darius. His right eye was slightly swollen and bruised. The male had always been jovial, sarcastic and sometimes fun, but no laughter shone from his eyes now. He looked perplexed, and slightly angered.

"I was walking through the woods after following the trail of a gnome and saw this asshole bothering Sam. He didn't leave with the others. He was aggressive and getting violent, talking about the challenge not being a fair fight and how his alpha should have won."

"So you killed him?" Nia asked, her voice a little shaky.

Darius shook his head. "He hit me and then I decked him. It was only a punch, yeah, a hard one, but he collapsed and never got up. And then his heart stopped beating."

She scanned the corpse. There, on his chin. Nia crouched down for a better look.

Upon first glance, the rough, scaly patch resembled an outbreak of Psoriasis, a common ailment among Skins. But instead of being red and silvery, this area of skin was black.

Hiding her fear, she pulled back the male's shirt collar. Nothing. Then she noticed a reddish brown stain on his jeans near his right boot. Nia fished her knife out of its scabbard and cut the cloth. Never had she been so relieved to see evidence of the other plague on her land.

"You didn't kill him, Darius." With the tip of her knife, she pointed to the jagged bite. "A gnome bit him."

Aiden squatted down beside her. "One gnome bite wouldn't be enough to make him drop dead."

"Maybe it was a diseased gnome." She slid the knife back into its scabbard and stood. Nia drew in a trembling breath. It was getting more virulent and contagious. It shouldn't have affected any males quickly. The gnome bite wouldn't have caused this kind of damage normally, but maybe the gnomes were infected, too.

"Even so, he shouldn't have died. It wasn't anything more than a glancing blow." Darius looked troubled and Sam snuggled against him, her arms wrapped around her mate's waist.

"There's something odd about the body," Aiden mused.

Dread filled Nia as Aiden reached out to touch the corpse on its chin, and the rough patch of skin.

"Don't do that!"

Aiden glanced up. "He's dead. He can't hurt me."

But he could. *More than you know.*

She wasn't certain if the parvolupus had mutated to transfer through skin contact, but didn't want him risking his life.

"If it was a diseased gnome that bit him, do you want to take that chance?"

Relief filled her as Aiden finally drew back. He glanced at his beta. "Is this the same one who's been spying on Niki's pack?"

Darius nodded. "He's been trespassing, trying to gauge her borders and the value of the land."

"What?!" She turned to Aiden, anger pushing aside her fear. "Why didn't you tell me?"

His gaze remained even. "I had no proof. Didn't want to confront Richard until I investigated the matter."

"Without telling me!" She drew in a trembling breath, deeply shaken by this news. "How long has he been sneaking onto my land?"

"Months," Darius said. "I finally got it out of him by threatening to beat the crap out of him. And then he got violent toward Sam…"

His voice drifted off and he slid an arm around his mate's waist.

Aiden shook his head. "Stupid bastard. Richard will have to be notified. He'll want to bury him."

Making a sound of distress, she pulled at his arm. "No. I'll call him, but he's not allowed back here. The rules of the challenge are clear and he knew them, as did every single person who stepped on my land. Respect the females, do not fight. Anyone who does, I have the right as alpha to dispense with as I please.

Especially now that I know he was trespassing on my land."

Their land had too many secrets that could kill. Nia looked at the body.

She narrowed her gaze. "I'm not allowing Richard or any of his males to set foot on my land again and start making trouble. Roxanne will take care of this. She has the equipment to protect herself."

Her beta looked scared, but nodded. Roxanne had disposed of dead bodies many times.

"I'll help you," Garth offered.

"No," Roxanne and Nia cried out at the same time.

"I use a Haz Mat suit," Roxanne said, glancing at Nia. "Please, go with the others. I don't want you taking a risk."

"I won't have you taking a risk either. Not with those dangerous gnomes around. Consider me your new bodyguard, Roxanne," Garth told her.

"No," Nia said, but the male ignored her.

Garth stared at her beta, smitten as a pup, but there was a determined arrogance about him. Aiden had it as well. It was the protective stubbornness of a male Lupine who'd staked a claim on his female. This one wouldn't take orders easily, she realized. As Roxanne headed for the barn to get the Haz Mat suit, Garth started after her.

Cutting him off, Nia stabbed him in the chest with a finger.

"Look wolf, this is my ranch, my rules and my land. Roxanne needs to take care of this. She'll be fine, she has a rifle! I'm giving you a direct order. You are not going with her."

Narrowing his eyes, he put his hands on his hips. "I

am going with her. I take direct orders only from Aiden and I'm not leaving her unprotected. You have no authority over me."

Then he added with a sniff, "Female."

The hell with this. If she let Garth disobey her, she'd never gain the respect she needed to make the Mitchell pack males listen to her, and get the hell out of here.

"Here's my authority."

He didn't see her knee, but oh man, he felt it when she made hard contact with his groin. Garth yelled and fell down, clasping his balls, wheezing.

"Stop thinking with your dick. I'm still the alpha on my land," she told him.

Dirty move, but necessary. Nia flexed her fingers, wishing she didn't have to do that. She stole a glance at Aiden, who gave a brief nod. Aiden fisted a hand in Garth's shirt, dragged him upright and shook him.

"Listen to Niki, you stubborn ass. That's *my* direct order."

With a sullen look, Garth nodded.

To her immense relief, the male turned and headed back to the lodge. Nia released a shaky breath. She had to get Aiden and his men out of here, quickly.

Because if they stayed, she couldn't guarantee they wouldn't suffer the same fate as the diseased dead man.

Aiden hated secrets. He'd spent too many years under the shadow of a domineering father who hid behind a lie. And now the female he planned to mate was hiding some very big secrets. He just knew it.

Patience eroding, he itched to shake sense into

Nikita and demand answers. But the wolf was stubborn as rock. Would not budge. He understood why she'd moved against Garth. The male needed to realize he would soon be under Niki's authority as well, and listen to her and respect her.

But he needed honesty from his mate. Nothing less.

They were all exhausted and hungry and on edge. Food would help with the frayed tempers. He hadn't eaten since gulping down a light breakfast of fruit at 5 a.m., not wanting to be sluggish for the fighting. But now his tired body demanded sustenance.

Aiden followed Nikita into the pack lodge, through the living room, into the enormous dining hall.

"I need you to show me where my men will be bunking for the night."

Was that panic flaring in her pretty blue eyes? Nikita headed for the counter holding a coffee pot, hot water and a box of tea. She poured herself a mug of coffee, gestured to the pot. He shook his head.

"I'm going to need fresh meat for my men." He gazed around the room with its square oak tables and bank of tall windows overlooking the mountains and the valley. "We can hunt in your forest. But I didn't see any big game. What happened to all the deer in your woods? I didn't even scent a rabbit. Or a squirrel."

Nikita seemed absorbed in her mug. "We have game. Just hard to find."

"Bull."

She looked up and he caught the fear in her eyes. Aiden roped in his frustration. Hoping his touch would sooth her, he settled his hands on her shoulders, alarmed by how much weight she'd lost. Niki had been much plumper only a few months ago.

"Send Darius home with Sam. Now," she told him.

Aiden stared. What the hell? Had she asked him to have sex with her here on the dining room floor, he couldn't have felt more surprised.

Pleased, oh yeah. But surprised as well.

"Aiden, he doesn't belong here anymore. Send him home with Sam." He could see her mind working like a clock, gears whirling. Making excuses?

"I don't want your beta here having sex with his mate and stirring up my pack. You saw what happened already with Garth. And you know the rules of the challenge. Until you and I consummate the mating, your men can't touch my women. No pairings until we're officially mates."

She set down the cup and leaned against the counter. "Your men are already cranked up enough. Last thing I want is them stalking my females, getting pushy and then I have to kick more in the gonads. I doubt you want that either. My knee's gonna get pretty damn sore."

Instead of answering, he studied his intended mate. With her dark gold curls, high cheekbones, pert nose and her full, lush mouth, she was lovely. But he didn't only see her beauty, he saw a female alpha with lines of strain around her pouting mouth, and smudges of purple beneath her sapphire blue eyes.

What had happened to her?

Clasping her hand, he led her to a table. "Sit."

Nikita bristled. "I'm not a damn dog, Mitchell."

Far from it, he thought, amused. "You're exhausted and look ready to topple over. Your wolf needs food."

After pulling out a chair, he gently pushed her into it.

"I have to tend to the livestock. I have chores."

What livestock? Nikita had once raised quarter horses and champion thoroughbreds. He saw only a few straggly mustangs in the pasture, cropping the scrawny grasses. And there were no crops of any kind that he could see.

How the pack was surviving, he didn't know. Aiden went into the adjacent kitchen, did a quick check of the pantry and refrigerator. The slim stores alarmed him. He pulled out his cell and called Darius.

"Aiden." Darius sounded worried. "Sam and I are hanging with the others outside. They want to know what the plan is."

Aiden made a prompt decision. "Get a few guys together to go to town to buy groceries. Lots of steaks, beef, the usual. Give them your corporate credit card."

"You already packed a cooler for the celebratory feast tonight. It's probably still in your truck."

Aiden frowned. He had tossed the cooler into his truck early this morning without anyone's knowledge. "How did you know?"

"You fight to win, my friend. What else would you have done?"

His beta's tone was dry. Darius knew him well.

"It's not enough to feed our guys and Niki's whole pack. Unload everything I brought, get dinner started and send the men into town for more."

"There's a grill downstairs on the lanai and a small kitchen and bar for entertaining. I'll get started grilling the food," Darius added.

"Good. Make sure to send enough men with the trucks to stock Niki's ranch for at least three weeks." He paused for a moment, thinking. "Tell them to buy plenty of beef, vegetables, staples, tea, milk, the usual. Oh, and a big box of chocolate puffs."

He knew Niki liked those, judging from what Lexie had told him. Lexie, Nikita's niece, was mated to Jackson and officially now a member of Aiden's pack.

"Then, after you and Sam eat, go home."

"What? No way. I'm not leaving, I'm your second in charge—"

"Exactly why you need to get home, and take Sam with you. Someone has to look after the home front." Aiden paused. "It's best if you leave, Dar. Things are tense enough now with all the men eyeballing the females—"

"Which is why you need me to keep them in line while you focus on Nikita."

"I can get Garth for that." He thought of what Nikita had done to the male. "He needs a distraction from Roxanne."

Silence.

"Go home, Darius, and enjoy Sam. I'll be fine here with Garth."

"Aiden, what's going on? You pissed because I hit that male from Richard's pack?"

He heard the faint undertone of worry. "Asshole deserved it for coming onto Sam. I'm more concerned with settling the guys down for the night, and making sure her females have enough to eat."

"There's no big game in the woods," Darius said slowly. "Things are pretty bad. Worse than what you thought."

He gripped the cell. "Yeah. Which is why I need to step in and take charge. Niki won't like it, but she'll have to live with it."

"Good luck, buddy." Darius laughed softly. "Wish I could be here to see you deal. See her tear into your sorry ass."

"Fuck you and the horse you didn't ride in on," Aiden said, smiling, and thumbed off the phone.

When he returned to the dining hall, Niki had rested her head on the table. Her eyes were closed.

Fast asleep.

She hadn't been eating properly, obvious from the weight loss and the exhaustion. And the strain of the challenge had taken its toll.

Aiden felt a mixture of longing, tenderness and something else he didn't quite recognize, nor want. He couldn't fall in love with this stubborn, strong female. Long ago he'd resolved to never fall in love and hand over his heart, like his dead and dear old dad had done with Aiden's mother. When his mother died, his father had fallen apart, neglected the pack and nearly killed his offspring. Aiden's fists clenched as he thought of his baby sister and the scars she'd suffered because of their father.

He would never allow his feelings to take over like his father had.

Oh, he'd become Niki's mate. Make love to her, long into the night. Treat her with the respect and caring she deserved. Make certain she never wanted for anything.

He'd do anything for her. Anything.

Except hand her his heart. *Love makes you a fool, and weak.*

He pulled out a chair, turned it around and straddled it. At the scrape of the wood against the tile, she raised her head with a dazed look. "I fell asleep. How long?"

"Ten minutes at the most. You didn't miss much." He ached inside at how vulnerable she looked. "My men are headed into town to buy supplies."

Niki sat up, yawning. "I have food."

And wolves can fly. He remembered her stubborn pride and quickly thought of an excuse. "A feast, to celebrate my victory. And my men are very hungry. You didn't count on having all of us stay for dinner."

Her eyes widened. She pushed away from the table. "They can't stay here. Send them home."

Aiden frowned. "Why? They'll only have to return tomorrow for the mating ceremony."

"Then let them return. I don't have room for them. And I don't want anyone sneaking off to bother my pack in the middle of the night."

"We could consummate the mating right here and now."

Something flickered in her gaze. "Rules are rules, Mitchell. I'm going by the book on this mating."

"True enough."

Niki stood and walked over to the doors leading to the wide balcony overlooking the rolling hills and sweeping pastures. He joined her outside as she sat in one of the wood rockers. Feeders hung from the overhead rafters as hummingbirds darted in and out, seeking the sweetness.

Like her. He remembered his gift. "I'll be right back."

When he returned, her eyes were closed again. Aiden suspected it was from hunger and lack of sleep. He gently placed the birdhouse in her lap. "Open your eyes."

She did and looked down. "What is it?"

Enormously pleased with himself, he chuckled. "What else? It's a birdhouse."

Niki lifted up the structure and examined it. "For what?"

"You mentioned you wanted to have a bird house for the hummingbirds to nest. So I got you one as my mating gift to you."

She sighed and shook her head. "Thank you. Ah, Mitchell. I appreciate the sentiment."

But she didn't look pleased. "What's wrong?"

"Hummingbirds aren't cavity nesters. This won't work." Nikita poked at the birdhouse. "It's very pretty, but useless."

Dumbfounded, he stared at the gift. "I went out of my way to get you a birdhouse for your birds and you don't like it? I thought you'd like it. It's your favorite color. Blue."

He studied her face. Nikita was complex and wild, like the animals roaming her ranch's forest.

"It's nice. As a decoration."

"It's a birdhouse!" Frustrated she didn't like the gift, he glared at her.

She sighed. "Listen Mitchell, no matter how pretty or ornate or strong the birdhouse is, it won't work. Hummingbirds like platforms. They nest in sheltered trees and in shrubs that make them feel safe. If you don't provide the proper nesting area, and food, they'll leave. You have to meet their needs if you want them to stick around. Pay attention to them."

And then it struck him that Nikita was exactly like her hummingbirds. Always darting around, fast and furious, looking for the proper spot to nest so she could care for her people, but no one paid attention to her needs. Aiden felt as if he'd been looking at her through a telescope, when all the time what he needed to see wasn't at a distance, but right in front of him.

He needed to address her needs or she'd fly away like her birds.

"Fine, pixie. I'll pay attention." He plucked the useless birdhouse from her lap and set it on a nearby table. "Right now I'm paying attention to the fact that you're half starved. You need dinner."

Niki looked guilty for a minute. "It is a nice birdhouse. Maybe another bird would like it."

"I have something else I know you'll like. For now, dinner."

At her protest, he put a finger to her lips, shuddering inside at the contact. Her mouth was warm silk. He longed to kiss her again.

"Hush. Stay here. Darius is rustling up a real feast to celebrate. I'll bring you a plate."

She didn't protest and that alarmed him. Niki must be hungry and exhausted if she allowed him to feed her. She had too much pride.

A few minutes later, he returned carrying a tray filled with silverware, plates, two cans of iced tea and a platter piled with thick sausage, four rare steaks, and hamburgers. He set the platter on the patio table. Niki joined him, pulling out a seat, her eyes huge at the sight of all the food. Hell, he could almost see her salivating.

It killed him to know she'd been going hungry. For how long?

Aiden cut into a steak and sat beside her. He forked

a piece and held it to her mouth. Niki shook her head.

Aiden brought the fork to her mouth, rubbing the steak against her lips.

"Eat for me, sweetheart."

Niki pressed her lips together.

"It's really good. I bought this steak with my own two hands. Slaved over the selection all day in the supermarket."

As she laughed, he popped the morsel inside her mouth. Aiden placed the piece just inside her lips. She flicked her tongue daintily over the steak, then closed her lips over the fork tines. As she chewed and swallowed, he gazed into her face with a primitive male hunger greater than his need for beef.

He fed her a few more slices of steak, instinct warning she had trouble shifting due to lack of fresh meat. After the fourth bite, she pushed his hand away. "I can feed myself, Mitchell."

But he felt a certain satisfaction, knowing she'd taken food from his hand. It was a traditional female acceptance of the alpha male's role in providing for her needs. Aiden wondered if Niki knew this.

Doubtful. If she had, she'd probably have taken the fork and stabbed him with it. Niki was not traditional in any sense. However, she was determined to play by the rules with the Mating Challenge.

Did she know the tradition for an alpha female to accept the male's role in caring for her sexual needs? Aiden's groin tightened as he thought of tomorrow night's ceremony. Oh yeah, he was most looking forward to fulfilling *that* need.

Aiden placed a thick hamburger on her plate. "Here. Try this. My specialty."

She poked it with a finger as if it were a roach. "What is it?"

"Rare hamburger, slathered with caramelized onions, Brie and bacon."

He could see her struggle with admitting her hunger. Finally Niki picked up the hamburger and bit into it. "OMG, I think I've died and gone to the afterworld."

"Not yet, sweetheart. I'm saving that for tomorrow night when we have sex."

He laughed as she rolled her eyes. Niki kept eating, making little sounds of pleasure. Satisfaction filled him. He liked seeing his woman happy and eating. He'd take good care of her. Very good care.

Aiden picked up another hamburger, bit into it with a sigh. Delicious. He popped open the tea, offering her a can.

Nia shook her head. "I don't drink iced tea."

She went into the dining hall and returned with a bottle of water. For a while they sat eating, watching the glowing sun slowly set behind the mountains, streaking the skies with pink light. Finally she pushed back her plate. "Thanks, Mitchell. Nice feast."

"I aim to please."

She cast him a sideways glance from those incredibly blue eyes. "Your men?"

"They're staying."

Anger touched her expression. "Send them home."

"No." He leaned forward, knowing this would be the first contest of wills as mates, but far from the last. "I want them here to look after your pack. Patrolling the grounds. I will not leave your females here unprotected, not with those damn gnomes roving the forest."

She glanced away, but not before he saw guilt

shadowing her expression. "Fine. They can sleep in the cowboy's bunk house."

"Because you have no cowboys left to sleep there," he said softly.

Niki whirled toward him. As she started to protest, he held up a hand. "Don't lie, Blakemore. No males. Not a single one, except a few boys who look prepubescent. What happened to your men?"

Cupping her face with one strong hand, he turned her to meet his penetrating gaze. "How long ago did they leave?"

He could almost see her mind working. "They didn't leave. They died."

"From what? Those gnomes?"

"You can't stay here, Aiden," she whispered and he heard a note of desperation in her silky voice. "I'll come to your ranch tomorrow and we'll hold the ceremony there beneath the full moon. I'll bring everyone, but you can't stay here, and your men can't, either."

Seeing the lines of strain on her face, the panic flaring in her eyes, he leaned his forehead against hers. "I will not leave you unprotected. And you know the rules. I cannot return to my pack and my territory without making you my mate in the flesh."

Not to mention his suspicion that Niki might bolt before he had the chance to do so. He didn't know what was happening at the Blakemore Ranch, but would find out.

Tomorrow. She was exhausted and needed sleep.

She fished her cell phone from her leather pants and called her beta, telling her to arrange sleeping quarters for Aiden's men, then thumbed off the phone.

"You can bunk down in the guest bedroom."

"You don't want me to share your bed?" He gazed at her, feathering his thumb across her plump lower lip, letting her see the intent behind the gesture. Gods, he wanted this female badly. Wanted to ravish her with slow, soft kisses, and strip away that layer of pride to find the woman beneath...keep her close to his side to rule...

As equals? Aiden shook his head free of the idea. He was naturally stronger and his instinct to protect ran deep. Pack needed strong, fearless leadership and one leader, not two. His authority was final. Niki would be his helpmate, and he'd need her advice to help integrate their two packs.

But rule at his side? Never.

"I need one last night alone." She bit her lip and he sensed her prideful struggle. "Please."

Aiden stood, silently resolving to find out what the hell was going on. "All right. But I'm putting my men on patrol. Fair warning, Niki."

He brushed a kiss against her forehead. "Tomorrow, when you're rested, we'll talk."

She eyed the leftover food. "Do you mind if I take that?"

Such a hesitant request. Aiden's heart turned over as he realized how much it took for her to ask. "You'd do me a favor if you did. I hate wasting food."

Throat tight with emotion, he stood and went into the kitchen to wrap everything. How long had she been living like this? Half starved, too proud and alpha to ask for help?

Never again, he silently vowed. If he had to beg, borrow or steal, he'd make sure she was well cared for.

Two hours later, a covered tray of food in her palms, Nia went to her cabin near the main lodge. She had a quick meeting with Roxanne and Mandy, instructing them to search for the chest when they could do so undetected. Nia knew she'd be too busy distracting Aiden Mitchell.

As she approached her cabin, four wolves prowled up the path leading from the pond to the lodge, their scent unfamiliar.

Aiden's men.

She waited until they passed. It would be almost impossible for her aunt and beta to search for Pandora's Chest tonight, with Mitchell's wolves on patrol.

She started for the walkway leading to the basement under her cabin. No one ever ventured here from fear of offending the alpha. This was her private quarters. A truck door slammed nearby. Nia stopped, her heart pounding.

Darius came toward her with his mate, carrying a box.

"Hi!" Samantha shifted the plastic bags in her hand and waved. "We were told to bring these to your cabin."

Nia's mouth went dry. "Sure, come inside."

She walked up the back steps, opened the door and stepped aside as Darius carried the big cardboard box. Samantha followed.

"Where's your kitchen?" he asked.

She led the way and the couple set the items down on her dining table. Darius opened the refrigerator and freezer and began stowing the items.

Groceries.

Nia set down the tray of leftovers, wishing the food wouldn't go cold. But Niki had cold food before. It was when her twin didn't have any food that she worried.

Samantha glanced at her and her smile was kind. "Aiden wanted to make sure your cabin was stocked. He's a big eater."

How kind. She knew Samantha was trying to ease her humiliation, for certainly the woman had seen how bare the cupboards were. Then Darius removed a big box of cereal. Pride forgotten, she took it from him.

"Chocolate puffs!"

He gave a crooked grin and she saw why Samantha was smitten. "Aiden's special request for you."

Mouth watering, she looked at the bags. Dare she hope...

Samantha withdrew a gallon of milk. "Of course we got milk. What good is cereal without the milk?"

"It tastes great without it," she admitted.

Samantha winked at her. "I know. Sometimes I love eating cereal straight out of the box, too."

When they finished unpacking, she shyly thanked them, wishing she could make friends. It was far too dangerous, no matter how nice the couple was. The last thing she wished for Samantha was for Darius to fall ill and die. Best they head back to their own home, where Darius would be safe.

Nia waited until their truck pulled away. Then she took the tray, added the box of cereal and the milk, and raced down the hill to the basement door.

Using the key beneath the cracked flower pot in the dead garden, she unlocked the front door and went inside.

The basement had been fashioned into an apartment,

complete with a kitchenette, full bath, living quarters, and a bedroom. There was even a lab where Niki worked, experimenting to try to find a cure for the disease. No windows, though. Nia shuddered. Her twin was strong to tolerate the lack of sunshine. All Lupines craved the outdoors.

What little fresh meat Nia had managed to scrounge up, she gave to her twin. Niki needed her strength. And she needed to run as wolf at night, the only freedom she truly could enjoy.

Nikita sat at the living room desk, absorbed in reading the ancient texts. She bent over a thick book, the green banker's lamp casting a glow upon the ancient parchment. Her twin glanced up from the desk as Nia set the table. "You eat. I'm not hungry."

"Liar. I already ate. Mitchell's men brought enough food to feed all of Montana. Want me to warm it up?"

Niki shook her head, her nostrils flaring. Nia watched her twin sit at the kitchen table and devour the cold steak. Her stomach tightened at her sister's obvious hunger.

Nia went to the refrigerator and fished out a can of iced tea, popped the lid and set it on the table. Niki loved iced tea, one thing she did not share in common with her twin.

Worry filled her as she sat at the table, chin on her arms, watching her twin eat. She was too damn thin. Nia had sold everything to pay for food, but it wasn't enough to provide for the pack.

When Niki finally finished, Nia dug out two bowls, filled them with chocolate cereal and milk. The twins sat on the living room carpet with happy sighs.

"Remember when Dad used to buy this for us? And

we'd eat out of the same bowl in bed while watching TV and he'd scold us for getting cereal between the sheets?" Niki crunched a mouthful of cereal.

"And Rick and Don would grab the box and try to hide it from us, and then pelt us with cereal, until we threatened to show Dad where they hid all their porn."

Niki giggled. "Remember how pale they got? They were so scared."

Emotion tightened Nia's throat. She set down the half empty bowl, her appetite diminished. Gone were the days of their little family, secure and hidden in their cabin, their older brothers fiercely protective of the girls and hiding the fact there were two. Oh how she longed for those innocent, carefree times when she could share things with her twin.

Share cereal, share clothing.

Share time.

All that's going away, she thought, tears pushing behind her eyelids. *I'm losing her. All these years I've fought to keep her, and now because of the Mating Challenge, I can't spend much time with her anymore.*

"How is your research?" Nia asked.

Her twin's expression shuttered for a moment. "I hit upon something that will guarantee a cure."

Her heart raced with excitement. "Niki! You sure? When?"

"Soon. I need to run more tests to be certain. I need time, Nia." Her twin looked at her, her gaze filled with determination. "Give me a little more time. I have to focus."

"I'll give you all the time you need."

"Keep Mitchell occupied, and everyone busy and distracted. That's all I ask. A week, perhaps."

Worry needled her. She hated deceiving Aiden. What would happen when the alpha found out the truth?

He'd be furious. *I'll deal with it later.* "Okay."

Niki pointed at Nia's bowl with her spoon. "You finished?"

"You eat it. I'm getting ready for bed."

Nia stood and gave her twin a critical look. "I know you're bored and cooped up here, sweetie. I don't think it's a good idea to run in the woods anymore at night."

"I'll be careful. I'm fast, and no one will see me."

Nia sighed. She worried about her twin getting caught, but couldn't deny her only pleasure.

After Nia finished in the bathroom, she climbed into the queen bed in green and pink polka dotted pajamas. Niki joined her a few minutes later, wearing a similar pair, only hers had pink pigs on them instead of polka dots.

She curled up on her side and her twin slid her arms around her waist, snuggling against her. They had slept like this in the womb, after their birth, and as infants.

When their parents separated them to keep Niki's existence hidden from the Silver Wizard, and Nia was alone in her crib, she'd cried for hours until falling asleep. Every once in a while, the twins shared a bed and held each other for comfort.

After tonight, she could never sleep with her twin again.

A tear trickled from the corner of her eye. Niki kissed her shoulder. "It's going to be okay, Nia. Everything's going to work out just fine."

She closed her eyes, wishing she could share her twin's optimism.

THE MATING CHALLENGE

Late that night, Aiden went for a run as wolf. The moon hung like a silver nickel in the sky. He headed for the pond and the circle of stones where ashes of old bonfires still lay scattered on the grounds.

Something was wrong on this land, and he needed to find out what. His wolf sniffed around the pond, but could only detect very faint scents of game, indicating the smells were perhaps weeks old.

Aiden sat on his haunches, panting, looking at the moon.

A gray timber wolf emerged from the woods beyond the pond. He caught a tendril of scent and his nostrils twitched. Niki. He wagged his tail, giving a big wolfish grin. They couldn't have sex until after the formal mating ceremony, but the rules said nothing about getting frisky.

And his wolf howled to get frisky with her.

Seeing him, the wolf raced past the pond, gaining the pathway leading up to the lodge. Eager for the chase, he followed.

The wolf bolted toward the lodge, and vanished behind a clump of bushes.

Slowing, he watched a woman emerge from the bushes. She waved a hand and clothed herself in sweatpants and a T-shirt and ran up the lodge steps leading to the dining room.

Intrigued, he shifted back to Skin, conjured clothing and then followed her into the kitchen.

Niki stood at the sink, her gaze wide. She looked like a cornered rabbit.

Aiden hung back, getting a whiff of her fear. He

didn't want to scare her. Why was she so frightened?

"I like to run at night," he told her. "It's peaceful. Quiet."

"I like to run at night sometimes," she admitted.

"Good to know you're back to form and can shift." He headed for the refrigerator and she watched him with a wary look.

"Drink?" he asked, opening the refrigerator. "I'm thirsty after that run. Thought I'd grab some iced tea. Want some water?"

"I'll take an iced tea. Love it."

He stared at her. How could she not like tea one day and then change her mind? He looked at her again.

There was only one can left. He grabbed it, popped the lid and rolled it over his forehead. "Nice and cold. We can share."

He'd stared at her mouth, thinking of consummating their bond. He'd thrust deep and hard inside her. Every inch of her soft skin he would know, every nuance…

"That's okay. You take it."

Aiden gulped down a long draught, then handed her the can. Niki shook her head.

Irritated, he shook the can a little. "Go on. I don't have dog germs. Hell, we've shared more with the kisses I've given you. And we're going to share a lot more, sweetheart, on our mating night."

With a shaking hand, she took it and sipped. Then blood drained from her face. Niki's mouth wobbled. She set the can down upon the counter, and ran for the sink and threw up.

Stunned, he started for her. She held up a hand like a traffic cop. "No!"

Niki ran water into the sink, and sipped some. She

tore off a paper towel from the nearby roll and wiped her mouth.

"I'm fine," she said. "Just need rest. Please, leave me alone. I need to get back to bed. Sleep."

Suspicion filled him. "Did you eat some bad meat?"

"No. It's nerves. I'll be fine."

Hmmm. Nerves, the woman who faced dangerous gnomes with a dagger and kicked one of his best fighters in the gonads?

He took a step forward and she backed off. "How about a good-night kiss?" he asked.

Now Niki looked like she would throw up all over again. Blowing him a kiss, she backed up toward the door. Then she turned and raced away, out the door, down the steps.

Confused, Aiden stared at the opened door. What the hell was wrong with his intended mate? Was she ill? Or did the thought of being intimate with him make her sick?

It wasn't a good omen.

And yet, deep inside, he suspected it wasn't him, but something else. Nikita Blakemore was hiding secrets on this ranch.

Sooner or later, he would discover every single one of them.

CHAPTER 6

Rose and purple streaked the sullen, leaden sky the next morning. A chill hovered in the air as birdsong filled the trees near her cabin.

Nia barely noticed the beauty of the sunrise as she headed down to the pond, shovel in hand. Dressed in old, grubby jeans, a gray sweatshirt, her long hair pulled back in a ponytail, she hurried down the gravel pathway.

Mandy had called and told her she'd timed the patrols of Aiden's men. Every hour they passed by the old well. Her aunt had managed to dig for the map, but found nothing.

Aiden's men would not return to the area of the well for another hour. Nia had exactly sixty minutes.

Forty minutes later, she had a series of small holes ringing the well. Nia sat on the ground, wiped sweat off her brow with the back of one dirty hand. Two minute break, and then she'd resume…

"What the hell are you doing?"

Aw hell. A shiver raced down her spine. Should have known Mitchell would look for her, but she figured he'd be exhausted from fighting yesterday.

Nia shrugged. "I buried a bone out here and my wolf wants to find it."

Aiden squatted down before her, picked up a handful of dirt. Thick waves of his ink black hair were brushed back from his face, still damp, as if he'd just showered. In his black T-shirt, tight jeans and faded Western boots, he looked rugged and every inch the alpha. Her female parts tingled and paid attention.

He peered into the holes. "Looks like you're searching for buried treasure."

As she looked away, he dusted off his hands. "Or looking to bury another body."

Suddenly weary, she sagged her shoulders. "There would be too many of those and not enough ground."

"Talk to me, pixie." He slid a hand around her neck, his warm palm chasing away her inner chill.

She relished his warm and drew closer. Aiden gave her a thoughtful look. "You feeling better?"

"I'm fine."

"You seemed pretty sick last night. I thought you ate some bad meat."

Puzzled, she shook her head. "The meal was terrific."

"Good. Now answer something else for me. Why did your males die? Why do you want me, and my men, off your ranch?"

Instead of answering, she studied his angular face, the darkness of his gaze, his sculpted cheeks and full nose, the firm, thin mouth accustomed to giving commands…

"You shaved off your beard," she said, realizing the difference.

Aiden gave a rueful smile. "For tonight. I told you, your skin is tender."

Tonight. The tingle between her legs intensified. She cupped his cheek, rubbing her thumb across the smooth flesh. With the beard and mustache gone, he looked younger, almost vulnerable. More approachable.

"I like it."

He closed his eyes as her thumb rubbed the corner of his mouth. "Had I known you liked it that much, I'd have done this sooner."

Nia smiled, liking how he seemed to almost purr as she stroked him. What other sounds would he make if she touched him all over? A shivery anticipation raced through her. Tonight they would make love and this big, handsome alpha would be exclusively hers.

Except technically, he belonged to Niki, the true alpha. Her twin.

Don't do this. Don't fall for him.

Aiden took her hand and brushed a kiss against her dirt-stained knuckles. He rubbed her hand against his cheek. "I can't wait for tonight, pixie. I've wanted you so long, it's driven me wild. I promise I'll make it good for you, despite the formalities. And after, we'll stay at your cabin, let the world pass us by for a few days. I'm going to keep you trapped in bed, feed you, pleasure you, and see to your every need. You deserve a rest from ruling the pack."

She indulged in the fantasy, the dream she'd entertained each night for the past year: Aiden making love to her every morning, and each night, his strong arms wrapped around her, making all her cares vanish…

Nia's gaze dropped to the ground littered with holes. Aiden couldn't make them vanish. Two boys who would soon celebrate their birthdays would die instead if she didn't find the chest.

"You can't stay here," she whispered, panic pushing aside her wistful dreams.

His eyes opened and he studied her with sharp intensity. "Why?"

"My people will resent it." She thought rapidly. "After tonight, take me back to Mitchell Ranch with your men, and let's settle in at your home. Roxanne can take care of things here. While your people are getting adjusted to my presence, it will give my pack time to adjust, too."

"They need to adjust together."

"You need to be home running things!"

"I have Kyle, Jackson, and Jake in charge, and now Darius. J.J. is there as well, helping out. He even brought Rafe, who left his new pack to help out. I have everything covered, Niki." He framed her face with his warm palms, searching her eyes. "Why are you so damn eager to get me the hell out of here?"

She resisted the temptation to close her eyes and bask in his touch. Aiden could make her melt with a single stroke of his finger.

"It's my ranch." She gazed up at him. "I worked hard to keep it together. I don't want you taking over."

There, a partial truth. If he discovered the full truth, would he leave her to protect himself? Or be furious that he'd been deceived?

He seemed to consider, and lowered his mouth toward hers. "I don't want your ranch. Just you, and your very tempting, very beautiful body."

The kiss was so sweet, so soft, his mouth silken as he rubbed it against hers. Nia's eyes fluttered closed as she parted her lips. But he didn't slide inside. Instead, he gently nipped her bottom lip with his teeth, then sucked it into his mouth. She moaned, clinging to his wrists, leaning into him.

Aiden broke the kiss and she opened her eyes. Stepping back, he tugged his shirt over his head.

Her gaze widened. "What are you doing?"

"Let's go swimming. You're dirty." He chucked the shirt aside and grinned. "I like you dirty. I get to wash you all over."

Nia didn't reply. She was too busy staring.

His chest was sculpted muscle, the dark hair stretching from one small brown nipple to the other. She wanted to run her fingers through that mat of hair, then downward, following that naughty line of hair dipping down to the waistband of his jeans... She'd unzip those jeans, tug them past his narrow hips, and then she'd reach for his very long, and very thick...

"Sausage," he murmured.

She blinked. Dear goddess, could he read her mind? Was this mate bonding between alphas?

"I'm not thinking of your needs. You haven't had breakfast yet. Sausage and eggs ok?"

She wanted to giggle. Nia rubbed her chin with her dirty knuckles. "It's fine, Mitchell. And you can't go swimming in that pond. It's filled with bacteria."

"I'm a wolf. A little bacteria won't hurt me."

"You don't know what's in there." She stepped in front of him, fear filling her. What if swimming in the pond accelerated exposure to the disease?

Sweat poured down her back as he stared at her. Could he guess something was amiss? But finally he nodded.

"I'd rather shower with you after we're mated," he

murmured, putting his shirt back on. "Come on. I'll make you a breakfast fit for the queen that you are."

As they trudged up the hill, she glanced over her shoulder. Maybe later, she could return to dig.

Because she was running out of time. And options.

She saw little of Aiden after they ate breakfast. He vanished to attend to the formal requirements of the mating ceremony, while she remained busy in the kitchen and dining hall, overseeing details of dinner. Truckloads of food for tonight's celebration had arrived, along with the finest Lupine chefs in the country. All courtesy of J.J.

J.J. was Aiden's best friend, a billionaire rancher in Colorado who had turned out to be Nia's ally. It was J.J. who had supplied her horses with quality feed for free, and when she finally had to face facts, J.J. had bought all the horses at a ridiculously expensive price.

Letting go of her beloved mare was one of the hardest things Nia had ever done. But at least she knew Windstorm would be well cared for.

Nia went to her sister's basement apartment and paced, too anxious to sit.

"Sweetie, you're making me nervous." Niki looked up from the ancient Lupine texts. "It's going to be fine."

"How can I say these vows, knowing I'm a liar? What if Aiden finds out?" Nia ran a hand through her hair.

"Eventually he will. We can't keep this up forever."

"If it means keeping you away from Tristan, I could playact for the rest of my life."

Niki stared at her. "You can't protect me forever, Nia. The truth will come out. But by then, I'll have found a cure for the parvolupus and our boys will be saved. That's what matters the most. And by then, my life will have finally gained meaning. I'll have contributed some good to our people, instead of hiding here...like a fungus."

Guilt speared Nia. She went to her twin's side and knelt down, taking her hands. "I'm so sorry. I never wanted you to feel like a fungus."

Niki smiled and squeezed her hands. "Actually, I do like mushrooms. I didn't mean to sound bitchy or ungrateful. You've spent your entire life caring for me. I'm just a little antsy because I'm so close to finding the answers. And I'm worn out."

For the first time she noticed her twin's paleness and her air of exhaustion. "What's wrong?"

Niki shook her head. "Nothing. I've been working extra hours, that's all."

She kissed her twin's cheek. "Then rest. I have some things I need to wrap up."

Late that afternoon, Nia held a meeting in the ballroom. She gathered the elders of her pack, the women who held influence among the younger set, the ten women who knew the truth about herself and Nikita. The women had lost their mates, their older sons, to the disease striking their lands.

They had protected the twins' secret fiercely over the years.

Usually these meetings were best handled by her twin. Nikita had a gentle manner and winsome way of talking with the elders. But Niki was hunkered down in her basement apartment, and switching places with her this close to the mating ceremony was not advisable.

None of these women knew the disease was caused by Pandora's Chest. Nia herself didn't realize it until last year, when she found her father's diary. Up until then, she thought it was an illness caused by toxic fertilizer her father might have used, or another environmental cause. Or even bad magick.

In folding chairs assembled in a circle, they gathered around her. Dolores, the eldest, sat in her place of honor to the right of Nia's chair. Gray hair tied back in a prim bun, her floral dress tugged over her knees, Dolores exuded a grandmotherly air that soothed raw nerves.

Dolores alone had lost two sons, five grandsons and her mate to the disease. Now she stood to lose her beloved great-grandson as well if a cure was not found.

Too tense to sit, Nia paced. Her lower lip wobbled tremulously as she studied their careworn faces, the worry in their expressions. These women had helped hold the pack together, and their loyalty was astonishing. When everything collapsed and their men died, they remained out of sheer determination and a spirit of survival. She adored these women. Among them, she could be herself, and not her twin. They called her by name, and it felt wonderful.

But now it was time to let go.

Because I can't take care of you anymore. I've tried and tried, but it's not just the land that seems cursed now. It's as if a pall has settled over the entire ranch. I can't do this alone anymore.

"I wanted to meet with you to ask your help over the coming weeks to integrate our pack with Aiden

Mitchell's," she told them. "And I need your help to keep guarding Niki's secret. She is getting close to a cure for the parvolupus and we need to keep her attention focused on the cure and her life as stress free as possible."

"Anything, honey. You okay?" Dolores asked.

Nia rubbed the tense muscles in her neck.

"I will be. The younger, unmated females will be selecting mates from Aiden's pack. They'll need level heads guiding them, and I can think of none better than the women in this room. Throwing a group of innocent, sexually frustrated females in their prime at a group of male Lupines who are, ah, filled with certain urges…"

"That they haven't been able to satisfy with their hands because they're horny as hell," Dolores quipped.

Everyone laughed and the ice broke. Nia smiled. "They've probably been too busy roping calves. But yes, they will be very eager, and while I trust Aiden to control his men, I am entrusting all of you with the control of the women."

For the next several moments, she talked with the women, hearing their concerns, trying her best to answer them. Finally, as conversation died, she looked around the group.

"That's about it, unless there's anything else you wish to add."

"Nia, honey, is there anything else you need our help with?" Dolores asked.

At her headshake, Dolores stood and went to her. "On behalf of all of us, thank you."

Nia blinked. "For what?"

The elderly Lupine sighed. "For being our leader, honey. For working your fingers to the bone to care for us, make sure we never went without, keeping us together when everything seemed to fall apart. For putting us first, even when you lost your own."

"I thought you were disappointed in me," she whispered so the others wouldn't hear. "We don't have much food, and we've lost nearly everything. We have no money. I nearly lost the ranch...if Aiden hadn't have bought the note and kept the bank from foreclosing..."

"But we have each other and that's what counts most. We're family," Dolores said, her hands soft and the skin like velvet.

Guilt shot through her. "You lost your boys and grandsons and Arlen."

Dolores' eyes grew misty. "Honey, I not only lost them, I nearly lost my mind. And that didn't happen because of you. You spent every day and every night at my side, telling me to never give up and keep fighting. You forced me to eat, to drink, to live for my daughters and my granddaughters and great-granddaughters. It's because of you I'm standing here today, instead of swinging from that old oak tree by the pond."

Nia gawked. "Are you serious?"

Dolores hugged her tight. "You kept several of us from making that terrible decision. You were there for us in our darkest hours, refusing to let us surrender to the dark nights of our souls. You are one hell of a leader, Nia Blakemore. We love you. Thank you for leading us."

The women stood and applauded. And then they came up, one by one, and engulfed her in a huge bear hug.

"I love you all," she whispered. Fighting tears, she looked away.

When the last Lupine hugged her, she scrubbed at

her eyes with a fist. "It's not going to be easy, and there will be adjustments, but it's for the best."

A noise from the doorway drew her attention. Roxanne hurried into the ballroom, her entire body tensing. "Niki, are you finished with the meeting yet?" she asked in an overly loud voice.

She wiped her face with a lace hanky one of the women handed her and stuffed it into her pocket. "I'm done. Why? Do you need me?"

"Not me. But he's been pacing outside for twenty minutes, waiting for you." Roxanne jerked a thumb at the double doors. "And I think he's getting a little impatient."

The doors burst open and Aiden walked inside.

Nude, he held a length of rope in his hands. A black Stetson tilted at a rakish angle on his head, Aiden walked toward her. Nia gawked as the women gave him several admiring glances.

The naked cowboy. Dear goddess, he was stunning.

Aiden twirled the rope as he advanced.

"Mitchell! Put some clothes on!" Nia snapped.

"Why? Everyone here has already seen me naked. And for what I plan, I don't need clothing."

She backed away until hitting the wall. Aiden looked at the women. "Goodbye, ladies."

They scurried toward the double doors. Dolores glanced over her shoulder and gave Nia two thumbs up.

"Things will be looking up soon, dear! Remember that!" Dolores called out.

Oh yeah, it was going to be all *up* from here on. For Aiden, anyway.

"What the hell are you doing here?" she snapped, her earlier melancholy gone.

"I'm tired of waiting, Nikita. Come here. Now. It's time." He advanced, determination in his hard gaze. She couldn't stop staring at those powerful thighs, the fluid way he moved as he walked, the rippled muscles of his abdomen. He was a beast.

A magnificent, noble beast intent on claiming her.

"Time for what?" She began to sidle toward the door.

"Time to make you mine."

"You plan to rope me and throw me down like a damn calf?!"

"I could. But it would be more fun to catch you instead. Tonight will be all ceremony and formalities. I want to have fun with you, first."

He raised an eyebrow. "I'll give you sixty seconds. Run."

His wolf wanted the chase. Well, then. She could run pretty damn fast. Nia took off for the door, her feet scrambling for purchase on the slick floor. Looking over one shoulder, she saw Aiden striding toward her, lazily twirling the lasso. Confident, as if he had no doubt of his conquest.

Nia dodged around a leather couch against one wall, leapt over a small table in front of it.

"C'mere, little Lupine," he drawled. "I'm in the mood for riding."

Nia saw the doors, the handles gleaming like a promise of freedom. He wasn't going to win. Not this. She'd beat him. Almost there, almost there…

A lasso sailed over her head and arms, and pulled. She stumbled and almost fell, but caught herself.

"Yee haw," he said in a deep voice.

The rope bound her arms to her sides. He gave a

gentle tug. Nia wriggled her arms as he approached, coiling the rope as he advanced.

"Half the fun is the chase." Aiden's dark gaze gleamed. "I figure I've chased you long enough."

"And the other half?" she whispered.

Aiden pulled her toward him. "The capture."

His mouth covered hers. He gave her no time to think, to reason, to speak. His lips nuzzled the curve of her neck, and he lightly bit, soothing the sting with a stroke of his warm tongue. Nia struggled to free herself from the rope. She needed to touch him, damn it.

"Let me loose, Mitchell."

"I like you like this, Blakemore. You can't fight me." He blew a breath into her ear. "You're a prize mare I'm going to ride hard later."

"I'm not a damn horse!" She shuddered as he cupped her breast, thumbing her rigid nipple through the fabric of her blouse.

"No, you're every inch a wolf." He lightly pinched her nipple and then licked the curve of her ear. "Wild and wanton. But I will tame you to my hand. And you'll love every single minute of it."

"You're an arrogant prick!"

He grinned, and kissed the corner of her mouth. "My prick is the least arrogant thing about me."

Nia stared. Laughter danced in his dark eyes and his lips curved with amusement.

"You're toying with me. Playing," she realized. "Not serious."

Aiden loosened the lasso and lowered it, allowing her to step free. "I'll be serious enough later."

"Why did you do it," she asked, her tone gentler.

"I was searching for you. Missed you." A hint of

vulnerability shadowed his expression. "Then Roxanne told me you held a meeting of the pack's elders. I figured it was an emotional goodbye and you'd need a diversion. Making you angry is better than seeing you cry."

His thoughtfulness stunned her. Too choked up to speak, she rested her head against his broad chest. Aiden stroked her hair.

Finally, she pulled away slightly, glancing at his erect penis. Her hormones screamed for more. Getting caught by Aiden Mitchell made her so aroused, she needed a cold shower.

Very cold.

"You definitely provide an uplifting moment, Mitchell."

He grinned. "Very much so. All I have to do is see you, you saucy, stunning wolf. You're a walking Viagra pill."

"You're no slouch yourself, Mitchell. When you walked in here naked, you made all those women probably rush out to buy new batteries for their nighttime toys."

Aiden winked. "I wanted to give your women a show. Let them know you'll be in good hands."

He cupped her ass and squeezed gently. "Very good hands."

As they turned and headed for the doors, Aiden slid an arm around her waist. She saw Garth and Roxanne standing outside. The male lowered his head in respect as he glanced at her, and then shoved a burgundy fleece robe at Aiden.

"Here you go, boss."

Aiden shrugged into the robe, and Nia noted ruefully

that Roxanne didn't even pay him attention. Her beta's gaze was soft as she studied Garth.

The two males fell into step as they walked down the hall, Garth filling Aiden in on the latest patrols. Nia accompanied Roxanne in silence, lost in thought. It would break her heart to lose this magnificent male. According to the rules of the Mating Challenge, he really did belong to Nikita, but a small part of her stubbornly wanted him for herself. Even if only for one night.

You may not have him for much longer, if you don't find the cure.

Her priorities were clear. Saving her twin had been paramount in her life.

And now saving Aiden from the same fate as her father and brothers became equally important.

CHAPTER 7

The time had come.

Nia had only attended two other Lupine weddings. She wasn't good at formal ceremonies and etiquette. Nikita had been happy to take her place and act as alpha representative for the pack, an irony not lost on the twins.

But tonight her twin remained in her basement, not daring to attend the ceremony lest someone discover her presence. How she wished her sister could be here! Nikita should be here, standing at her side with a bouquet of red roses, lending her support. Witnessing her transformation from single alpha leader to a mated one.

Or taking her place, for Nikita was the true alpha leader.

Dressed in a long, flowing white gown, a circlet of white roses upon her head and white satin shoes upon her feet, Nia stood with Aiden in the pasture by the barn, the only area large enough to accommodate the 400-plus wedding guests. His men had worked hard to transform the area, hauling in chairs and placing them before a white trellis covered with hothouse roses and wisteria. J.J., the alpha Aiden had chosen to officiate, handed Aiden the ceremonial knife.

If only she could stop shaking inside, but that was impossible, because this entire ceremony was a lie. And if Aiden discovered she was not the true alpha, he would be furious.

She and Aiden then sliced their palms with the blade and clasped hands, their mingled blood dripping to the earth and sinking into it. J.J. bound their right wrists together with a leather cord. "May you always be tied together by the bonds of loyalty, courage, strength, and love."

Nia stared at Aiden, her heart pounding so hard she knew he could hear it.

She forced her voice to remain steady as she spoke her vows to Aiden, wishing with all her heart she could honor them to her last dying day. "I, Nikita Blakemore, alpha of the Blakemore pack, take you Aiden Mitchell, of my own free will, as my mate. I promise to honor and respect you, to love and cherish you with my body and my spirit, to stand by your side as our alpha leader and support you above all others, and to be yours, forever."

Misery filled her. The vows were sacred to their people and she violated them with her lies. If he found out, Aiden could declare the mating annulled. Maybe he would foreclose on the ranch and leave with his men. And she and her females would be left alone once more.

But as Aiden stared into her eyes, his expression soft, she pushed aside her fears. Tenderness filled her as she noticed his hand shook a little. Then he gathered her hands into his, his palms strong and warm, such lovely warmth.

Perhaps he did care for her, the real her, not the image of her as an alpha.

"I, Aiden Mitchell, alpha leader of the Mitchell pack, take you Nikita Blakemore, of my own free will, as my mate. I promise to honor and respect you, to love and cherish you with my body and my spirit, to stand by your side as my alpha female and support you above all others, and to be yours, forever."

His gaze remained steady. "I promise to protect you with my body, your honor with my spirit, and defend our packs and you to the last drop of my blood."

To the last drop of his blood. It wasn't a vow made lightly, and far as she knew, only alphas fully committed to their mates uttered it at the ceremony.

Guilt wrestled with joy as she thought of the horrific consequences of impersonating her twin. She could not speak, only close her eyes as he kissed her, his mouth firm, warm, and authoritative.

When he pulled away, he signaled to Darius and Garth.

They headed across the lawn, where tables and chairs had been set up beneath an enormous white tent. Aiden stated he was fully committed to her. But how could she state the same, when this whole ceremony was a farce?

Oh, she had plenty of good reasons, and the foremost one was to protect her twin, not to mention save her pack. Raids from gnomes and the drain on their finances left them desperate. But those rationalizations wouldn't make this wrong right.

Aiden thought he mated with the alpha female leader of the Blakemore pack. Not her twin sister. But the moment she unveiled her sister, she put Nikita in danger of exposure to the Silver Wizard. Nikita was terrified of Tristan. And after spending her entire life hiding her sister's existence to protect her, Nia wasn't about to tell the truth.

Her new mate guided her to the head table, decorated with white and red roses. A cool wind blew through the trees, rustling the leaves, raising gooseflesh on her bare arms. The thousands of tiny blue-white bulbs strung on the tent ceiling sparkled like fairy light. It gave the tent a mystical, ethereal touch.

Covered with red linen tablecloths, each table bore a squat glass vase of red roses, white hyacinth, and honeysuckle. Aiden sat and then pulled Nia onto his lap to feed her the ceremonial first bite of their wedding dinner. Her mouth curled into a smile as she noticed what he'd chosen for her to eat.

Sausage.

"You're never without surprises, Mitchell," she told him.

"I always aim to make you laugh, Blakemore." Aiden speared the sausage and held it to her mouth.

"So you may never go hungry. I will always keep you satisfied, in every way possible," he murmured as she ate it.

Their hands still tied together, Nia lifted the silver cup filled with water to his mouth, trying to control her shaking hand. Sweat trickled down her back. With every ounce of her strength, she controlled her nervousness.

"So you may never thirst for another's touch except mine. I will always quench your spirit," she told him in the traditional vow.

He kissed her then, his mouth moving over hers.

Fear filled her at the thought of this powerful male taking her in the traditional way later. They must consummate their union before members of the pack to assure their people their union was sealed.

But Aiden didn't know he had mated a liar.

"Niki." Aiden lifted their joined hands and settled his palm on her face. "Don't be frightened. I'm going to take very good care of you, sweetheart."

Then they untied the leather cord and settled in for the wedding feast.

After a while, Aiden stood and excused himself. Nia sipped champagne and watched the dancing.

Upon a raised wood dais, a band played as the guests danced. The wolves laughed and twirled and stomped upon the wood platform. All the cheerful energy filled the air and chased away her morose thoughts. She sipped champagne, relishing the tingle of it against her tongue. A glass filled with green liquid sat by her plate, along with a slotted silver spoon and a bowl filled with sugar cubes. She would not drink the absinthe, the traditional mating drink of Lupines. It made females amorous, but also dulled their wits and she needed all her wits to keep up the masquerade of being the alpha leader of the Blakemore pack.

Beth, Aiden's niece, and her mate Dale came over to wish her congratulations. She liked Beth, who was smart and funny. Dale, Aiden's chief of security, was quiet, and clearly devoted to his mate.

Shortly after they left, Aiden returned, ignoring the slightly bowed heads as he passed, and sat beside her. He wore a well-tailored black silk tuxedo, which looked elegant on him. He was so handsome, whether in evening clothes or in dusty blue jeans.

Or naked.

He looked at her plate. "You need to eat, darling."

"I'm not that hungry."

He pulled her onto his lap and then pushed a hand through her hair, his calloused fingertips stroking her scalp. It felt so damn good. She didn't want this, didn't want his touch. Because she could get accustomed to this, and when he left her after finding out she was the wrong twin, she'd miss him too damn much.

Not to mention what consequences she might face, oh hell, the entire pack might face. What if Aiden became so infuriated he foreclosed on the ranch, leaving them all homeless?

Aiden slid a hand over her neck, feeling her galloping pulse. He smoothed back her hair. "You're nervous as a scared filly. It's all right, darling. Formalities and then it'll be over with, and we'll return to your bedroom. I'll take very good care of you, sweetheart."

The rules of the Mating Challenge required them to mate before their combined packs to consummate their union. Then they would shift and run as wolves. The mating would be hard enough. Nia felt his erection press against her thigh. Oh yeah, very hard. But shifting in front of the pack when she'd had so little fresh meat over the past few months?

She didn't like being humiliated.

Nia climbed off his lap, sat in her chair, speared a piece of meat and ate it. Aiden looked up and signaled to someone. Beside him, Darius dug into his steak.

A waiter in a white jacket and black pants hurried over with a plate. On the plate was a raw slice of liver.

Sam, sitting beside Darius, craned her head. "What's that?"

"A special treat for my bride. Her favorite meal," Aiden said.

Sam made a face. "Yuck."

Darius grinned at his mate. "Hush and eat your veggies. If you're good, maybe Nikita will give you all hers."

Aiden thanked the waiter and set the plate down, pushing aside the pretty china filled with vegetables, sausage and steak.

"Raw liver is the best thing for Lupines who need fresh meat. It gives us energy and empowers our magick," he said quietly.

Nia looked at the meat, her wolf senses clawing to the surface. She looked at the man who was now her mate and saw the concern in his gaze.

He knew. He knew she had trouble shifting, and wanted to amend it without embarrassing her. Emotion filled her throat.

"Thank you," she said quietly.

"I'll always take good care of you," he said in a husky voice.

She picked up her knife and fork and began to delicately cut the treat.

When the last slice was finished, she felt new strength fill her. The protein had infused her body with energy, just as Aiden had promised.

Nia sipped her water. At a nearby table, Carl flirted with Lucy, one of Nia's pack. Lucy smiled, but seemed tense.

Nia detested Carl, who owned a grocery and supply store. She owed him thousands of dollars. Angular and skinny, he had a thin oval of a face and bore a constant sneer, as if his tighty whities were way too tight. He always found an excuse to visit her ranch to point out how much she owed, and Nia had ensured he never stayed long. He reminded her more of a troll than a Lupine. When he'd found out she was mating Aiden, he'd conned her into giving him an invitation. She had run up too much credit at his store to snub him.

Tempted to rescue Lucy, she was relieved to see Carl distracted by the arrival of his food.

Aiden squeezed her hand. "It's good to see everyone here. Have to admit, I'm a little disappointed. I thought Tristan would show up."

Her heart fell to her stomach. "The Silver Wizard is a friend of yours?"

"Not exactly. But an event this significant, a mating between two alphas, is something he'd seldom miss." Aiden grunted. "Besides, that silver devil once told me I'd never claim you as my virgin mate. I'll never forget that. He said, 'Nikita will surrender her virginity to me.'"

Breath fled her lungs. Oh gods, oh gods. *Does he know? Does Tristan know?* Whipping her head around, she searched the guests in case the wizard hid among them. Nia fought the urge to bolt from the table and run to the basement for her twin.

She managed to find her voice, though it was shaky. "A-and what does that mean?"

Aiden shrugged. "He's a sly wizard, always talking in riddles. I believe he was testing me, see how far I'd go to make you mine."

He picked up their joined hands and kissed her knuckles. "And now you know how far I'd go, sweetheart. You okay? You look a little pale."

Her stomach knotted painfully. Nia licked her lips.

THE MATING CHALLENGE

"Maybe he didn't have a mating gift for you. That's why he didn't show up."

The feeble joke made Aiden glance at her. "Sometimes a gift from one of those wizards has a double meaning."

"And sometimes a gift is just a gift," a deep, disembodied voice said.

Nia gripped Aiden's hand so hard he winced. Please no, please no....

"Show yourself," Aiden demanded.

A cloud of white smoke appeared. Out of the cloud stepped a dark-haired man well over six feet tall. Dressed in a black silk tuxedo, with a white shirt with white crystal buttons, he was quite handsome and looked to be about her age, but she knew he was ancient.

A well-trimmed dark beard shadowed his square jawline. His dark hair curled at the edges, each strand tipped with a shiny white crystal. His eyes were a clear blue-gray. An aura of immense power shimmered around him, making her very afraid.

Not Tristan. She knew this from childhood and her father's grim tales about the powerful wizard with the black hair tipped with silver. Nia wondered what this particular wizard wanted.

J.J. sitting near Aiden at the head table, stared at the newcomer. "Xavier? What are you doing here?"

"Hello J.J. Good to see you." His gaze softened as he looked at Alexa, J.J.'s mate, "Alexa. Congratulations on your baby."

Alexa colored and smiled, placing a hand over her rounded belly.

Then the wizard turned back to Aiden. He gave a

little nod. "I am Xavier, the Crystal Wizard, one of the four wizards of the Brehon who rule over Others. I came to offer you both congratulations from Tristan, your guardian and your judge. He asked me to send his regards on his behalf."

Xavier looked directly at Nia. "He felt it would not be appropriate to show up on this joyous occasion since his appearance has the tendency to cause Lupines distress."

Distress? How about a heart attack?

The Crystal Wizard reached into his jacket and withdrew a quartz crystal the size of a man's thumb. It was filled with red fluid. He tossed it upwards and it spun in the air, above his outstretched palm.

"Tristan wished me to give you this as a mating gift. This magick crystal contains the tears of the dragon. A most rare, and precious gift. It enables you to bring someone back from the brink of death. But beware. The price can be deadly."

Aiden looked at the spinning crystal. "Interesting. Never heard of it. How does it work?"

"You hold the crystal next to your heart, and it drains your magick and infuses the tears. Then you place the crystal into the mouth of the dying person. It will dissolve, releasing the potion." The crystal spun faster, tossing off brilliant sparks of light. "It can only be used once, and the one using it to save a life risks his..."

The wizard focused his burning blue-gray gaze at Nia. "Or her life, for a Lupine without magick is doomed. A Lupine without magick cannot live with other Lupines, for he...or she...will be seen as a weakness in the pack."

Nia almost felt as if this wizard could see inside her soul. She gripped Aiden's hand, wishing she could flee. Sooner or later the deception would be unveiled. And then what?

"Thank you," she managed to say in a somewhat steady voice.

The crystal stopped spinning and Xavier placed it on the table before them.

"Yes, thank you." Aiden's dark gaze sharpened. "But why did Tristan send you instead of one of the other wizards?"

Xavier gave a humorless smile. "I offered to do this for Tristan because I wanted to check on one of my people. A troll."

Nia turned in the direction of his pointing finger and saw Carl, who was eating his food as if it were his last supper. "He's a troll? He told me he was Lupine."

More surprises. And please, no more. She wasn't certain her racing heart could take any more shocks.

Xavier nodded grimly. "He has mixed blood, but is more troll than Lupine."

The band struck up a slow dance. His mouth tight beneath his dark beard, Xavier watched as Carl tugged Lucy onto the dance floor. Nia tensed, seeing how unhappy the girl looked. Leaning against the bar near the dance floor, a cowboy named Stephen sulked as he glared at Carl.

"Lucy is far too young for Carl," Aiden murmured.

"And she likes Stephen from your pack. I tried to seat them together, but that rat bastard Carl switched places." Nia sighed. "Aiden, will you rescue her?"

But before Aiden rose, Xavier gave a grim smile. "Excuse me. I am in the mood for a dance."

Suddenly Carl stumbled over his own feet, and released Lucy. Xavier cut in smoothly and began dancing with her.

Aiden grinned as he looked at J.J., who grinned back.

"Oh, this is going to be good," J.J. said. "Xavier doesn't mess around."

Xavier whirled Lucy around, who looked immensely relieved to be rid of Carl. He danced her over to the glowering Stephen, practically throwing her at the cowboy. Stephen recoiled and caught Lucy in his arms. She looked up at him with a wide smile.

Xavier gave a little bow. "My apologies, fair maiden, but I am exhausted. Perhaps this handsome young man can take my place."

He winked at the blushing Lucy. Grinning, Stephen led her onto the dance floor. Carl started toward them, but then Xavier blocked his way.

The wizard suddenly flicked a finger and Carl's trousers vanished, leaving him clad only in his underwear. Red-faced, Carl bolted, fleeing as if the hounds of hell pursued him.

Xavier returned to stand before the head table, his smile grim. "It appears Carl will not be able to dance with Lucy nor eat dinner next to her any longer. He suddenly remembered he was not properly dressed."

Aiden and J.J. laughed, but Nia felt confused. All her life she'd been told the wizards were cold, uncaring and dangerous. This kind gesture contradicted everything her father had said.

"Why did you set up Lucy and Stephen?" she asked.

"Because Lucy wants Stephen, but she is too shy to admit it. Stephen wants Lucy, but he's bashful as well.

Sometimes young love must be coaxed to blossom." Xavier's gaze twinkled. "We wizards are not all bad, my lady."

"I'll say," J.J. put in. "If not for you, my cousin would have died a terrible death."

The Crystal Wizard nodded at J.J. Then he turned his attention back to Nia, his gaze softening. "Do not fear me…Aiden's mate. I am here to help you. Again, my congratulations on your union. May you have a long, happy and fruitful mating with the one your heart desires. Cherish each other and always be truthful."

The irony of his words was not lost on her.

Aiden stood and offered his palm. Xavier shook it.

"Will you stay and have something to eat and drink?" Aiden asked.

The wizard gave a formal bow. "Thank you, but I am required elsewhere."

"Stay," J.J. urged. "You're dressed for the occasion. And we never did formally thank you for saving my cousin."

Xavier shook his head. "I have a car show to attend. There is the sweetest red Mustang convertible I've had my eye on for some time."

He waved a hand and the formal wear vanished, replaced by a black leather jacket, white T-shirt and blue jeans with the cuffs rolled up, exposing white socks and shiny loafers. His hair was slicked back and the beard had vanished. He looked like a teenager instead of an ancient wizard shimmering with power.

"The Fifties was a wonderful era. My favorite. Tristan accuses me of living in the past. But at least I am living in the last century, not the Dark Ages like he does."

Then he winked at Nia, and some of the tension fled her tight muscles.

Waving a hand, the wizard disappeared.

Nia dragged in a deep breath and then gulped down some water. Gods, that was intense. Aiden shook the crystal, and the liquid inside it seemed to glow.

"Interesting gift. Hopefully we'll never have need of it." He placed it inside his jacket.

She managed to take several bites of her dinner. Then Nia brightened as her niece, Lexie, approached the head table with her mate, Jackson. Nia stood as Lexie rounded the table and then engulfed her in a tight hug.

"Congratulations, Aunt Niki. I hope you'll be as happy with Aiden as Jackson and I have been." Lexie's gaze grew troubled. "You should have more family than just me to celebrate your special day.

Nia's throat tightened and she squeezed Lexie's shoulders affectionately. Nia had never known her older sister, who had left the pack before the twins' birth in order to mate with a wild, rugged Lupine their father disapproved of.

Nia held out her hand to Jackson, watching him with a guarded look. "Welcome to my ranch," she told the tall, lean cowboy.

Jackson pushed back his black Stetson and shook Nia's hand. "Thank you for having us," he said in an equally polite voice. "I hope you'll be happy."

Nia smiled, and her expression softened as she gazed at her beloved niece. She tucked a strand of hair behind Lexie's ear. "You've taken good care of my niece, Jackson. That makes me very happy."

As Jackson and Lexie returned to their seats, Nia sat

and watched the dancing. Suddenly Aiden stood and pulled her to her feet as the band played a slow song. She went into his arms and everyone respectfully walked to the side to give them the entire dance floor.

Closing her eyes, she rested her head on his broad shoulder, moving against him in time to the music. Aiden held her close, humming along.

Being in his arms threatened to make her lose all common sense. Nia felt the pressure of pretense slip away.

Aiden began to sing in a low tenor. Nia's entire body relaxed. She moved in rhythm to his swaying hips, cherishing his touch.

And then she realized how dangerous this was, how she was letting down her guard. Bad idea. Would she next start blabbing secrets?

Hey, my sister is the eldest twin, but my father told everyone she died and only the younger twin survived. I've pretended to be her since birth to protect her from the Silver Wizard. See, there's a prophecy in our family that the eldest girl twin will be spirited away by the Silver Wizard, who will take her away to the afterworld and then she'll die. So my parents hid Nikita from birth and I just pretended to be the only female all these years. No twins. Just me.

And as a nice bonus prize, our whole damn pack is cursed because of Pandora's Chest. All our males die when they reach puberty. Guess you didn't realize all this was part of the package, huh?

Nia lifted her head and looked at him. He stared down at her, still singing the love song. She didn't love him, couldn't love him and this was a match of convenience and power, not feelings. Gazing around the room, she saw several satisfied smiles that told her several Lupines thought she was smitten with Aiden and he had her wrapped around his finger.

No way.

She threw back her head and released a long, mournful wolf howl.

Everyone laughed. Aiden's expression shuttered but not before she glimpsed the heat in his gaze and a promise.

"I'll get you for that later, Blakemore, when I make you howl for a much different reason," he murmured.

Finally the music ended and they returned to their table. Nia wriggled her toes inside the white shoes.

Now that she'd had plenty of raw meat to consume, she felt the influence of the full moon coaxing out her wolf. Who needed absinthe when one was fully Lupine, and the moon caressed them with her silvery glow?

Careful. Don't drop your guard lest he find out who you really are.

Darius and Kyle came to their table. "Aiden, it's time," Darius said, giving him a significant look.

Aiden picked up her hand and kissed the back of it, his lips warm and firm against her knuckles. "Stay here, enjoy. I have some matters to attend to. I'll be back soon."

He rose, all power and grace, and walked off with Darius and Kyle. Watching him, she felt desire, and apprehension, flood her body. Privacy for an alpha was rare in a pack; she had guarded hers with zeal over the years. Now she would have to share her bed, her home and her body with this big alpha.

And mate with him before their combined packs. Nia fingered the glass of absinthe. Maybe she should indulge. Take the edge off her nervousness. She picked up a cube of sugar to place on the slotted spoon, put the spoon over the glass and then reached for the nearby pitcher of ice water to dilute the mixture.

Hair rose on her nape. She turned her head, noticed there were several males from Aiden's pack watching her carefully.

A real alpha, like Aiden, would not dilute the mixture. Neither would a female alpha determined to match her man's strength when they consummated their union.

Nia removed the spoon and the sugar, set them aside. She took a small sip, grimacing at the sickly sweet licorice taste. She set down the glass.

Holy crap. The tables before her began to grow blurry. This was a sip? What would happen if she downed the entire glass without diluting it? Would the tables and their occupants start whirling around like spinning tops?

She couldn't risk it. But she had spent her entire life pretending to be something she was not and knew she could continue to pull this off.

Nia poked at the glass with a little sniff. She said in a loud, clear voice, "No wonder Mitchell didn't touch his. It tastes like old socks mixed with gasoline. And they call this Viagra for Lupines? I don't need this. If Mitchell can't get my motor running, no drink is going to help."

Someone snickered and out of the corner of her eye, she saw a few male nods of approval. Sitting nearby, Sam shook her head, then moved over to sit next to her.

"Those guys," she said, waving at the males in Aiden's pack, "think that they are walking Viagra. It's a trait in the Mitchell pack. But they're good men, all of them. They work hard and they will fight to the death for Aiden, and now that you are mated, they will do the same for you."

Nia thought of how her brothers and father would have done the same and a lump rose in her throat. Her family should be here at her mating day, and most of them were buried beneath the cold, uncaring earth.

She traced a line on the tablecloth, trying to remember the last time she'd attended a festive pack event. Unfortunately, those had been rare over the past few years. "It's a challenge, leading a pack. I'm certain it's been even more of a challenge for Aiden with struggling to control his males. You always have to consider your people's welfare before your own."

The absinthe was making her tongue loose. Yet for once she longed to confide in a female friend. Her twin didn't understand the burdens Nia carried, and Nia never wanted Nikita to worry about anything. Nikita had spent her entire life in the shadows, hiding, and her twin's lack of a real life was a burden enough.

"I know the main reason Mitchell wanted me was for my pack and all the females in it. This is a mating of convenience more than anything." She lifted her shoulders. "And you can tell that we have no males in our pack. I miss having them around, miss their humor, and how protective they were of us, their wisdom and their caring."

Sympathy filled Sam's eyes. "Did you lose your father?"

The lump in her throat threatened to choke off her breath. Nia nodded, struggling to maintain her composure. "And my two brothers. They were good Lupines."

She bit her lip, knowing she must not say more. "We fell on very hard times."

"And you kept your people together. That takes tremendous strength," Sam said, touching her hand. "I'm glad you have Aiden now at your side."

Nia gave a small smile. "I don't really 'have' him. He's very much an alpha who will do as he pleases."

The half-Lupine, half-Elf looked solemn. She gazed around the tent at the couples on the dance floor. The males from the Mitchell pack had begun to pair off, a fact Nia planned to use for getting them off the ranch. The fewer males who were on her property, the fewer worries she faced.

"Aiden is a good male," Sam said quietly. "He's tough, but fair. I'm sure it won't be an easy adjustment, but it never is with a male of great worth because they all come with their own traits. I hope he will make you as happy as Darius has made me. Aiden's suffered a lot in the past, and he never talks about it, but you can see it in his eyes."

Nia's heart softened. She had seen the same torment shadowing the alpha's eyes once in a while, but he always masked it with cool indifference.

Sam smiled. "I can also see how much he cares about you."

That wasn't affection. It was lust, but she could handle lust. Primitive, carnal desire. Love? She loved her twin, and her pack, and had sacrificed too much in life to share her heart with Aiden. Love was selfish. It demanded attention, and falling in love with a powerful alpha like Aiden could be her downfall. Love would derail her fierce devotion to her twin, her desire to save her pack, and maybe even loosen her tongue, unveiling the deception necessary to keeping her twin's existence a secret.

Nia took in a deep breath. She had lost every single male she'd ever loved. She had to mate Aiden to save her ranch, but she could not love him and risk her heart. The emotional demands of love were a trap. You fell in love and then grieved when you lost that person.

Still, a small part of her longed to know what it was like to be cherished and cared for the way Darius cared for Sam.

Sam squeezed her hand. "Let your inhibitions go and release your inner wolf. Darius and I had a very, um, primitive first time together. We had to endure a Mating Rite. It was savage."

Nia stared. A Mating Rite was brutal, even for a full-blooded Lupine. "You're very brave."

"No." Sam glanced up and her expression softened. Nia watched her look across the tent as Aiden approached, flanked by Kyle and Darius. "I'm very much in love with my man. Love makes all the difference in a very public and primitive ceremony like a Mating Rite. Or a Mating Challenge."

But Aiden didn't love her. Nia's heart squeezed tight in her chest as Darius reached the table and picked up Sam's hand, gently kissing it. His eyes were filled with tenderness and desire as he gazed at his mate.

Aiden's gaze was filled with heat as he held out a hand to Nia. "Come. It's time."

She rose, took his hand, knowing her duty, knowing this was another role she must fill. Deep inside, she wished she could glimpse a little of the love and tenderness in Aiden's eyes that Darius showed for his mate.

His palm was strong, yet his grip gentle as Aiden led her into the main lodge. Nia had read about this for many months, had mentally prepared herself for the eventuality of the challenge.

Mandy had turned a guest bedroom into a dressing chamber for the event. It was carpeted, had pegs for clothing, a small bathroom with a shower, and a dressing table with a lighted mirror. When she went into the forest to mate with Aiden, nothing could be on her skin. No lotions, powders or scents other than her own.

The rules were quite specific. If she violated them, she risked someone from Aiden's pack complaining, perhaps even enough to draw the attention of Tristan, the Silver Wizard.

No thanks. She'd play by the book.

But now as she and Aiden entered the room to shed their clothing before they would walk to the forest for the consummation of their union before their packs, Nia felt no confidence.

All she felt was a terrible sense of loss.

Her twin should be here, reassuring her. Her mother. Someone from her family who would make her laugh, ease her apprehension.

Instead, she faced Aiden, her new mate, who turned and closed the door behind them. Lights from the overhead fixtures filled the room with glaring white light. Nothing to hide. Mandy had tried to make the atmosphere softer by burning several candles in jars upon the shelves, but the lighting made the room cold and impersonal.

Nervousness churned inside her stomach, which felt as if she'd swallowed ground glass. She hated this. A mating should have love and tenderness, not this ritualistic formality.

Aiden leaned against the closed door. "I thought you'd be more comfortable if we changed into these for our walk to the forest."

He pointed to the white robes hanging on the pegs.

Nia blinked. "Isn't that a violation of the rules? I thought we were to be bare skinned."

"The rules can be bent." His dark gaze was unwavering. "I want you to feel as relaxed as possible, Niki."

Relaxed? She'd never felt this awkward before. She'd never even undressed before a man. Nia's insides quivered. Maybe if he didn't call her by her twin's name, it would feel better and she could pretend that there was love between them, pretend Aiden cherished her.

"I wish we didn't have to do this," she murmured.

"I don't like this either. But we have no choice. We have to adhere to the rules of the challenge. As much as I want us to have privacy for our first time together, we can't. We have to set the example as alphas."

If only I were the true alpha of my pack.

Aiden seemed larger than life, sucking up all the space in the dressing room. The scent of him overpowered her senses. Musk, spices, and pine. All man.

All wolf.

And soon this wolf would lay claim to her body, taking her in the traditional Lupine manner of an alpha claiming his mate. Only the consummation of their union would be done before their united packs.

She could barely look at him, couldn't even summon

a flicker of desire at this moment. Nia was too nervous.

He jammed his hands into the pockets of his trousers. They were such nice trousers, and he'd ruin them.

"Honey, what's wrong?"

She hugged herself. "I can't do this."

Aiden approached, his manner relaxed and easy. "It's just the two of us now. You've already seen me naked. Undress for me, darling. There's no one else here to see. Only me."

She'd have to remove her clothing either here or in the forest. The forest would be darker, but this was far more private.

Nia swallowed hard, and turned around. "Unzip me, please."

She felt his fingers brush against her back as he slid the zipper downward. Aiden stepped back.

Nia wriggled out of the white gown and let it puddle at her feet. She slipped out of the white satin pumps.

She had not worn stockings. Only her satin bra and the white matching panties remained between herself and total nudity.

Steeling herself, she slid the panties down, past her wide hips, wriggled out of them and tossed them aside. Last, she fumbled with the heavy bra. Nia unfastened the hooks and let it drop to the floor. Air brushed against her skin and her sensitive nipples. She stared at the wall, a flush igniting her face as she crossed her arms over her breasts.

Never had she felt this exposed.

Aiden stepped close, slid a thumb beneath her chin. He tipped up her face to meet his eyes. Warmth, and deep tenderness lingered in his smoldering gaze.

"You're so beautiful," he said hoarsely. "So damn lovely. Better than all my dreams."

Very gently he took her hands and removed them from her breasts. Nia stared at his solemn expression.

"You have an unfair advantage, Mitchell. You're still wearing clothing."

"True, that."

Aiden sat on the bench to remove his shoes and socks. Standing, he tore off his tie, shrugged out of his jacket and then unbuttoned his shirt, shrugging out of it. He hung both on a clothing peg. Nia's breath hitched at the sight of his warm, tanned skin. Muscles rippled below his skin. She studied his ridged abdomen and felt her arousal kick up several notches.

Then he unbuckled his belt, and unzipped his trousers and pulled them down, along with his boxers. He stepped out of the clothing, and hung both trousers and boxers on the pegs.

Nude, he stood before her, his erection nearly reaching his belly button. Nia licked her lips, not sure if she should quiver with fear or rejoice at his size.

Wow.

He was alpha. No doubt about that.

He stepped forward and looked down at her. "No one here but us, Niki. Only you and me."

This big male desired her, only her. And soon he would be exclusively hers in bed, just as he'd make her his own.

She would not think of the consequences if anyone discovered she wasn't the true alpha. Tonight, she wanted to think only of Aiden, and fulfilling the sexual desire she'd held for him ever since she first saw him years ago.

"Niki," he said thickly. "I've wanted you for so long. I couldn't wait any longer, wolf. You drove me crazy. If I couldn't have you, I'd die."

It wasn't a declaration of love, but passion filled his voice. Tonight, passion would suffice.

She wanted to run her hands up his back, over the thick muscles, and then downward, touching the slope of his firm ass. Nia thought about him pumping that ass as he took her and her arousal sharpened. The forest would be dark and she would ignore the packs, focusing only on Aiden and his fierce need for her.

But the rules of the challenge were clear. No sexual touching after they had spoken their vows, then they would consummate their union before the packs.

Ever since she'd set eyes on Aiden, she'd wanted him, wanted him with a ferocity that she'd never claimed. Nia denied her feelings, concentrated on her people, and pushed aside desire. Nervousness rippled over her body. When you wanted something for so very long, and the very thing you wanted stood, larger than life before you, it was hard to believe it was real.

Aiden took her hand, guided her over to the dressing table. "Sit. Face me."

She did.

A small smile played on his full lips. "Relax. I'm not going to eat you."

"Pity," she murmured.

His smiled turned wicked. "Vixen."

"Wolf," she corrected.

All those fantasies she'd had late at night, pleasuring herself and thinking of Aiden as she did so, now surged to the surface. This was real and intimate. Too intimate.

As if he read her mind, Aiden walked over to the

light switch and flipped it off. Candlelight played over his honed muscles, danced over the chiseled angles of his face.

He dominated the space in the room, sucked it up by the sheer power of his presence. Dominated it as he would soon dominate her.

But there was a smile lifting the corner of his mouth, a smile filled with wicked promise. No trace of the big, arrogant alpha. Except for the desire always on the surface.

Feeling shy again, she covered her breasts.

"You are perfect. You have nothing to hide." Aiden took her hands and placed them at her side.

A lick of scent threaded through the air, her desire and his intense, male smell of forest and spices. Nia drew in a breath.

"Spread your legs."

She bit her lip and balked.

"Do it." He gentled his voice. "Please, honey."

Flushing with heat and embarrassment, she opened her thighs wide. He sank to his knees before her, like a supplicant. It made her feel more relaxed, instead of him towering over her. He was a big man.

She resisted looking at his groin. In more ways than one.

Aiden drew in a breath as he stared at her center. "You're so perfect. Wet and glistening, like dew on a rose."

Nia trembled.

"Did you ever touch yourself at night, thinking of me?" He rested his hands on her thighs.

She said nothing, not wanting to give him that power.

"I stroked myself a lot at night, thinking of you."

She stared at him. "Really?"

That same, intimate smile filled with heat. "Really. I'd take my cock in hand in the shower, and think of you. Dreaming of this moment when we'd be alone together, naked."

His voice deepened. "Ever since I saw you, pixie, I've wanted no one else but you as my mate. And I knew I had to have you. Until I claimed you, I had to be content with my fist."

Only her? Or did he want the alpha of the pack? She licked her lips. His crude words evoked an image that made her body pulse with need. Aiden alone in the shower, his head thrown back, his eyes closed as he pumped a fist over his erection, thinking of her…

"Only me? Why me? Because of my looks?" she whispered. Gods, she needed to know it was really her in his mind, not the image of her as alpha. Or her twin. They looked alike. What if it was really Nikita he desired?

His gaze became filled with heat and a fierceness she didn't understand. "You're a fine-looking Lupine, sweetheart, but that's not it. It's you. Your passion, your spirit, what drives you…" he pointed to her chest, "as much as it drives me. Pack. Everything for your people. When I first met you that day in the pasture, I recognized a kindred spirit. A woman who would not hesitate to do anything for her people. Make sacrifices and put her own personal needs aside for the sake of pack. I saw that in you, and I said to myself, 'That is the only woman for me.'"

Damn him, Aiden Mitchell. He'd said the only thing that she'd ever longed to hear…that she was special and unique. Not her twin. Just her. Perhaps some women needed reassurances of their beauty or their intelligence. Nia did not.

She wanted someone to recognize she was different from her twin.

His voice dropped a notch. "I'm no saint, Blakemore. I saw you, a strong alpha female who would make a perfect mate, and all I could feel was this need, this intense fucking need that I've never felt before. It took all my control not to chase after you on my horse, tumble you to the ground, strip you naked and fuck you senseless. I'm dying here, because I want you so badly I'm shaking."

Nia could barely breathe as his chest heaved in and out and she saw him quiver, like a restless horse eager for a gallop.

Or to mount a filly…

Aiden drew in a deep breath. "Relax, baby. Breathe in and out for me."

She did.

"Now imagine my hands on your legs, sliding up your thighs. Your soft, warm skin. You're trembling because you know what I'm going to do."

His voice deepened to a husky rumble. "I'm going to touch you. You want me to touch you there."

Tiny muscles in her sex throbbed and pulsed, as if he'd stroked a finger over her wet folds. Nia squeezed her vagina tight, knowing she grew wetter at the heat in his words.

"Do you want me to touch you?" he asked in a husky voice.

She nodded.

"I can't." Real regret sounded in his voice. "The

rules are I can't touch you sexually, not until we are in the forest, surrounded by pack."

His gaze darkened to pitch. "But there are no rules about me watching you touch yourself."

Breath left her lungs in a whoosh.

"Do it, Niki. Touch yourself, baby."

He took her hand, kissed the back, then guided it between her opened legs. "Close your eyes and see me caressing you."

Nia closed her eyes and leaned against the table.

"First, I'd touch your thigh. So warm and soft. I've been dying to touch you there. You have amazing legs and your skin is like velvet," he murmured, his deep voice like a brush of dark chocolate against her tongue.

Nia slid her hand up her thigh.

"Then I'd work my way up, making certain you were slick and ready for me. I'd want to taste you, feel the wetness of your juices beneath my tongue, like the sweetest, syrupy fruit."

Her fingers trembled as they made contact with her soaked folds. With a butterfly touch, she slid a finger through her cleft, feeling the slippery evidence of her desire.

"Do it," he ordered. "Feel yourself and imagine it's me doing it...teasing, light, just the barest touch."

Nia dragged a finger through her soaked folds and touched her swollen clit. She trembled with need and excitement.

"I'm stroking you, oh so slowly, gentle now. And then harder as your body begins to tense and the pleasure starts to mount. You need this, you beg me for it, wanting me to touch you, making you come. Only me, baby. I'm the only one who will ever do this, will ever know the sweet perfection of your body, will feel your perfect little tightness around my cock."

Her hand moved to the sound of his words, as if obeying the inherent command in his deep voice.

"Come, sweetheart. Come for me. Let me see you come," he whispered.

She arched back, obeying the husky command in his deep voice, and let the tension overtake her. Nia cried out as her body tensed in climax.

She bucked back and forth, gasping as the orgasm seized her. Nia panted, her legs trembling, the space between her legs damp with arousal.

Aiden drew in a deep breath. She opened her eyes.

"So beautiful," he murmured. "I can't wait until we're alone together to watch you do it again."

Still breathing hard, Nia felt her sex pulse from the aftershocks of her orgasm. Never had she felt anything this intense, this shattering. She struggled to regain her senses and her control. She'd become a slave to desire, and he had taken her there without laying a finger on her.

This was bad, oh so bad. One orgasm and she craved more, many more. Aiden was intoxicating and she hadn't even kissed him. She must regain her composure.

Or he'd shatter her in a different way. Sexually, the man could easily dominate her in bed.

But out of it? Never.

Nia pushed her thighs together and gave him a teasing smile. "Lazy, Mitchell? I'd rather watch you do it to me."

He grinned, his gaze filled with heat. "I plan to wear you out, Blakemore. I hope you have a mirror in your bedroom for watching."

"Installed one special just for you. It makes everything look bigger. But now that I've seen you in the flesh, I wager you don't need it."

He chuckled. "You are a minx."

"Wolf."

Aiden glanced at the flickering candles. "We have to go. It's time."

She took his outstretched hand and stood.

"But we're not leaving here until I kiss you." He framed her face with his hands, and his scent made her drown in desire all over again.

"Breaking the rules, Mitchell."

"Fuck the rules. One kiss won't hurt."

His kiss was light, gentle. Then she slid her arms around his neck and deepened the kiss.

He broke away with a slight smile. "We'd better stop here, or we'll both be in trouble."

Aiden handed her a robe. Nia slipped it on, relieved to have the cloth covering her nudity. He found two pairs of sandals and she slipped on the smaller shoes.

"The gravel is hard on your soles," Aiden told her.

"More rule breaking, Mitchell. I like it."

As they left the lodge, she felt the dampness between her thighs. It served as a reassuring reminder that they had shared an intimate, private moment outside of pack.

Soon, she would lose her virginity in a moment that was far from private. Nia reached deep inside her for her wolf and found her staring back, pawing for release. She was Lupine. Wild and powerful, and savage as her mate.

His equal.

They walked down the pathway to the pond, where silver moonlight shimmered upon the still water. Aiden led her to a grassy clearing near the pond. The wide, open space was ringed by hills and whispered of ancient secrets. Several granite boulders formed a ring. Nia had held pack meetings here before.

And now here she would mate Aiden.

Assembled around the ring were the combined members of their packs. No visitors. Not tonight for this formal ceremony.

The Lupines surrounding them were clothed in the traditional black ceremonial robes.

Aiden gave her hand a reassuring squeeze. Drawing in a deep breath, she slipped off her robe as he did the same.

Cool air brushed against her naked skin, caressing her breasts and teasing her nipples. She dragged in a deep lungful of air and scented Aiden. Her mate. Nia let her wolf rise. It clawed, eager in its demand to mate.

Nia faced him, her courage spiking with her arousal. She took his hand. It was large, warm and bore the callouses of hard labor.

Aiden was not a lazy cowboy who let the others on his ranch do all the work.

Boldly, she slid his hand downward, until it covered her breast. She stroked his hand over her warm flesh, the friction making her nipples erect.

A groan fled his lips.

"I want you, my mate Nikita. As an alpha desires his mate," he stated.

"I want you, my mate Aiden. As a female alpha desires her mate," she said aloud.

Eyes widening and darkening, he drew back. Nia watched his penis lengthen and thicken. She felt her vagina grow moist and ready to take him.

"Turn around," he said hoarsely. "Kneel and place your palms flat on the ground."

Obeying, she flung her long hair aside, and peered over her shoulder. In the moon's silvery glow, Aiden stood tense, his hungry gaze stroking over her body in a heated caress.

His swollen, red penis grew even longer and thicker. A Lupine reaction.

Trembling, she dropped her head down and waited. She felt his hot, wet tongue part the soft folds of her vagina and delve between them. Aiden began lapping at her soaked core, each stroke creating unbearable pleasure.

And then he seized her hips with his large, callused hands. She felt the rounded tip of his cock probe her soft feminine flesh.

Fight him. She had to prove she was a tough female, and at least try to fight him, for this was part of the challenge as well. If Aiden proved weak and she could best him, the mating would become void and she would be free once more.

Other alpha females would prove their strength, and test his to see if he would prove himself strong enough to father their young. She must try to throw him off as other alpha females would. Nia's arms felt shaky. With all her might, she reared backwards, and snarled. But Aiden pressed her downward easily with his muscled weight.

A growl of approval rippled through the crowd.

Nia tried again and bucked upward. She heard Aiden give a groan as his penis slipped through her cleft. He put one palm against her back and murmured softly. "Easy, now, Niki."

Even in this most intimate moment, she would not

have the satisfaction of him calling her real name. This troubling thought, more than his physical strength, subdued her.

He pressed his penis against her entrance once more. The thick hardness of him felt like a steel bar. Her wet flesh shuddered as it tried to accommodate his huge length as the tip of his cock probed inside her. Aiden's big body hovered above hers. Discomfort increased as he began to enter her tight passage.

Aiden bit his lip. Tight. So tight. He didn't want to hurt her, but ahh, she felt so damn good. Had to make this good for her, make her feel pleasure as well, but this first time required a necessary pain of breaking her innocence.

It will get better, sweetheart, he silently promised, sweat streaming down his temples as he tried to hold back.

Tension thickened the air. The rules of the challenge were clear. The male must take the female in the traditional mating position. Prove to their packs that he was virile, prove he was a powerful alpha capable of impregnating their female alpha and siring an heir.

Aiden gritted his teeth at the raw pleasure, and knew the time had come to brand her in the flesh.

Nia tensed as she felt the head of his thick penis push harder against her soaked folds. He slid partly inside, then retreated. Again. Then he slid deeper. The pressure became real pain. She closed her eyes, culling all her feminine Lupine senses, drinking in his scent, feeling his hands grip her hips, holding her steady for his possession.

Then he bent over her, licking the curve of her spine and he whispered into her ear.

"Hold onto me, sweetheart. Everything's going to be all right. It's you and me here. Only us. No one else."

With a powerful flex of his buttocks, he thrust deep inside her, breaking the barrier of her virginity. Nia stifled a startled cry, squeezing her eyes against the burning pain. Blood trickled down the inside of her thigh.

Nia went still, her swollen vagina tight around his thick cock. The pain eased, leaving only a delicious pressure.

Tenderly, he brushed back her hair, and kissed her neck. "You okay?" he whispered.

She rotated her hips. "Fuck me like the wolf I am."

A low, triumphant chuckle rumbled in her ear. Aiden drew back, then pushed his hips forward. His enormous shaft throbbed inside her tight channel, binding them together in the flesh.

Then he began plunging deep inside, stretching her wet, swollen cunt. Eyes closed, her long hair curtaining her face, she pushed back against every delicious surge. Aiden dug his fingers into her hips as he thrust and their flesh slapped together. He bent over her ass, reaching around to cup and knead her breasts. Thick, silky hair on his chest rubbed against her back. With each relentless thrust, she arched her ass upward, eager for more. The position did not bind her to submissiveness, rather it gave her a heady sense of feminine power as her mate took her.

A deep growl rumbled from Aiden's throat. She felt his engorged penis swell as an odd roundness pressed against her wet, sensitive tissues.

His wolf's knot.

As the protrusion thickened, it rubbed enticingly

against nerve endings enriched with blood. Nia moaned at the exquisite pleasure.

Aiden gave a final, deep thrust, his knot swelling and tripling her erotic bliss. Orgasm seized her loins, shooting up through her body as Nia screamed. Rearing back, he seized her hips and released a long, low howl as his cock thickened, streams of semen spraying hotly against her womb.

For a few minutes, his big body shuddered behind her. Finally his climax slowed.

They collapsed to the ground, his heavy weight pinning her down. Murmurs of approval rippled through the air.

His breath bellowing in her ear, Aiden ran a hand over the curve of her hip. "I've dreamt of doing that to you for a long time, sweetheart. Both of us bonded together in flesh."

His knot securing them together loosened.

Tears stung her eyes behind their closed lids. Not at the ghost of pain where they were intimately joined, but at the surrender of her innocence and power. She wasn't losing only her virginity, but her very self. From this moment on, her life was Aiden's to command. She'd ruled her people and carried the weight of heavy responsibility on her shoulders.

No longer. Fear rushed through her body. They were one, according to Lupine law. But he had mated a liar. And if he discovered her deception, what would he do?

Aiden pressed a kiss to the curve of her spine. And then he pulled out of her body and lay down next to her, smoothing back her hair. The rich tenderness of the gesture shattered her more than her deflowering.

"You okay?" he whispered. "I'm sorry it had to be like that."

She nodded. "And now, you'll give me your mating mark."

The bite all male Lupines gave their mates to claim them, and let other males know they were taken.

"No mark. That's for later, when we have privacy." He kissed the side of her throat. "Are you up for round two? I promise I will make it very, very good for you, sweetheart."

Relief filled her. The mating mark was equally as intimate as the sex. He rolled over, and she noticed he was still quite erect. Was this the power of an alpha? Maybe, but she scarcely had time to think because he patted his groin.

"Climb on, sweetheart," he said in a husky voice. "Ride me and let them see what a female alpha can do. You're as strong as I am."

Nia stared down at him, trembling, her throat tight. The laws didn't require this kind of submissiveness on his part. Only the male was to be dominant. But fierce determination shone in Aiden's dark eyes.

"You can do this," he said encouragingly.

She straddled him as he held his cock upright. Very slowly, Nia sank down on it, wincing a little. Gods, he was big. But the pain had faded, replaced with a delicious sense of being utterly filled.

He caressed her breasts and then toyed with her clit, his thumb creating an exquisite friction as she rose up, fell down. Each rhythmic stroke sent ripples of pleasure through her, a tension that began building higher and higher. He let her set the pace, let her ride him to the stunned gasps of the assembled Lupines.

This wasn't about sex. It was about regaining her dignity and pride, and asserting her leadership before the women. Nia felt an alarming tenderness for this powerful, big alpha.

She rode him harder, faster and then the tension gathering low in her loins exploded as another orgasm slammed into her. Nia tilted her head back and howled into the night as Aiden joined her, his hot seed once again flooding her womb. Each spurt of semen sent new little waves of pleasure shooting through her. Finally he stopped ejaculating.

Hanging her head, she braced her hands on his powerful chest, feeling his cock pulse inside her, knotting and tying them together. She collapsed atop him as he stroked her hair.

Everyone began to howl with victory.

Gradually he pulled free, his eyes glowing amber in the darkness.

The Lupines surrounding them on the circle's edge watched them silently. Waiting. It was time to complete the ritual and run together as the new alpha pair with their people. The others would not shift until she and Aiden did.

Aiden signaled her with his gaze. *You okay?*

Nia drew in a calming breath. She had survived all this so far. Nodding, she took his hand as he helped her to her feet. He tilted his head upward at the moon's caress and howled.

She joined his cry, and willed herself to shift into wolf. Nia lifted her hands to the sky and called upon all her senses as wolf. *I am Lupine. I am strong.* Power flowed through her, strong and sure. She felt a tingle rush down her spine, a tickle in her belly, and the power increased. Suddenly she found herself transformed, standing on four legs.

Wolf.

Beside her, Aiden stood in wolf form, the black and white markings on his muzzle marking him as a pureblood alpha. She had no such markings, but her father had taught her to have the bearing of one.

Aiden trotted over and rubbed his muzzle against hers in great affection. Then he licked her nose and nodded at the woods. The pack shifted into wolf form, howling in great abandon.

They ran as wolves, Aiden racing at her side as she bounded over dead logs, feeling freer and more energized than she had in months. This Lupine had branded her in the flesh and given her new life.

If she wasn't careful, she could fall in love with him.

Chapter 8

She'd had the most delicious dream; someone cared about her. Her, the twin who held the pack together, who lived for her people.

A man who would see to her every need, and keep her safe and warm when the shadow of cold, dark winter crept onto the land.

Nia snuggled down further into the covers. Someone stroked her back in long, soothing caresses. A deep murmur; words she didn't understand, but spoken with such tenderness. Nia drowsed in bed. She should get up. But the hand stroking her felt so good. It had been years since a masculine hand touched her with such loving care. Her father had hugged her, caressing her hair, whispering how she would always be his little girl, but she had to stay strong for her sister.

"I hate putting this burden on you, Nia," Edward Blakemore whispered as he hugged her so tight she knew she was loved. "But you're our only hope. Stay strong for your sister."

She didn't want to think of his death, or the sickness. She wanted to cling to the memory of those wonderful, rough hands holding her with such care, such love.

"It's okay," a deep voice murmured into her ear. "Sleep. I'll take care of everything."

Someone to take care of everything. No responsibilities for her, no worries. She sighed and burrowed deeper into the covers. She wanted this, needed rest and a worry free morning. But who could lift this burden?

Nia rolled over into the muscled arms enveloping her and opened her eyes to see a rugged face, framed by jet black stubble and two piercing dark eyes.

Aiden.

They were mated now.

She closed her eyes. She heard Aiden's deep voice, tinged with amusement, rumble in her ear.

"Okay darling. I'll get breakfast ready. You sleep."

He dropped a warm, soft kiss on her cheek as she snuggled deep into the covers. Such luxury.

Nia opened one eye. Sluggish gray light peeked through the gauze curtains at the window. She'd always loved dawn, loved watching the sun rise over the mountains. It was her favorite time, to steal a few precious moments for herself.

She had no time for luxury. Time to face the world. She heard Aiden in the kitchen, a low curse and "Where the hell does she hide the coffee?" Nia smiled, remembering last night and the thrill of racing through the woods as wolf.

Her smile faded.

She stripped and headed into the bathroom, twisting the brass knobs for the hot water. In the shower stall, Nia sagged against the wall, sighing. Every morning she allowed herself fifteen precious minutes to shower. In those minutes beneath the spray, no one bothered her, no worries were permitted, no phone calls or thoughts about feed running low, the horses growing skinnier...

Her sister growing more delicate and frail as Nikita spent more time locked in her lab, trying to find a cure for the disease.

Nia started to reach for the soap. Her arm fell to her side. Her muscles felt sore and the space between her legs pulsed with an unfamiliar ache.

She had been well loved. No, not loved. Aiden didn't love her. Needed her, yes. Desired her, definitely. But he didn't love her.

The shower curtain jerked back. Opening her eyes, she shrank against the tile, covering her breasts.

"What the hell are you doing here, Mitchell? Can't you wait your turn?"

"No." Hands on lean hips, he grinned. "I came to ask where you stashed the sugar, but the view looks much sweeter right here."

We don't have sugar. It's one thing I cut out to save money.

His bold gaze swept over her body. "You don't have to hide yourself from me, sweetheart. We're mated now."

Her eyes widened as he tugged the tight gray T-shirt over his wide shoulders, and then reached for the buckle of his jeans. "What are you doing? Can't I have fifteen minutes alone?"

"Not this morning. Maybe sometime in the future." Aiden tugged the jeans past his narrow hips and kicked them aside. Nude, he was as magnificent as she remembered, his penis standing erect.

As he stepped into the shower, he studied her face and frowned. Aiden touched her left cheek. "Was I too rough on you last night?"

"No." A flush ignited her entire body as she remembered. "It was...great."

His thumb stroked over her cheek. "Did I do this? No, I couldn't have. It's old. I never noticed this before."

Panic flared as he thumbed her scar. She'd forgotten. "I usually cover it up."

Aiden pulled the curtain aside. He reached for the soap and stepped beneath the shower spray. "Just relax," he murmured.

He began washing her. Aiden ran the soap down her back, soaping her bottom. His touch was gentle for such a big guy. Nia didn't want this, but she felt the tension ease as he massaged her shoulders. Then he ran the soap between her legs and she flinched.

"Easy," he murmured. "I'll make it good for you."

Foam popped and bubbled as he washed her groin, then his fingers lightly teased her, sliding between her cleft. Nia threw back her head and moaned as he slid a finger inside her.

The sex last night had been so good, so mind blowing. All those fantasies she'd harbored about Aiden during those long, lonely nights when she sought relief, tossing and turning in her bed, rubbing herself against a battery operated boyfriend, had been nothing compared to the reality. He'd taken her body, wrung her inside out and for a little while, she'd forgotten the world and all its sorrows.

When he pressed a hand against her back, gently urging her downward, she braced her hands on the shower seat.

"Are you too sore for this?" he asked, sliding another finger deep inside her.

"No." The word came out as a bare whisper.

His thick cock nudged her slick folds. He slid his penis between her cleft, light and teasing. Oh, he was very, very bad. Nia gripped the seat, her nipples hard, her body tense with sweet anticipation.

"Just do it, Mitchell."

"Patience, Blakemore. You must learn patience." Aiden rubbed his cock back and forth, creating an exquisite friction.

"You're so fucking beautiful," he breathed.

"Very eloquent. A man of few words." Nia smiled and then gasped as he pushed against her opening, then grunting, he slid deep inside her.

That first moment her inner muscles always resisted him, the same as she had resisted him all these years. And then as he nestled deep inside her, her body surrendered, as if it knew resistance was futile.

Nia moaned as he grasped her hips and began rocking inside her. Not fast and hard like last night, but slow, oh, so slow.

"You like that, sweetheart?" he murmured.

Her only answer was a whimper of pleasure.

Aiden pressed a soft kiss against her back, his tongue tracing a trail up her spine. "I'll make it good for you. I'll always make it good for you. But I'm afraid I'm going to have to do this now. It will only hurt for a moment."

Twisting her neck, she saw him open his mouth, and watched his incisors sharpen and lengthen. Excitement and dread pooled in her belly. The mating mark.

Aiden gently turned her head aside, nuzzled the side of her throat.

"Now," he breathed against her skin.

Sharp teeth sank into her neck. Pain surged, along with an erotic throbbing in her loins. Aiden licked the wound, his tongue dragging slowly over the bite. Stinging pain faded, replaced by growing arousal. Nia moaned as the arousal sharpened, wetness gushing between her legs.

He began moving once more. Deep inside, then slowly out. The exquisite pressure left her panting. During these moments, he went into her so deep she couldn't tell where she ended and he began. The thought should have scared her. She'd been independent and strong for so many years. But it didn't. It felt comforting, like having a soft bed to collapse into at the end of a long, tough day.

Soft? Nia whimpered as he began thrusting harder. There was nothing soft about Aiden Mitchell. Every muscled inch of him was hard as granite.

Now he was panting, his breathing ragged as the water beat upon them both, matching his deep thrusts. "Come on, Niki, come for me. Come for me."

His hand reached around, touched her clit and with that one bit of pressure, she felt the tension explode. Crying out, she shattered as he shouted her name, his penis pumping hot semen deep inside her. The tremors lasted as she kept climaxing, sweet little orgasms with each spurt. The bonus of being Lupine, she thought, dazed as he finally stopped ejaculating. Nia drew in tremendous lungfuls of air.

As his wolf's knot diminished, Aiden very slowly slid out of her and helped her to stand. He turned her around and pulled her into his arms. She felt his heart hammer beneath her ear, felt the silky, wet hairs of his firm chest against her cheek.

For some odd reason, the feel of him holding her wanted to make her cry. He did this, this big, strong male. Made all her defenses drop, made her into a vulnerable little girl all over again.

She couldn't afford tears. Nia willed them away and stared up at him. She squeezed his penis.

"Thanks, Mitchell. Now if you don't mind, I'll take breakfast. Eggs sunny side up, whole wheat toast and a big, thick," she squeezed his penis again, "sausage."

A small smile touched his face. It made him look younger, less growly. "You are one demanding female, Blakemore."

She stroked a finger down his penis, feeling hardness beneath velvet soft flesh. He groaned and it made her feel less vulnerable. "I plan to be much more demanding if you don't hustle your pretty ass and make me breakfast."

After she dried her hair and dressed, she went outside to her private balcony, sitting at the black wrought iron bistro table. Nia sipped the coffee Aiden had poured for her, and listened to the bird song in the trees on the hillside below her cottage. She adored this time of day, when the world awoke, and the ranch came to life.

It was the only safe time during the day she and Nikita had to share together. The only time they dared to be together during the day, before the rest of the pack stirred.

But with Aiden sharing her bed, she didn't dare bring her sister here. Nia stared at the mountains, the sweep of dew-soaked pasture, and wished she, not Nikita, had been first-born. Her sister had suffered too many years in hiding, with too few precious reprieves of enjoying life.

A life hidden away. What kind of life was that?

Never to find a mate, mother children? Always hidden in darkness?

She turned her cup around slowly, staring into the liquid as if trying to divine the future.

A noise below. Her stomach clenched. Gods, no, could she...

Nia peered over the balcony. Her twin climbed the steps leading to the private suite and then sat at the table with a defiant look.

"Got coffee?" Niki asked.

She whipped her head around, listening. Only birdsong, the distant whinny of horses and the murmurs of the two trusted ranch hands who fed them. Dear goddess, Aiden was only a few feet away.

"Sweetie, Aiden's in the kitchen. You can't risk it!"

"I'm lonely. So lonely." Nikita bit her lower lip. "I miss you and wanted to make sure you were okay."

Guilt pinched her. Before, they'd traded places: a few days of Nia taking the basement suite, a few days of Nikita pretending to be her. But with Aiden here, Nikita was forced to hide away.

She slid her hand across the table to grasp her twin's. "I miss you, too."

Nikita studied her with an astute look. "Are you happy now that you are mated to him, Nia? You look different. I want you to be happy."

Happy? Satisfied, yes. But she'd never be truly happy until the curse was lifted from their people. And it would take a tremendous act of sacrifice on her twin's part to accomplish that.

"Aiden's been good to me." True enough.

Nikita tilted her head, a gesture Nia had learned to mimic. "What's it like?"

Nia smiled, knowing the question beneath the question. "It's wonderful. A little frightening at first, because Aiden is so intense…powerful…"

"Big," her twin finished.

They laughed. Nia leaned forward, tracing the rim of the coffee cup with her finger. "It's everything I expected, and more. Beneath the open sky and the cool air, it was like being bathed in starlight."

She talked about the experience for a few moments, delicately omitting details, focusing on the thrill of changing into her wolf and running through the woods.

Torment swirled in her twin's blue eyes. "I should summon the Silver Wizard and present myself to him, and that would break the curse."

All of Nia's relaxed enjoyment vanished.

"No!" Panic clogged her throat. "You'll die. You can't be with him. He'll take you to the afterworld and I'll never see you again. You know you can't go there and return to earth. You'll die!"

Tristan would take her beloved twin away, and she'd vanish like the mist rising over the mountains.

"There has to be another way," she told her sister.

Nikita looked at her with eyes that had seen too much. Wise, sad eyes, much like her own. "There is no other way. Unless you want Aiden to die. And he will die if he remains here, Nia."

"I'll return with him to his ranch. I just need a little more time to talk him into it. The disease won't touch him there."

"And he'd never leave here, not until he feels this ranch is safe and operational again." Nikita gave a rueful smile. "The pride and honor of a real alpha male.

Never leave a job half finished, or your mate's home and pack in jeopardy."

Her nostrils twitched. "I'd better get back to my place before your mate comes out here and thinks he's seeing double."

Her twin stood and dropped a kiss on her head. "Congratulations, little sister. I'm happy for you."

Nikita leapt over the railing and Nia watched her land on her feet. She waved and went into her room just as the door to Nia's bedroom opened.

Aiden walked onto the porch, carrying a tray filled with two plates and more coffee. "Who were you talking to?"

"No one. Just myself." She sipped her coffee, relief spilling through her as she heard the downstairs door quietly shut. "It's the best conversation I can have."

"You were quiet this morning. Everything okay, Nikita?"

She set down her cup, trying to hide her shaking hands. "Don't call me that. Please. Call me Pixie. Or Blakemore."

Aiden raised his dark brows. "All right. But answer my question."

She thought of her twin safely tucked downstairs in her luxurious prison and swallowed past the lump in her throat. "Everything's fine."

He sat on the chair Niki had just left. Nia held her breath, hoping he would not notice her sister's scent, or the fact the chair was warm. She was starving, and her stomach grumbled, but until she sensed that Aiden didn't suspect anything, she could not eat nor relax.

Aiden blinked a moment, then set about slathering

his toast with butter. Nothing wrong. Everything was okay. Nia dug into her eggs with a happy sigh.

"I'm so hungry." She ate a forkful of eggs.

"You hardly ate anything last night at our mating dinner, except for the liver. And sex makes you burn calories." Aiden winked at her.

"You're just saying that because you want a good excuse for another workout," she teased.

"I don't need an excuse, not with you. I wanted to serve you breakfast in bed, but if I did that, there'd be no breakfast for me. I'd be too busy nibbling on all your delicious parts."

A flush lit her face. She took a bite of sausage and then pointed to it. "This is good. But I bet you can whip up something that tastes equally delicious."

He grinned, poured honey over his toast and licked it off with his tongue. Her entire body clenched with need.

Aiden ran his tongue around his lips. "I know something else I can do with honey."

Oh wow, there was a promise in his seductive smile, in the way his dark gaze twinkled.

"So do I." Her gaze dropped to his lap. "I think I'll try it out later when I'm hungry for…an Aiden sausage."

He grinned and she grinned back.

This was what she'd always dreamed her mating would be like; a close intimacy between two Lupines who vowed to remain together forever, sharing their lives, dreams, and secrets.

Secrets. She had quite a few big ones. Nia set down her fork. She should tell Aiden what was going on.

The memory filled her mind, clear as water. Her

father, lying on his deathbed, a rare moment of clarity when the horrible seizures and convulsions hadn't affected him. His blue eyes, dulled with pain, but still sharp with intelligence. His withered hand reaching for hers, the fingers gnarled and claw-like, while her twin stood outside the bedroom, weeping.

He'd wanted to talk to her alone.

Promise me, pumpkin. Promise me you'll never betray our people to outsiders and tell them of this damn disease. Promise me you'll do everything to protect your sister from being carried away by the Silver Wizard, and keep her hidden from everyone. It's a lot I'm putting on your shoulders, but you're the strong one and I'm counting on you to hold it together.

Nia blinked away the memory. For five years, she'd faithfully held to her father's promise. She could not break it now, not even for her mate.

She watched Aiden eat his breakfast. For such a big male, he had impeccable manners. A lump formed in her throat. Her father had been like that, setting the example.

Promise me you'll never betray our people to outsiders...

Deathbed promises were sacred. If she broke her oath, she violated everything that had ruled her life since her father and brothers had died.

Aiden and his men seemed safe—for now. The disease only struck males who had contact with the land for at least two weeks. But it was best to get the males off her ranch, away from danger. After seeing one of Richard's men with symptoms of the parvolupus, she couldn't be certain the disease hadn't mutated and shortened the incubation period.

"What are our plans for today?" she asked.

He sipped his coffee, his dark gaze holding hers. "First I'll tour the grounds, get an idea of how much work your ranch requires in repairs so I can give orders to my men on what to fix first. After that, I'll hold a formal meeting with your people to let them know my expectations, and what they can expect of me."

Acid churned in her stomach, ruining the delicious taste of the eggs. "Must they remain here?"

He gave her a curious look. "Of course."

"Wouldn't it be better to send them back to your ranch? I expect I'll be living there, with all the females your males want to mate with."

Aiden's gaze did not waver. "Not when your ranch looks like shit. I want my men, hell, *our* men now, to start pitching in with repairs. You have them at your disposal."

"This ranch is falling apart. I'd rather just go to your place."

Please believe me. I can't risk you getting ill.

"After all you've done to keep your home together, you want to abandon it?" Aiden shook his head. "No. We're staying here."

She slammed down her cup, making the china rattle. "Damn it Mitchell, don't I get a say in this? It's my property. And what gives you the right to dictate this?"

"The ranch isn't yours until I deed it back to you, which I will do when it's properly fixed." He ate a piece of bacon, his face brooding. "You're used to doing everything your way, and that's going to end now."

"And do everything your way? I don't think so."

"Eat your breakfast. We'll talk as we tour your

ranch." His mouth thinned. "And maybe then you'll level with me and tell me what happened to all the men. Not even a damn cowhand working your stock. Or any stock to speak of. Why did you sell it all?"

Nia pushed back her plate. "I'm not hungry."

He set down his fork, his body rigid. "You will eat. You're my mate now, and I'm going to care for you. You're lacking in protein. Eat."

"Fuck you, Mitchell."

"You already did that last night and in the shower, Blakemore." Unsmiling, he regarded her. "There are some things I'll learn to compromise on, but your health and welfare aren't among them. Eat."

Sullen, she picked up her fork and began to eat. When they finished their breakfast, Aiden cleared the table.

Then they walked outside the cottage. On her front porch, Darius, Kyle, Dale, Jackson, Garth, J.J., and Raphael lounged on the steps and in the faded, rusting furniture. They stood upon seeing them, nodded in respect.

Dismay filled her. "What are you doing here?" she asked them.

"We're here to help assess repairs. Aiden asked us," Raphael said.

"And run any intruders off the ranch so they'll never return. I'm leading the team to track every inch of this land. I'm Aiden's best hunter. If there's a gnome lurking in your woods, I'll find it." Kyle cracked his knuckles.

More males exposed, in danger of catching the disease the longer they remained on her land. And these were mated males. Hadn't she heard enough sobbing and wailing as the mates of the dying expressed their sorrow? She couldn't bear to see it happen again.

Nia threw Kyle a cool look. "Anything with a nose can track down a gnome. Even Aiden could do it. They smell as bad as your feet, Kyle, only they don't stink as much. I'll stick with my females hunting them down."

Maybe if she insulted them enough, they'd get the idea and leave.

Far from looking insulted, Kyle laughed. Dale punched his arm playfully. "You forget to shower again, wolf? Damn, I thought Arianna cured of you of that little problem."

"Kyle's feet smell like roses compared to yours, Dale," Darius put in.

"Want to hold a contest? My feet are bigger and smell way worse," said Jackson.

Nia stared, trembling inside. These males were determined to do as their alpha asked. They had a loyalty that ran as deep as her females had for her. She looked at J.J. and Raphael, and instead of seeing two strong alpha males whose friendship bonded them to Aiden, she saw their coffins, and their mates weeping over them.

She thought fast. The disease seemed to strike faster in unhealthy males. And it was concentrated in the areas frequented by the pack. Maybe she could buy time in sending them to the furthest borders of the ranch.

Nia glanced at Aiden, who folded his arms across his chest and looked cold and stiff. She'd hurt him with her words.

Better to hurt him with words than to watch him die...

"If you're going to stick around, then go to the west and northern borders. Lots of territory. The gnomes have been sneaking in by using the mountain pass. I can't cover that ground because it's remote, rocky and dangerous to access on anything but foot and I have too damn much to do around here. There's a dirt road leading from the lodge to the mountains you can use to access the pass, but you'll need a four wheel drive."

All of them looked at Aiden.

Aiden growled deep in his throat. "Do it."

The males jumped off the porch and headed to their trucks. Aiden didn't look at her. "Let's go. We'll start with the barns."

CHAPTER 9

Five hours later, she and Aiden returned to her cottage. Exhausted, Nia sat out back on her balcony as Aiden showered. A cool breeze played with her hair, drying the sweat on her body.

Aiden was furious.

To his credit, he said little, but judging from the tension in his broad shoulders and the lines bracketing his firm mouth, he was pretty pissed she'd let things slide this long. When he'd seen the main barn, with its weathered exterior, withering floorboards, rusty farm equipment and leather harnesses going to rot, he'd turned away and muttered.

"You should have let me know. I'd have sent my men sooner."

Sorry honey, I was too busy trying to hold things together and save my pack from dying. Didn't have time to host a barn raising.

The shower shut off. Nia went back inside. Aiden left the bathroom, a towel wrapped around his lean waist, his black hair wet and curled at the edges. Water beaded in the hairs on his muscled chest.

She glanced away, not daring to want him all over again.

"You should have told me." He sat on the bench near the window and scowled. "One day that damn stubborn pride of yours will get you in trouble, Blakemore."

"Not as much as your pride will, Mitchell. Did you think you could bring your men in here and steamroll over my pack, acting as if you could save the day?"

"Someone had to save your pretty little ass because you were too damn proud to ask for help! Did you want to wait until everything was at the point of no return?"

"Why are you yelling at me? I did the best I could, considering I had nothing!"

"I'm yelling because I don't want you to live like this anymore, damn it! I don't like seeing you hungry and alone, and hurting!"

She stared, her stomach working into nervous knots. He cared. But that could turn disastrous. "Then don't stay here. You got what you wanted, so go home."

"Never without you," he growled. "You're mine. Where you go, I go."

She stared up at him. "You won't like where I'm going, Mitchell. Straight to hell."

"Then I'll join you."

He backed her up against the bed and when she fell upon it, he covered her.

Their lovemaking was fiery, filled with all the anger and the passion she felt.

Aiden's cell phone rang. He rolled over and thumbed it on. "Report. We're both here."

He switched the phone to speaker and Darius' worried voice came over the line.

"No signs of gnomes on the outer borders. But

there's some dead wildlife that we found, two deer, a few squirrels and about three rabbits. Looks like disease got to them."

"Damn," Aiden said softly. "Did you save any of the carcasses?"

"One of the rabbits. Bagged it with gloves and put it on ice when we got back to the lodge. We burned the corpses. If it's some kind of wildlife virus, we don't want it spreading."

"What was the sex of the animals?" she asked.

Aiden threw her a puzzled look.

"Male, least the deer were. Didn't examine the others too closely. All we saw was they had fur missing, placed by these weird black scales, like a fungus."

Her heart slipped to her stomach. No wonder the gnomes had fled. They were too smart to stick around because the parvolupus had begun to mutate, affecting other life forms.

Could it get any worse?

"Thanks Dar. See you at dinner."

Aiden shut off the phone.

She slipped out of bed, dressed and went outside. So many conflicting emotions and feelings. She didn't want to have Aiden Mitchell in her life. She'd spent years running everything, thank you very much, and now he'd charged into her life and took over.

They butted heads like two fighting rams. And yet the lovemaking left her breathless and craving more.

And they faced a disease that could kill even a strong male like Mitchell. Nia closed her eyes, remembering the pain etching her father's face as he gasped his last…

Promise me you'll never betray our people to outsiders...

She needed clarity.

Aiden poked his head out the door. "Where are you going?" he asked as she descended the steps.

"For a short walk. Alone."

Nia raced down the stairs, then followed the gravel pathway down to the pond. A short while later, she jogged through the woods, pushing past the overgrown brush. Dry leaves and twigs crackled beneath the soles of her boots. She climbed the hill until reaching a wide, open space. Mountains rose in the backdrop, jagged and proud peaks that had guarded this land for centuries.

Her parents had always wanted to be buried here.

She dropped to her knees beside two plain marble headstones engraved with their names. Her family was gone, except for Nikita. First their mother during childbirth. Then they'd lost their eldest brother to the disease, then their second brother.

Dad followed him to the grave ten days later.

Nia stared at the gentle curve of each headstone. She brushed dead leaves away from them and touched the marbled engraving of her father's name.

"I miss you," she whispered to the cold stone. "I miss you hugging me and calling me your princess. I miss how you used to make us pancakes on Sunday with little smiley faces drawn in syrup. I miss how you propped your feet on the coffee table and ate all the popcorn when we watched movies. I miss how you used to hunt with me, always behind me to watch my back.

"I miss you so much. Dad, I wish you were here to tell me what to do. I feel like I'm walking in a fog."

Burying her face in her hands, she sobbed for all she and her twin had lost. Their family. Their innocent childhood. Most of all the love of the parent who was fiercely dedicated to guiding them through life.

She didn't hear him behind her, but detected his warm, rich scent of pine. The masculine aroma made her feminine senses tingle amid the misery. Or perhaps it was because they were mated now, and her body recognized her man.

Two gentle hands settled on her shaking shoulders, massaging as he murmured to her in his deep voice. Then she felt him settle on the ground beside her, and Aiden pulled her into his arms. Nia cried against his chest, releasing the flood of grief she'd stemmed for years, grief she'd refused to show because there had been too much to do, the crisis paralyzing all her pack. Someone had to take charge.

So she had.

But now it felt too damn good *not* to be the strong one, the one who didn't weep when they buried yet another once-strong male, or the ranch's stores of food and supplies ran low. Now she could finally cry for her family, lying beneath the cold earth.

She lifted her wet face and he wiped away her tears with his thumbs. "Don't cry, sweetheart," he murmured. "I'm here now. Tell me what's wrong."

"I need to be alone. Please. I'm sorry, but I need time with my dad." She pulled away from him and touched the gravestone. "Just for a little while."

He traced a tear with his finger, two lines indenting his forehead. "Nikita, I'm your mate now. I'm here for you, whatever you need me for. I wish you'd open up to me."

Oh, she was sorely tempted. But the years of disciplining herself to keep everything shut inside her had honed her control. And her twin had begged for a few more days so she could focus on finding the cure.

"I'm the alpha. They can't see me break down. You understand. This is the only place I can truly be alone, have privacy to mourn."

He closed his eyes for a moment, and then squeezed her shoulder. "I understand. I'll be at the cabin. But if you're not back in thirty minutes, I'm coming after you. I don't like you being out here by yourself. There might be more gnomes who decide you'd make a lovely wolf snack."

"I'll be fine. I've taken care of myself for years, Mitchell." She scrubbed her face with a fist and added softly, "Thank you."

He dropped a kiss on her forehead. She heard him heave a deep sigh and then walk away, shuffling his feet in the dry, dead leaves.

Aiden couldn't believe it. He'd been mated for less than a day, and his mate wanted to be alone in a graveyard.

He swore quietly as he returned to her cabin. Niki was supposed to be lounging in bed, pampered by him, not weeping by a grave. He felt helpless at the sight of her tears. Hell, he'd do anything to make her happy, but she still remained guarded and cautious.

Except in bed, where she turned into a wildcat, eager and clawing in her need. Oh yeah, no problem in that area.

But outside of bed, she was still prickly.

When would she open to him?

He reached Nikita's cabin, walked up the back steps, opened the door and went through the hallway into the living room and ground to a halt.

Niki sat on the sofa, leafing through a magazine. She looked up, and blinked in apparent surprise. Then a smile touched her face. No tears. No signs she'd been crying.

He looked around, stunned. How had she beaten him back here? Yeah, he'd made a few detours, checking out the barn and the pond, but still...

"Hi."

Aiden's nostrils flared. He felt confused and off kilter. Hell, Niki had made him feel like that ever since he'd met her five years ago. But not like this, as if he didn't know her.

It was her fragrance. Her scent, it was different. Just a little. A touch of the fragrant lilies and spring flowers he loved, laced with vanilla. Vanilla was the essence of childhood Lupines and Lupines who'd never had a lover. But Niki's scent should have changed by now. Certainly they had made love enough to warrant such a change.

"What are you reading?" he asked.

She held up the magazine. "Wildlife journal. Habits of wolf packs."

He grinned. "Because of all that howling you did an hour ago?"

Niki stared at him as if he'd spoken a foreign language. Aiden rubbed his chin, puzzled.

He studied her face, really looked at her, and noticed for the first time that her upper lip formed just a little more of a bow. Odd. No scar, either. What happened to her scar? Did she cover it with makeup?

He peered at her face. No makeup. Fresh, wholesome skin. That was all.

"Are you happy?" Niki asked him.

Taken aback, he stared. "With you?"

She nodded.

"I would be happier if you weren't so damn close-mouthed about everything and you'd open up to me."

"But are you *happy*?" The magazine trembled in her grip. "Happy having me as your mate. Making this kind of forever commitment. Promising to care for me as long as your heart keeps beating."

Never had he seen Niki this uncertain. Aiden sat down beside her and took the magazine, tossing it aside. He clasped her hands, wincing at how cold they were, and looked into her eyes. She swallowed hard and pulled her hands away. Blood drained from her face. Startled, he frowned. She looked too pale. What happened the rosy cheeks? The healthy pallor that his mate had since he'd stuffed her full of food?

"I've wanted you for five years, Niki. No other woman would do. Mating you was a commitment I'm damn glad to have made, and I'd promise to care for you into the next lifetime, or whatever follows this one. No regrets."

A tremulous smile touched her mouth. "Good. I'm glad of it."

He pulled her into his arms.

"I'll be even happier if I can taste you instead," he murmured, and covered her mouth with his own.

She stiffened, her fingers tightening on his arms, digging into the muscles like claws. She tasted of cherries and sharp, tangy spices, not the sweet honey and fresh peaches of his mate. The kiss was flatter than two-day old beer, missing Niki's fire and passion.

Aiden immediately released her. Shock, dismay and then disbelief filled him. How could he have not seen?

Niki stared at him, her face paling. "I have to throw up."

She raced for the kitchen sink and began vomiting. Aiden stared at her, feeling all kinds of dismay. His kiss made her sick? What the hell?

But when they made love, it was all fire and passion.

Maybe she was pregnant. No, she hadn't yet gone into heat. Aiden shook free of his thoughts and grabbed a bottle of water from the refrigerator. He uncapped it and handed it to her as she wiped her mouth with a paper towel.

Niki took the water and drank deeply. Sweat dampened her hair. "I'll be all right. Thank you."

"I make you sick," he said slowly. *Way to go, Mitchell. Talk about an ego deflator.*

"I have to go. Fresh air." She set down the bottle and started for the door.

But he hadn't made her sick before…it was as if this Niki was an imposter. And then he recalled Tristan's prophetic words: *"You may win the leader of the Blakemore pack's hand, but never her heart. She belongs to another who has claimed her first and she will surrender her virginity to him. It is in her destiny."*

He'd thought the sly wizard had been yanking his chain, testing him to see how far Aiden would go to claim Nikita. But what if there were two…

Aiden's gaze sharpened as if he saw his mate for the

first time. The scar. The way she got physically ill around him. One way to tell.

"Let's go." He started toward her.

She gave him a wary look. "Where?"

"The bedroom. You promised to do something very interesting to my anatomy." He scanned the kitchen. "Where did you put the honey? You said only organic would suffice."

She gave him a panicked look. "I'm not in the mood."

Of course you're not. You won't be around me. Because you're not my Niki, my mate.

Maybe this Niki will give me answers.

Aiden leaned close as she backed up against the door. "What's going on here, Niki? Why are you so secretive and why are you so eager to get me out of here and send me packing to my ranch?"

Those blue eyes widened in apparent surprise, but she quickly recovered and shrugged. "I'm sure you have a lot of work to do back on your ranch."

"Sure there isn't another reason?" He kept his hands to his side and his voice gentle. "I'd never hurt you, or betray you."

A flash of vulnerability on her face, then her expression shuttered. "I'm fine. And I don't need your help. I need fresh air."

Right.

He reached for the zipper of his jeans. "You sure, sweetheart? Because about twenty minutes ago, you were raring for another shower with me."

Red suffused her cheeks. "I've showered enough for one day. My skin is wrinkling."

He considered. "Maybe. Have to check for myself.

Come on, darling, get undressed and let me see that gorgeous tattoo you got for our mating day."

Now her eyes nearly popped out of her face. "Tattoo?!"

Aiden threw up his hands. "What's wrong with you? Were you drunk when you got it? It's so cute. Just a little old heart with my name on it. Stamped right on your pretty little ass. Remember how I kissed it last night?"

She began backing up against the door. "I have a headache."

He heaved an exaggerated sigh. "Damn. Mated one day and already the little woman pleads a headache. I could pound on you all night and never stop."

Raising his brows, he winked. "Want an aspirin?"

Blood draining from her face, she ran out the door.

Aiden's smile faded as he looked out the window after her. She walked down the pathway snaking down the hill and ducked out of sight.

He hoped she'd be okay. She truly had looked ill.

Anger filled him, cold rage shoving aside his concern. His Niki had a lot of explaining to do when she returned.

And yet, for all the questions racing through his mind, he knew he had to tread delicately. For Niki hid a huge secret she'd been hiding for years...

Her identical twin sister.

Chapter 10

Nia didn't know what had gotten into Aiden.

She returned from the graveyard, her eyes swollen, her face blotchy, Aiden took one look at her and kissed her hard. She kissed him back, needing his touch, needing connection. For years she'd distanced herself from everyone but her sister, and even with her twin, she'd kept part of herself hidden.

But with Aiden, she could find abandon in sex, and release her emotions through touch. The kiss had been long and left her breathless and panting for more. He pushed a gentle hand through her hair and gave her a long, thoughtful look.

Nothing more.

Then he swept her into his arms and kissed her soundly, then framed her face with his big hands and kept staring at her.

As if seeing her for the first time.

"You okay?" he asked roughly. "I hate seeing you cry."

She nodded.

"Is there anything you want to tell me? I don't want secrets between us."

Oh boy, that was a good one. She had secrets leaking out of her ears.

"We're alphas, Mitchell." Her voice softened. "We wouldn't be good ones without having secrets that protect our pack."

To distract him, she slid her arms around his neck and pressed a gentle kiss against his mouth.

"Let's go into the bedroom," he said in a husky voice as she pulled away. "I missed you."

She touched his arm, feeling the warmth of his skin. Aiden got warmer when he was sexually excited. She didn't need to look down. All she needed was the heat in his gaze, caressing her.

Nia felt an electrical charge pass from his skin to hers, a current of erotic promise. Her groin tingled, and the space between her legs grew wet.

They made it into the bedroom.

Her panties were soaked as he kicked the door closed. He stared at her, his gaze hot amber, and he growled deep in his throat.

She knew he could scent her.

Her breathing turned ragged with need as he pulled her into his arms, nostrils flaring, his mouth unsmiling. This wasn't love. It was pure carnal need.

They were made for this.

She kneaded his muscled ass, reveling in the firmness of his buttocks beneath her exploring fingers. Nia stared up at him, her core pulsing with hot need.

He pressed close, letting her feel his enormous erection.

Nia dropped to her knees and unzipped his jeans, freeing him. He was huge, hard, engorged with blood. A clear droplet wept from the red tip of his Lupine penis. His penis was slightly triangular. It made penetration easier. She shivered with anticipation.

Nia took him into her mouth, working her tongue over the shaft as Aiden gripped her shoulders. He tasted a little salty and spicy. He threw back his head and groaned.

She liked hearing him like this, knowing she caused it.

His erection grew larger, stretching her mouth. Then he pulled out, his penis bobbing and covered with her saliva, as he stared down at her with those incredible wolf eyes.

"It's time," he said in a guttural voice.

Nia stripped off her clothes, tossing them aside, and lay upon the bed, her legs spread wide open in invitation. Aiden stood at the bed's edge, ready to take her.

He guided his penis to her soaked center, and pushed, entering her slowly. She winced, for each time he entered her, Aiden met resistance, as if her body didn't want this submissive invasion. But she tilted her hips up and he surged forward.

The friction was incredible as he gently thrust, looking down and watching his penis enter her body, as if this claiming fascinated him. He kept thrusting forward, then he growled deeply.

Aiden pulled out, flipped her over to her stomach. He climbed upon the bed.

She felt his penis push between her soaked folds again as his hands gripped her hips, holding her still.

His whole length was inside her, filling her, and she moaned. She could not move in his steely grip, nor did she want to move. Nia let him control the pace, let him take her, wolf that he was, and fisted the bedspread in her hands. She lowered her head and pointed her ass upward, desperate to come.

Panting, he drove into her as his flesh slapped against hers. Aiden fisted a hand in her hair as he thrust into her. He bore down, penetrating deep and deeper still. Then the tightness blossoming in her core spread, and she cried out. The orgasm rocked her so hard she nearly saw stars.

Craning her head, she saw him go still and stiffen. Aiden groaned came, spurting hotly inside her. This wasn't mere sex. It was hot, baby-making sex, the alpha determined to impregnate her so his line would continue.

They both collapsed to the bed, Aiden's heavy weight resting upon her. He tossed aside her hair and kissed her damp neck.

Gradually, he pulled out and lay beside her. After a little while, he made love to her again, this time each movement gentle and filled with tenderness. For a little while, he made all the nightmares fade away.

But she knew they would return soon enough.

The meeting with her pack didn't go quite as Aiden expected. He'd thought Niki's people would be relieved to know he planned to stay while he and his men fixed the ranch and restored it to its former glory. Relieved that they didn't have to move to his ranch, and leave behind everything familiar.

Instead, they kept looking at him with worried eyes. One or two even voiced their preference for leaving.

"There's nothing here for us anymore," a woman said, holding her young son in her lap. "We need a fresh start."

Niki had remained silent, letting him do the talking. But his mate's earlier preferences echoed that of her people: fresh start, let's all move.

He wondered about that.

Dinner that night was awkward. He said little, watching her, wondering if she was going to finally admit the truth. She cooked him a fine steak dinner, grilled to perfection. After the dishes were washed, she sank onto the couch and fell asleep.

Seeing the strain on her face, the smudges of exhaustion beneath her eyes, he let her alone, though inside, he wanted to wake her, demand answers.

So he found a fleece blanket, put it over her and watched her sleep. Tomorrow, he'd confront her.

Niki, or whoever she was, looked young and vulnerable in her sleep. She had grown up without a mother. It must have been tough. Hell, he'd lost his mother and it turned him inside out.

But to watch her father and two protective brothers die, and then be left with the responsibility of protecting her pack, hiding her twin? And why the deception?

For a few minutes he sat there, watching the dying fire and his sleeping mate.

He sensed the great ripple of power in the air and stiffened.

Tristan appeared before him, standing by the fireplace. The Silver Wizard had black hair down to his shoulders, the ends tipped with silver. He wore his customary outfit of a black tunic, black pants and soft doeskin boots.

"Go away." Aiden's gaze shot to his sleeping mate and his protective instincts surged. "You're not welcome here."

"Relax alpha, I am not here to take her from you."

He thought quickly. Maybe he could coax answers from the wizard. "Take who away?"

Tristan's dark gaze gleamed. "Your mate."

"Who is…"

Tristan's mouth curved in a sly smile. "The one you have chosen for life."

Aiden blew out a frustrated breath. "Her name?"

The wizard blinked. "You have taken this woman as your partner for life and you don't know her name?"

"Damnit Tristan," he said in a low voice. "Stop messing with me. Why are you here?"

Tristan pointed to the chair opposite Aiden. "May I?"

Aiden shrugged. The Silver Wizard could blow up the entire sofa with his powers. Aiden's acquiescence didn't mean squat.

The wizard sat, his manner relaxed and unthreatening. "I am here check on things. To see how you're doing with your newly mated status."

"I'm terrific," he muttered.

Tristan's gaze darkened. "Be gentle with your mate. She has reasons for what she does. Your understanding and kindness will go far. If you win her heart, you will win your heart's desire."

Aiden's head began to throb. "I'm understanding as hell. You came just to give me relationship advice?"

"I also wished to check on how the one who was promised to me long ago is faring."

His head began to ache from the non-answers. "What one? Is she here?"

Tristan nodded. "In due time you will know. I will take her with me, and she will become mine, as it was destined."

"Why do you want her? You like abducting reluctant women?"

He stiffened, expecting Tristan to fling an energy bolt, or at the very least, a stinging zap of power. But Tristan shook his head. "When she joins with me, she will do so of her own free will."

"What the hell is going on?" Aiden demanded. "What's wrong with this place? It feels cursed."

Tristan studied him with his dark gaze. "Does it?"

"Tell me."

"Things must develop according to plan." The wizard shook his head and regret seemed to shine in his dark eyes. "I will tell you this. Your mate's father paid for the consequences of not allowing me to help him. I could not stop what he unleashed."

Damn. This was worse than Aiden had thought. "But you can stop these consequences now. You're a wizard."

The Silver Wizard stared as if Aiden were three years old and trying to decipher quantum physics. "No. But the consequences may be reversed. It must come from within."

Gods, he was so frigging tired. "Why is it every time I talk with you, Tristan, I feel like I'm listening to someone babble in Latin or another dead language?"

"My Latin is a little rusty. It has been many centuries since I used it."

Aiden blinked.

"I am from the Dark Ages." Tristan stood, and gazed at the sleeping Niki. "All will be revealed when the time is right. Know this, wolf. You must remain strong, no matter what ails you. And be weak when she needs you to be weak."

Aiden blinked, but the wizard vanished.

"Bastard," he muttered.

The following day, Nia managed to convince Aiden to send his males back to the Mitchell Ranch. It had been easier than she'd thought, for all she had to do was make a few suggestions to her pack. That morning, a group of twenty-five females tracked down Aiden and begged him for permission to visit his place and hunt as wolves.

There was not much large game to be found on the Blakemore Ranch lands.

Aiden not only granted permission, but he sent all his men back with the women. Only Garth insisted on remaining behind. The Lupine had grown fond of Roxanne, and was courting her to be his mate, and Roxanne refused to leave the ranch. "We'll make lists of the needed repairs, and if necessary, hire a crew," Aiden decided.

Now, in addition to herself and Aiden, Roxanne and Garth, the only ones remaining on her ranch were 30 older females whose children were grown. Nia felt as if someone had lifted a huge weight from her shoulders. Aiden's guys were safe.

But she still had to convince Aiden to leave, and that would prove a challenge.

That afternoon, after she'd helped Aiden repair fences in the pasture, she took a long, leisurely shower and then dressed in jeans, a long-sleeved pink Western shirt, and boots.

As she headed outside to visit the lodge to check with Roxanne on the day's needs, she caught a familiar scent on the porch. Sharp pine, old leather and the enticing smell of the forest.

Aiden.

Nia glanced at the shadows on the porch. One moved. Aiden stretched out a long leg.

"Hey there, pixie," he murmured.

Grateful he wasn't as snarly as last night, she smiled. "What are you doing out here?"

"Waiting for you. I have your mating gift ready."

She thought about the birdhouse and sighed. "The hummingbirds…"

"No birds. Something you'll like much better." Aiden stood and stretched, the muscles of his wide shoulders rippling along his tight checked shirt.

She bit back a sigh of desire, mingling with sharp longing. He wasn't truly hers, no matter what the mating ceremony had said. Or the long, passionate lovemaking sessions. And when he found out he'd formally mated the wrong twin, what then?

Maybe she should start scanning the real estate section of the local paper for places to live.

Aiden stretched out his hand. "Come on, pixie. You can take a break from being in charge for an hour."

Deeply curious, she took his hand, allowing him to lead her down the steps, to the gravel path past the lodge, to the golf cart waiting there. The barn was a short drive away.

Aiden powered up the golf cart as she sat beside

him, and they took off. A short distance from the main pasture, he parked the cart by the pathway leading to the barn.

Gravel crunched beneath their boots as they trudged along the path. It was oddly quiet.

When they reached the weathered barn near the main pasture, he put a warm, calloused palm over her eyes. "No peeking."

Nia had no desire to peek. The empty pasture had felt like her heart; cold and bereft. The ranch once boasted the finest thoroughbred horses this side of the Mississippi. No more. All their stock had been sold to finance Nikita's lab, and feed and keep the pack.

Her twin's expensive lab, where Niki worked desperately to try to find a cure for the disease killing their males.

So deep was her longing, she could still scent the horses, their earthy aroma of dung and mud and flesh. Could still hear them nicker in greeting…

"Ok." Aiden kissed her temple and removed his hand. "You can look now."

Nia opened her eyes and stared.

Two horses stood in the fenced pasture. One was pure black, with an arrogant air, trotting around the grass as if he owned the pasture. The other was a gentle chestnut mare with a star shape on her forehead, and four white socks. The mare ran over to the fence, nickering at Nia.

Tears filled her eyes. "Windstorm. But how…"

"J.J. suspected this was your personal mare, because of the way you were reluctant to say goodbye to her. I bought her back for you."

Emotion churned in her stomach. She couldn't find

the words. Aiden Mitchell had a reputation as a tough, arrogant alpha, but this generous gesture had shown her a different side of him. Nia reached up and kissed him hard and then dashed toward the fence as the mare trotted over to greet her, flicking her tail.

The mare lowered her head and Nia stroked her nose, her heart filled with joy for the first time in months. After losing so much, she could hardly believe she had her beloved friend back.

Aiden joined her, putting his hands on her shoulders. His touch was absolutely gentle and she felt the warmth of his breath as he lowered his head to whisper into her ear.

"I want you to be happy. I had Kyle bring over Chance so we could ride together. He brought tack and supplies as well."

Nia continued to stroke her mare's nose. "Pretty arrogant of you, Mitchell, thinking you're a real cowboy. I thought you were a wolf."

"Wolves can be cowboys. And cowgirls, too." He turned her to face him and his expression made her still. No trace of the usual Mitchell arrogance. Only a flickering of wistful longing, as if he knew what it felt like to be lonely, surrounded by an entire pack who would do anything for you, yet could not do anything for you because of the secrets you hid inside.

Nia reached up and framed his stubbled face with both hands. "Thank you," she told him.

She needed this male, needed him at her side, needed him deep inside her body in the dark of night.

She must learn to let go. *I will, soon. A few more days. Niki said a few days and she'll have the cure. She's so close.*

But for now, she would indulge in the fantasy that Aiden could be hers forever.

"Prove you are a cowboy, Mitchell. Let's ride."

He grinned and picked up both her hands, kissing the palms. "Thought you'd never ask, Blakemore."

They brought the horses into the barn and saddled them quickly. The tack Kyle had left in the barn was oiled and glistening and sturdy. No more cracked leather bridles, or saddles with frayed straps.

After leading the horses out of the barn, they mounted. Nia admired the way Aiden swung a long, muscled leg over the leather saddle. He looked fine on a horse.

That is one cowboy who knows how to ride, and ride well.

The thought coaxed a fierce blush to her cheeks.

Morning dew layered the thin blades of grass in the pasture. The air was still and quiet as she and Aiden followed the trail in the pasture paralleling the mountain.

As they rode past the split-rail fence dividing the pasture from the dirt roadway, she glanced at him. In his black cowboy hat, tight jeans, and checked shirt, Aiden made a rugged and handsome cowboy, as if the ranch had always been his home.

Suddenly he stopped the stallion and shifted his weight in the saddle. With the slightest pressure on Windstorm's flanks with her knees, Nia halted her mare.

"Do you feel it?" he asked. "Something isn't right. The air is too…quiet."

Nia looked around. Little hairs on her nape saluted the air. Though it was chilly, the breeze usually sweeping down from the mountains wasn't present.

Tension knotted her stomach. Nia gazed around, looking for signs of disturbance.

"No wind. No birds, wildlife. Everything is too…still," he mused. "And that smell…it smells like burnt rubber and acid. Something metallic."

"Blood," she said, stricken. "The blood of everything it scourges."

She whipped her cell phone out from her jeans pocket and dialed the lodge. When Roxanne answered, she barked out an order, her voice crisp with fear. "Secure all quarters. Get everyone inside and bar the doors. Storm warning, level one."

Fear tinged her beta's voice. "I was going call you. Rickie is missing. His mother went to his room to take him with her to the Mitchell Ranch and he was gone."

Terror snaked down Nia's spine. Rickie. One of the two young boys who would soon experience the first shift into wolf.

Her wild gaze swept over the pasture, her wolf howling at the silent menace churning in the distance. "Since when?"

"This morning. His mama told me he'd left a note. He's run away." Roxanne lowered his voice. "His birthday is next week. He's so scared he'll die next and he didn't want to go to a strange new home at the Mitchell Ranch."

"I'll find him," Nia promised. She thumbed off the cell, her heart hammering in her chest. Damn it, she'd been too absorbed in the challenge and other affairs. She should have seen this coming. Poor Rickie, the oldest male in the pack…

"We have to get to shelter before the storm hits. But

Rickie, one of our young, is missing. He could be anywhere. I have to find him," she told Aiden.

He gave her a level look. "Storms in Montana this time of year? What the hell is going on, Niki?"

"It doesn't matter. Rickie's gone. He's only 12, almost 13. If he's caught out in this…" She drew in a trembling breath. "He's my responsibility. I have to find him."

Aiden slid off his horse. "I'm a damn fine tracker."

Then he gave her another level look. "We'll find him. But later, damn it, I want answers."

Later, fine. She could deal with later, had been dealing with it her entire life. Nia jumped off Windstorm, tugged on the reins as Aiden shifted into wolf.

As she led the two horses, she followed the big timber wolf. His nose pressed to the ground, he sniffed the dry earth, the withering grasses, for some trace of the boy's scent.

And then he lifted his head, his ears pointed forward. Aiden released a low howl. The eerie cry sent a shiver down her spine.

He bounded off for the forest. She tied Chance's reins to her mare's saddle, and then leapt back upon Windstorm and followed.

True to his word, Aiden proved to be an excellent tracker. In fact, he made her strongest trackers look as if they had the noses of Skins. After a chase of about two miles, Aiden raced over the pasture, into the woods, and began to howl, pawing at a patch of brush.

Nia recognized Rickie's sweet vanilla scent of childhood, mingled with something sharper, and the sour stench of fear. She dismounted and let the reins drop.

Aiden lowered his head and whined, wagging his tail. She recognized the almost submissive pose of the wolf; indeed, she had done the same when dealing with terrified young who thought they were about to get punished. Silently thanking him, she called out softly.

"Rickie, honey, it's me, and Aiden. We were looking for you. We won't hurt you. You're not in trouble. Come out."

A young boy, dressed in a worn sheepskin jacket, sneakers and faded jeans, emerged from the undergrowth, straps of a bulging backpack upon his thin shoulders. Aiden loped forward and rubbed his muzzle against the boy's thigh. With a trembling hand, Rickie touched the big wolf's head.

"Rickie!" Nia ran forward, sweeping the boy into a tight hug. She looked down at his pale, freckled face. "What the hell were you thinking?"

His mouth wobbled. "I don't want to die, Aunt Niki."

"Rickie…"

"Not like Timmy did. We celebrated his birthday and six weeks later, he was dead. I don't want to die!" He fisted his hands and his body shook.

For the first time she noticed the peach fuzz on his cheeks, and how his once-thin shoulders had taken on bulk. A rill of fear stroked her spine.

"Rickie, did you experience your first shift into wolf?"

He looked away with a guilty expression. Nia bit back a moan. Oh gods. He was now at risk of becoming infected with parvolupus.

"Why didn't you tell me? Your mother?"

Rickie's haunted gaze met hers. "Mom's been so

worried about me, I couldn't tell her. I tried to stop it, I did. But I had to do it. That's why I ran away. I didn't want anyone else to know...I am now fully Lupine."

She soothed him, stroking his hair, feeling guilt and regret spear her insides. *My fault. I should have taken them all off the ranch, should have done something...*

Aiden looked at her, and even as wolf, she could read his expression. *Forget it. The kid comes first.*

Then he rubbed his muzzle against the child again, as if marking him. Aiden lifted his head to Rickie and licked his hand.

Rickie touched him, fear evaporating from his expression. "He's a big guy. Alpha."

Hearing the awe in his voice, she smiled. "Rickie Turner, meet Aiden Mitchell in wolf form."

Rickie rubbed Aiden's head and the alpha wagged his tail. Totally non-threatening, his manner cool and calm. Her own pulse slowed a little. Aiden was a good male. Good with children.

He'd make beautiful babies.

Nia fished out her cell phone and called the lodge, ordering her beta to tell Rickie's mother he'd been found and he was safe.

She glanced covertly at the timber wolf and the boy rubbing his ears and lowered her voice. "I'm headed for the cabin. We'll be safe there and spend the night. Secure the quarters and make damn sure to clean up after the storm hits. I don't want to scare Rickie further. Poor kid's terrified enough."

As she hung up, Aiden loped over to a nearby tree and lifted his leg. She could almost be amused at his territorial gesture. "Please, Mitchell. Must you?"

Aiden turned with a wolfish smile. *Oh yeah*, she

could read in that smile. *Around you, I always have to mark my territory.*

"I haven't seen a real alpha male in years." Rickie held out his hand to Aiden, who licked it again.

She smiled. But now was not the time to make friends. "We have to go, sweetie. Your mom is really worried about you."

Then she heard a distant wailing, like a banshee.

"We have to get to shelter. Any kind of shelter." Nia whipped her head around, gauging her bearings. "There's a cabin nearby. It's stocked with winter provisions. But we have to hurry."

Aiden shifted back to Skin and conjured clothing. Well over six feet, he looked down at Rickie, who suddenly backed away, his expression filled with wonder.

The alpha ruffled the boy's head. "Come on, Rickie. Let's do what your Aunt Niki says."

They ran for the horses. Rickie looked up at Aiden. "Can I ride with you?"

Without words, Aiden lifted him up into the saddle, then swung up behind him. Nia mounted Windstorm.

"The cabin is about quarter of a mile north. Follow me!" She dug her heels into her mare's flanks.

She took off at a gallop, hearing him close the distance behind her. Nia gulped down fear as they rode. The winds seemed far away, kicking up fallen leaves and dust on the horizon. Miniature tornadoes swirled and bounced in the distance.

Now the sounds echoed over the sweeping pasture, and she could see the wind.

Swirling colors of purple, magenta, and deep indigo smoke swept through the dry grasses. Beyond the pasture, she heard an eerie, distant cry, haunting as a train whistle echoing through the mountain. Terrifying as the approach of a tornado.

And much deadlier.

The second joy of the curse. The Banshee Winds, magick winds that carried the strains of the disease and spread it like dandelion wisps floating through the air.

Nia spotted the cabin with its adjacent stable large enough to accommodate four horses. She'd ensured it would withstand the weather when she'd had the cabin wired for electricity and built the stable.

After losing her male cousin to the Banshee Winds, she never wanted anyone to be caught out here without protection.

"Hurry," she cried out, pulling Windstorm to a halt and jumping off.

But Rickie had already slid off Chance and grabbed the stallion's reins. "We have to take care of the horses!" he screamed.

Aiden slid off his mount and let Rickie run toward the barn as Nia followed, her heart pounding hard. She could taste the metallic stench of blood in the air that heralded the magick winds arrival, sense the whirling, sharpened pieces of obsidian rock embedded into the winds eager to scrape and cut and hurt. If they were caught outside, she would bleed.

But Aiden would die and Rickie would sicken and eventually die as well.

Aiden opened the barn door as Rickie led his stallion inside and Nia followed. They stabled the horses and ran outside. Nia closed the door firmly. The Banshee Winds hadn't affected the livestock, but with the new mutation affecting the wildlife, she wasn't taking chances.

A low howl cut the air, making them both wince.

"What the hell is it?" Aiden demanded.

Nia grabbed Rickie's hand. The boy practically tugged her toward the cabin.

"Come on, come on, let's go!" he screamed.

Aiden didn't ask another question. Instead, he herded them toward the cabin. The eerie howling grew closer, stabbing her sensitive Lupine eardrums like knives. Warmth trickled down her cheeks. Her ears bled from the horrible wind's high-pitched squeals.

They reached the cabin, but she could feel the wind at her back, know it had come for her, would make her hurt.

Rickie tripped and fell. The wind was nearly upon him, and it would cut him until he died.

Terror lodged in her throat and for a moment she could not breathe. If she died, so be it, but Rickie was young and he needed to live. Deserved to live.

"Aiden," she screamed, her voice high and reedy. "Help him!"

Aiden picked the boy up, flung open the door and threw Rickie inside. Mitchell understood. The welfare of the children always came first. Always.

Then he turned, grabbed her by the waist and pushed her inside as the wind battered him. Aiden raced into the cabin, slammed the door as the wind hit it with a furious howl. He leaned against it, struggling to keep it closed.

Nia pressed her weight against it as well, and slammed the thick oak bar down in place. Aiden straightened, narrowing his eyes as he quickly scanned the cabin, as if assessing it for danger.

"The windows," he began. "We should shutter them."

"We're safe now." She braced her hands on her knees, panting. "The winds can't touch us here because they can't sense us. The windows are strong."

The cabin had a living room with a fireplace and a faded sofa set before it. Rickie perched on the sofa, shaking, his hands wrapped around his middle.

He was crying, and trying hard to hide it.

The children came first. She went over to join him as the sky darkened to indigo and the winds pushed with shrieking force at the cabin.

"You're okay, sweetie. You're safe."

Rickie pulled away, his lower lip jutting out as he hung his head. She understood, could feel the shame radiating from him. Dear gods, the kid was only 12 and he was ashamed of being afraid of losing his life.

No child should have to harbor fear like that.

She pointed to Rickie. Aiden sat next to him, giving him a solemn look. "You okay, big guy?"

Rickie managed a nod.

Aiden released a deep breath. "Glad you're holding it together, because I was damn scared."

The boy glanced up, his dark eyes wet. "You were? But you're alpha."

"Being an alpha doesn't mean I don't get scared, especially of magick I can't control. It means I have to work harder at overcoming my fear, and at doing the right thing." Aiden gave him a solemn look and scrubbed a hand over the dark stubble on his face. "You'd make a good alpha."

Rickie narrowed his eyes. "Yeah, right."

But Aiden nodded.

"Alphas have to look after pack, and on a ranch, it means looking after the livestock. That was some quick thinking, telling us to stable the horses first. You're a good cowhand."

Rickie beamed at the praise. He'd stopped shaking. "Really?"

"Really. First rule of the ranch is see to the livestock. You did well."

"You guys want to make a fire?" Nia suggested. She left them doing so and talking as she went into the tiny kitchen and opened a cupboard door. There was only canned food, but all of it safe to eat. She'd warm stew for dinner and they'd bunk down here.

They would not take chances outside, and risk exposing Aiden and Rickie to the punishing force of the winds.

She poked her head out the kitchen. "There are several cans of stew in the pantry. I'm starting dinner."

Aiden glanced at the window. "We'll stay here for the night. When the winds die down, I'll call Garth and let him know we're safe."

"Not necessary. I already told Roxanne we're here for the night."

Aiden smiled at Rickie. "Stay by the fire a minute, son. I'll be right back. Have to have a little chat with your aunt Niki."

Nia's heart raced as Aiden joined her in the kitchen, his massive body taking up all the space in the tiny room. He leaned against the counter and folded his arms.

"Level with me, Niki. I want to know what the hell is going on around here. Now."

CHAPTER 11

She had survived so much in her 25 years. Nia wondered how she would survive this interrogation by Aiden Mitchell, one of the most feared and ruthless alphas in the west.

She decided to tell a partial truth.

"The Banshee Winds are one reason this ranch has suffered financial ruin. They started about a year ago, and have grown progressively worse."

Aiden didn't even blink. "I've never heard of such winds. Not in Montana or anywhere else."

"That's because they're confined to a specific geographic area." She fished in the refrigerator for a bottle of water and uncapped it, drinking deeply. Sighing, she set down the bottle. "My ranch."

Aiden picked up the bottle, put his lips over it. Such a firm, warm mouth. She watched as he drank, his strong throat muscles working. Aiden finished the bottle and then he wiped his mouth with the back of one hand and tossed the empty into the trash. "Go on."

"The winds are attracted to places filled with magick and are like a weather system. In the right atmospheric conditions, in this case, the right conditions filled with magick, they converge."

Nia bit her lip to prevent it from wobbling. "They appear when male Lupines have just experienced their first shift, for those males have the new, powerful magick of their wolves. The winds killed my cousin Ivan shortly after his first change."

His expression softened. "I'm sorry, pixie."

Nia stared at the darkened window, willing herself to remain strong. Gods, how many times had she refrained from grieving because she had to be strong for her people, for the pack's children, and be the leader everyone thought she was?

"He was a good kid. Ivan had just turned 13. He was such an optimist, so upbeat we nicknamed him Happy. He was running as wolf near here when the winds came down the mountain, and he was caught in the open."

Ivan had been reckless, and refused to listen to reason. Filled with confidence, he'd gone riding, and planned to run over the fields as wolf.

Nia squeezed her hands, her nails biting into the tender skin of her palms. "We found his body a day later. Ivan was dead, cut to ribbons. His face…"

She closed her eyes, trying to recall the smiling boy who had placed his trust in her, that she would find a cure for this damn disease.

Aiden stepped close, pulled her into his arms. He said nothing, only stroked a hand down the curve of her spine. It felt so good to be held. But her composure hung by a thin thread. Nia scrubbed her faced with her hands and stepped away from her mate.

"I had the cabin reinforced and wired for electricity for those riding on the range in winter, and for anyone caught by the Banshee Winds. The winds, as far as we can tell, only target adult males or males approaching puberty. The Lupines killed by the winds were all adult males. Females aren't killed, but you can get hurt, sliced by tornadic activity. The winds kill the males by settling on him until he dies."

Aiden didn't let her put distance between them. He stepped close, stroking a thumb over the scar on her face. "Is that where you got this?"

Startled, she nodded. "The winds have attacked here twice before. I got caught in the first storm, looking for Ivan. I didn't get too badly hurt because I got to this cabin in time. I did get cut, and it took a long time to heal, and then it scarred."

Lupines seldom bore scars. They had amazing healing powers. But not when faced with a terrible wind that destroyed with such brutal force.

Nia flipped on the wall switch. Warm, welcoming light flooded the cabin, the glow settling her raw nerves. A small table and chairs took up most of the space beneath a bank of windows next to the postage-sized kitchen.

Aiden turned and began to investigate the contents of the kitchen. Nia's jaw dropped.

"You're bleeding!"

She raced over to him, and looked at the three slashes on his shirt. "Take off your shirt."

"As the lady commands," he murmured, but shrugged out of it.

On the thick muscles of his back were three distinct lines caused by the winds, all oozing blood. Fear surged in her throat. Nia found a dishtowel and wet it. "I have to disinfect these."

"I'm fine. They've already stopped bleeding."

Sure enough, he was right and the cut had begun to close, testifying to the enormous healing power of a natural born alpha. Nia reached up and kissed the scabs, her mouth trembling.

If Aiden hadn't thrown Rickie inside, the child might be dead by now.

Aiden turned around, his gaze solemn. "You okay, pixie?"

She nodded, managed to regain her composure. "There are a few shirts and other clothing in the bedroom. See if you can find something that fits. The magnificent sight of your naked chest threatens to bring me to my knees."

He grinned. "Sounds like my wildest dreams, except there's a young child in the house."

When he left, she found a box of instant cocoa and started boiling water. Rickie would need something hot and soothing after what happened.

She poured two mugs, and set them at the kitchen table and called Rickie over as Aiden returned to the room buttoning a blue chambray work shirt. The shirt was slightly tight, and stretched over his thick shoulders and bulging biceps. He winked at her and joined Rickie at the table.

Then she began to heat up the cans of stew on the stove.

Aiden leaned back against the chair, watching Rickie drink the hot treat. He sipped his, his gaze thoughtful.

"I'll set the table," Aiden told her.

He began, hunting through the cabinets for bowls. His long, strong fingers brushed against her hand as she stirred the stew. The heat of sexual awareness made her shiver and she drew in a deep breath, struggling with a sudden surge of want.

A short while later, she poured the stew into the bowls Aiden had set upon the table.

Suddenly ravenous, Nia spooned up her meal. She'd been used to this kind of fare for a while, since the pack couldn't afford fresh meat and game was scarce in the woods.

"Aiden, you're not hungry?" she asked.

Something wild and dangerous flashed in his gaze. "Not for stew. I'll satisfy my appetite later."

With you, that heated glance added.

After dinner, Nia found Rickie a pair of pajamas that had belonged to Ivan. A lump in her throat, she gave them to the boy and joined Aiden in the living room.

When Rickie emerged in the hallway, they escorted him into the bedroom. Hands stuffed into the pockets of his jeans, Aiden watched as she tucked Rickie under the covers.

Rickie looked at Aiden with wide eyes. "Is it safe here? Will the bad thing get me here?"

"You're safe, son. I won't let anything happen to you," Aiden assured him.

"But you can't stop the disease, even though you're an alpha. Uncle Ed tried, but it got him, too, in the end."

The alpha sucked in a breath and glanced at her. But he went to Rickie and touched his head. "Don't worry about that now, Rick. Get some sleep."

Rickie gave a huge yawn. "Good night."

Nia went into the living room, listening to the storm outside. Her stomach knotted as she thought about how they might have been caught outside. She'd been so focused on riding Windstorm and having fun she'd forgotten to remain alert. If not for Aiden's warning...

He went behind her, slid his arms around her waist. "It's going to be okay, pixie."

But despite his reassurances, she could not relax. They sat near the fireplace, listening to the howling winds. Finally the keening wails slowed, and then died to a whisper. And then, blessed silence.

Raising her head, she listened.

In the distance, a bird sang, and the horses in the shed whinnied.

"It's safe now. The storm has passed. It won't be back.'

"How can you be sure?"

"It's the nature of the winds. They arrive, target a Lupine, and then leave. They won't be back for a long time."

She looked at him. "I'll go out and water the horses. There's a little hay for them. I use the stables as a storage place for hay for the winter months. Can you please stay here with Rickie in case he has nightmares?"

Aiden nodded.

When Niki returned, Aiden gave his mate a long look, his temper simmering. Secrets and more secrets. And she wasn't opening up and sharing any information with him.

Now was the perfect time to talk with her, make her confess.

But seeing the smudges of exhaustion and her

slumped shoulders, his anger faded. He didn't have the heart to pry her with questions now. She needed a real meal. She'd been so busy caring for everyone else, she didn't care for herself.

That was his job.

When they returned to the lodge, he'd demand answers.

"Are you sure the winds are gone?" he asked.

She nodded.

"Okay. Stay here, bolt the door after me. I'm going hunting to find you fresh meat."

As she opened her mouth, he gave her a stern look. "No arguing."

"The wildlife could be affected by that fungus that Darius found on the deer."

"I'll be careful. If there's disease, my wolf can detect it." He frowned. "I don't like leaving you here alone, unprotected."

Niki went to a kitchen cabinet, and brought back a small safe. She dialed the combination and fished out a handgun. "I'm not unprotected. I can take care of myself."

He left her loading bullets into the gun. Aiden went outside and shifted into wolf, relishing the feel of power rushing through his body. His senses exploded, his sight sharpened as the moonlight draped the land. He raced into the woods, listening for the sounds of wildlife. A soft wind rustled in the overhead pine boughs, but other than the wind, the forest was quiet. Odd how the winds targeted Lupines, but left the forest and the cabin untouched.

Surely on this land there must be a rabbit or other game he could flush out.

He loped through the forest, scenting the ground, and caught the days old of smell of rabbit. Aiden padded through the woods, following the trail.

He headed east until reaching a small clearing in the forest, about one quarter of a mile behind the cabin. His wolf whined, not liking this glen. It smelled of dark magick and power. But the rabbit was close and he salivated for the kill.

Aiden spotted a flick of movement and prowled forward, the tasty scent of rabbit flooding his nostrils. Suddenly another glimmer of movement.

A silver wolf emerged from the forest. Aiden growled, his fur on edge, every sense surging to protect his territory and his mate and the young back in the cabin.

But then his nostrils flared as he caught the wolf's scent. Man and wolf struggled for control as wolf wanted to charge forward and attack. Man won out, for Aiden knew this wolf.

He kept a respectful distance, but a wary eye on the intruder, knowing the wolf could shift into a wizard at any moment.

The silver wolf lowered his head sniffed a nearby tree. Then he looked at Aiden and wagged his tail. Suddenly he lifted his head and began to chase.

Rabbit. Two rabbits. Both healthy. Aiden followed, tracking the rabbit on the left, ignoring the other wolf. They chased the rabbits for a short distance. The kill was swift and merciful. Kill in his mouth, Aiden loped back to the glen and dropped the rabbit. Suddenly ravenous, he ate, keeping an eye on the silver wolf. The wolf did not eat.

Instead, as Aiden finished, the silver wolf trotted

over to Aiden and dropped the rabbit at his feet. He wagged his tail.

Aiden licked his lips, uncertain of this gift, and the wolf's motives.

Tristan, you sly dog. What do you want?

A foul, dangerous smell drifted into the glen. His ears pricked back and he growled, suddenly very afraid for those he'd left in the cabin.

A troll, standing about seven feet tall, entered the clearing. His eyes gleamed red and his skin was covered in a thick, ugly black fungus.

Aiden stared, his body poised in the flight or fight mode. He could fight the troll, perhaps even win, but if there were more…and the dark magick ringing this glen worried him.

The troll stank like rotting mushrooms, as some kind of disease had claimed him. It moved forward, dragging a heavy club.

The silver wolf growled and pinned the massive troll with his glowing blue stare. The troll backed away. Then the wolf snarled and blinked.

In an instant, the troll vaporized, leaving behind nothing but ash. Damn, that was powerful.

The silver wolf shifted into a tall, dark-haired man clad in black. Tristan leaned against a tree trunk.

"I would never let him hurt you, Aiden. You're a good leader, and she needs you." The wizard sighed and Aiden blinked in surprise. Tristan seemed almost weary.

"This is not a good place for you. For anyone. Return to your mate, give her the second rabbit. She will need all her strength soon."

Aiden licked his lips and nodded. He didn't know

what the wizard wanted, but his wolf sensed no threat.

He picked up the kill and began to leave the glen.

But not before stopping at a tree Tristan had sniffed and lifting his leg. Sniff *this,* wizard.

As he raced off with the dead rabbit, he heard Tristan's amused chuckle float on the wind.

CHAPTER 12

When Nia, Aiden and Rickie finally returned to the lodge the next morning, Carol, Rickie's mother, ran outside to greet them, screaming with joy as she hugged her son.

Rickie, who'd seemed to mature in the last day, pulled away. "I'm okay, Mom." He looked at Aiden, who nodded.

"I'm sorry I upset you by running off."

Carol hugged her son harder. "Don't ever do that again. We'll find a way to deal with whatever problems we face. As long as you're with me."

Rickie looked up at Aiden. "You going to stick around? You're not going to leave us like my dad did? My dad ran off five years ago and said he'd be back and he never came back."

Her heart turned over.

Aiden smiled and ruffled the boy's hair. "I'm not leaving. I promise."

Then he gave Carol a respectful nod, and took Nia's hand, leading her back to her cabin.

Aiden herded her inside, until they reached the bedroom. He swiftly undressed her, and then ripped off his shirt. Buttons popped as he tore it off. He sat and tugged off his boots, and then removed the rest of his clothing.

As Nia climbed onto the bed, he joined her, kissing her and tumbling her backwards onto the mattress. She curled her fingers around his broad shoulders as he moved inside her. Aiden's gaze glittered fiercely.

Her hands rose up, fisted in his thick, silky hair. Nothing else mattered at the moment but having him inside her, now. Her aching, wet pussy squeezed with need.

He kissed her, his mouth moving over hers in desperate, frantic intensity and she knew he felt the same frenzied need. After the horror of the storm, she needed to get lost in him, feel him so deep inside her Nia knew he would never leave.

Feel him imprint himself on her flesh, brand himself upon her body so days later, she would walk and feel him inside her still.

Brand him with her flesh, so she would stay with him, forever.

All those fantasies she'd had of Aiden were girlish dreams compared to his hard body moving swiftly on top of hers, his strong hands pinning her wrists against the mattress.

He sucked on her lower lip, releasing it with a slight popping sound. Nia writhed and moaned, eager to have him join his body to hers.

Aiden growled again. She recognized his possessive need to claim her physically, to mark her as his own. To merge them so completely they could not tell where one began and the other started.

This was Mitchell, her Mitchell, the alpha male who

beguiled her, vexed her, wooed her and made her sweat and scream and beg in bed. She wanted no other. Her mate.

He devoured her mouth in hot, hungry kisses and she gave it back to him with equal intent. Aiden's palms skimmed up her belly, to her breasts and he flicked his thumbs over her hardening nipples. Then he bent his head and sucked her right breast, his tongue whirling over the pearling bud. Nia wrapped her legs around his narrow hips and opened her thighs wide.

"Take me," she ordered, panting.

Lifting his head, he stared down at her, his gaze dark, a pulse beating strongly in his neck.

"Please," she begged.

"Ask me again, nicely." Aiden fisted a hand in her hair and stared at her. "You're mine. Tell me you're mine."

Beneath the arrogant words, she heard the faintest hint of loneliness, as if he needed her as much as she needed him. Not merely for sex, but something far bigger than themselves, to usher aside the dark moments when it seemed they were the only ones holding it together, the leaders whom everyone assumed would have all the answers, even when there were none.

"I'm yours. Do it, now!"

He entered her in one single deep thrust, and she stiffened beneath him. Pleasure and pain shot through her at the force of his entry. Nia squeezed her legs around his hips and pumped upwards to meet his demanding strokes. Panting, he stared down at her, his fingers laced through hers, his gaze wild, sweat beading his forehead.

His scent wrapped around her like a blanket, intoxicating her more than any drug ever could. Aiden took her in hard, almost violent strokes, his balls slapping against her flesh, his cock rigid and slick with her juices.

"More," she demanded.

They began a rhythm, male and female, a dance older than time itself. Nia's throat closed tight as she stared into his eyes, darkened to onyx. She could have lost him to the Banshee Winds, and the mere thought made her want to weep. To see this magnificent, virile and proud alpha with the tender heart die, his heart forever silenced, his eyes vacant as they stared at the sky as the others had...

A sob wrung from her throat. Tears filled her eyes as she clung to him, her fingers digging deep into the thick muscles of his shoulders. *Don't leave me, don't ever leave me, please...stay here, love me....*

Tiny muscles in her sex throbbed and pulsed around his thick cock. Give and take, she thought in a haze of sensual pleasure. Male and female, each needing each other. The way it was meant for Lupines.

He fucked her hard and fast, making her sob and plead. Then he drew back on his haunches, wrapping her legs around his waist. Aiden leaned over her, pushing into her, playing with her clit. The friction of him sliding over her, combined with the light flicks of his fingers, brought the tension to an explosive burst. Nia screamed as she climaxed, her body bucking and shaking. Waves of pleasure slammed into her again and again.

Then he stiffened, giving a loud groan, his cock growing thicker inside her. The wolf's knot, tying them together. He kept climaxing and each jettison of his semen sent her into fresh waves of orgasm all over again.

His heavy weight pressed her deep into the mattress as he eased his body onto hers. Perspiration slicked their skin. Nia felt his cock throb inside her as Aiden rested his head on the mattress beside her.

Aiden rolled to the side, taking her with him, their bodies still tied together. Finally his penis returned to normal and he slid out of her body. Cuddling against him, Nia toyed with the damp curls on his chest, her breathing ragged. She had never imagined making love with Aiden Mitchell could be this intense and exhilarating, and emotionally draining.

He did not let her leave the bedroom for the next six hours. He brought her food, and drinks, and made love to her non-stop.

She'd sensed Aiden would be fantastic in bed, judging from his confident manner, the graceful way he moved, those muscles moving fluidly beneath his tight jeans. But nothing prepared her for the reality. Not even her wildest sessions with a vibrator.

The alpha's lovemaking contained an element of pure animal intensity, all wolf. He was gentle, but once she'd displayed her own ferocity, he met her evenly. His eyes glowed amber, showing his wolf surging to the surface, displaying an eroticism she found impossible to resist. He'd coax her to the brink of climax with his gentle hands, and then urged her to turn over onto her knees, and then he'd enter her from behind. Dripping wet, ready to receive him, she'd moan as their bodies became one, the sweat slicking them as his male flesh thrust hard into her, his body slapping against hers.

He'd touch the back of her neck with his tongue, licking her skin, flicking over the sensitive part of her throat where he gave her his mating mark. And then just as she exploded into rapturous bliss, he'd gently clamp down on her neck, his big hands holding her still as he nipped at her skin, the ultimate alpha move of a male claiming his mate.

It was if spending time with Rickie had sealed his own longing for a son.

Nia lay in bed, exhausted as Aiden went into the kitchen for more food. She rolled over and hugged the sweat-dampened pillow.

It was nice to stay here and dream they could have a normal life.

For in a short time, she knew reality would intervene once more.

Two nights after the Banshee Winds, all of Aiden's pack returned to the Blakemore Ranch and joined with her people in the large dining hall of her lodge for the first formal, celebratory dinner between their two packs.

Thanks to Aiden, she felt energized and more alert. He'd kept feeding her fresh, raw meat and for the first time in months, she felt Lupine.

Now as she sat beside him, she felt ready to tackle whatever came her way. After the dinner, she would talk with Aiden and tell him the full truth about the disease. He needed to know.

The thought of breaking her father's promise had torn her apart, but she couldn't risk any more lives.

Rickie had refused to leave the ranch. He was in awe of Aiden, and wanted to stay close. And every minute the boy stayed on the ranch, he was more in danger of catching the disease, especially now.

Tonight's dinner was a joint celebration, served by both their packs. To show their loyalty and appreciation for the newly mated alphas, their people had joined together to cook dinner. The prime rib, new potatoes and mixed vegetables smelled terrific, but she had no appetite. As they ate dinner, surrounded by the one hundred and forty-seven members of their pack, she felt the ruse she'd woven begin to crumble, the mortar of the foundation of secrets turning to mud. How much longer could she continue to hide her twin?

It had been a delicate balancing act with her pack alone, but they had respected her privacy and obeyed her edicts. Aiden's pack?

They respected her, but they were everywhere since arriving for the dinner.

Nia touched Aiden's hand. "After we eat, send all your people home."

To her surprise, he didn't protest or question why. He simply nodded. "Good idea. But I'll keep Garth here with me. He and Roxanne are showing a deep interest in each other."

Relief filled her. At least she'd get the guys out of here. Most of them. She glanced at her beta, who was leaning toward Garth, her face alight with interest as he talked. It would be lovely to see Roxanne settled and happy.

"Maybe you should send Garth back, too."

"No. He's one of my best hunters outside of Kyle

and Arianna, and the best cowhand I have at assessing repairs. I need him to work on the barn."

Aiden gave her a steady look. "Dale's also staying. And so is Beth."

She craned her neck, looking at the pretty, dark-haired Lupine who was a biologist. "Why?"

"I want her to examine the rabbit carcass Darius and the others found. If your land is stricken with disease, she can determine what kind." He rolled his shoulders. "She'll need a place to set up a lab, put her equipment. I thought that basement beneath your cottage would suffice."

Panic clogged her throat. "No!"

Heads started. She smiled at everyone and lowered her voice to Aiden. "If there is something dangerous that could affect Lupines, shouldn't the lab be someplace where the specimen can be quarantined?"

Aiden raised his brows, considered. "Of course. What do you recommend?"

Goodness, the alpha was actually asking her advice. "I'll find a private cottage for her. Maybe the old one by the barn."

Aiden slid his hand over hers. "Thanks."

She gave a relieved smile and returned her attention to the food she didn't want.

When the plates were cleared and they awaited dessert, the speeches began. Most were brief and courteous, acknowledging Aiden and Nikita's new roles among both packs. Then Aiden stood and told them how they would take time to assimilate both packs together, but for the meantime, they would still operate under the old system each alpha had set into place.

Nia stood to make her speech. She gazed around the room and then cleared her throat.

The door to the dining hall burst open. Nia's heart dropped to her stomach as Carl Chandler strolled inside. She had not seen the troll since her wedding day.

Aiden frowned. "What the hell?"

"Excuse me, everyone! I hate to interrupt your little feast, but I have a matter of importance to address with the alpha." Carl looked at Aiden. "The male alpha."

Nia's pulse raced. Aiden frowned as her pack gave questioning looks. How could she tolerate such rudeness?

It was easy when she owed the man five figures for the past six months' worth of groceries.

"I hope that now that Nikita is mated, you'll pay the little lady's debts. Finally, I'll get the money I'm owed."

Face flooded with heat, Nia stared at the floor. Could she be any more humiliated?

Aiden tensed. Oh hell, he looked ready to beat the crap out of the troll. If she let him interfere, she'd lose what little respect she'd had among both their packs.

Nia put a calming hand on Aiden's arm, feeling him tremble with rage. "I'll take care of this."

She stood back up and faced Carl. "You're rude and boorish and trespassing on my land. I'll give you two minutes to get your hairy ass off my ranch."

She glanced at the clock. "I'm counting."

Cheers went up from her females.

Carl sneered. "You can't order me around, Blakemore. You owe me $45,000 for the unpaid bills you ran up for your groceries. If I weren't such a generous male, I'd demand you give me the cash right now."

He headed over to Lucy, who shrank back. Sitting next to her, Stephen growled at Carl, the sound rippling through the room.

Carl ignored him. "But the real reason I'm here now is to make an offer. Give me Lucy here as my mate and I'll forgive the debt. She's a young, pretty thing. Should be good at warming my bed."

Stephen jumped out of his seat. Red-faced, he looked ready to slug Carl.

"Stephen, stop it," Nia ordered. "This is my business."

She raced over to the table, and put a comforting hand on Lucy's shoulder. The poor girl looked pale and ready to retch at the thought of mating with Carl. "You're not going to mate anyone you don't want, sweetie. Especially not this hairy-assed troll."

With a nod of thanks, the younger Lupine seemed to relax.

Carl began to tremble, his bony shoulders shaking. "How dare you—"

Nia looked at the clock hanging on the dining room wall, thinking of all the insults she could pile on Carl. Perverted troll came to mind. "One minute. You have one minute left."

"You're a loser, Nikita Blakemore. You couldn't succeed at running anything, let alone this ranch. If not for mating with Aiden, you'd kill your pack. I wish you'd shut the hell up and let your man talk for you, bitch."

Aiden stood so quickly his chair fell "You bastard. That's it. You're going down."

Carl's insult stung the heart of her. Nia trembled, fisting her hands, struggling to leash her temper. As

Aiden advanced, she went to him and put a hand on his chest.

"Please," she said in a low voice. "Let me handle this. I must."

The alpha's face grew red with rage, but he took a deep breath and steadied himself. Nia faced Carl, lifting her chin.

"My pack is my business. My people are loyal, and they will stand by me, as I will always stand by them. As for you... I wish you'd drop dead, you bastard."

Shaking his head, Carl laughed. He opened his mouth as if to speak. Then suddenly his face went pale. Staggering backward, he groaned deeply.

Then Carl dropped to the floor with a groan and lay still.

Darius, nearest to him, bent down and felt his pulse. The beta looked up, shock rippling over his handsome face.

"He's dead."

Carl had done exactly as she asked. He'd dropped dead.

Chapter 13

Pandemonium erupted. Several members of Niki's pack and his started for the door.

Aiden whistled, and his pack went still. He held up his hands. "Everyone! Calm down and go downstairs to the living room while we figure this out." He glanced at Darius. "Dar, you, stay here with me. J.J., Rafe, get them all settled downstairs."

"What about her?" One of his pack pointed at the pale-faced Niki, who kept staring at the dead Carl. "She has dark magick in her words."

"You've had too much damn whiskey, Paul. For that remark, you'll repair all the north fences for the next two weeks."

"Paul's right," said John, another of his pack, who gripped the hand of an attractive female. "How do we know Nikita didn't wish him dead?"

Aiden growled and John shrank back. "You'll join Paul in repairing those fences. Now get your damn asses downstairs and see to the others."

They scurried away. Aiden went to Niki and settled his hands on her shoulders, turning her to face him.

"You okay?"

His first concern was his mate. A hundred obnoxious males could have dropped dead before him and his first concern would always remain Niki.

She gave a little laugh. "That's the first time I actually wished for something that came true. Maybe I should have wished for other things, like money to pay the damn grocery bill or for the barn to get magically fixed by itself."

He gave her shoulders a light squeeze. "That's my girl. Always putting up a brave front."

Niki went to the sideboard, grabbed a tablecloth out of a drawer.

"What are you doing?" Aiden asked, glancing at Darius, who shook his head.

"Covering the body. I know that he's probably not worth it, but—"

She gasped and dropped the cloth as the "body" began to stir.

"He's not dead!"

Darius went over to Carl with a thoughtful look, then glanced at Aiden. "I could arrange it."

"No." Aiden crouched down by the "body."

"Don't touch him," Niki shouted. She bolted over to them, and hunkered down. "He could be very ill. And contagious."

She lifted the Lupine's arm. Aiden felt his blood pressure drop.

On Carl's arm was a large black patch of what resembled fungus.

"Damn," Darius muttered. "The same stuff we saw on the wildlife. What is that?"

"It's contagious. We have to get him into quarantine.

But only the females can touch him." Niki whipped out her cell, called her beta.

"Roxanne, I need you, Mandy and Carol up here, stat. Carl's not dead. He's got the disease."

As she pocketed the phone, Aiden gripped her wrist. "What disease?"

She looked at Carl. "I have to take care of this."

"Forget him for now." He signaled to Darius. "Help the women with whatever they need, but keep it quiet! I don't want anyone else panicking. It's a goat-fuck already."

Aiden guided her out of the dining room to the porch outside. She plopped into a rocking chair and gripped the armrests, her face pale, sweat beading on her forehead.

"What made him this sick?" She shook her head. "He had a compromised immune system. Carl was weak."

"How do you know?"

"I like to check out my creditors. When I found out he'd been sick on and off, I learned to time my visits to the grocery store to avoid running into him."

He had a bad feeling her creditors weren't limited to Carl. And why? There was little overhead on this ranch. No stock anymore. Mouths to feed, Lupines to shelter, yes, but none of the expenses his ranch incurred.

None of that mattered now. He searched her face. "Do you know what sickened Carl?"

She said nothing for a minute, but torment flickered in her deep blue eyes. "Mitchell, you and your men need to leave here. This place isn't safe for you. It's filled with darkness and death."

"Tell me what you know. Something in the water,

the lodge, the air? What the hell is going on at this place?" He struggled to leash his temper.

Niki's shoulders slumped. "It's time you know the truth. The full truth about why I want you off my ranch."

"Well, it's about godsdamn time you told me the truth. After you've been fucking lying to me all this time. You can start by telling me who the hell you are."

Nia paled. "What?"

He drew in a deep breath, tempted to pound his fist into the wall from sheer frustration. "I know your secret. You have a sister. A twin sister."

Nia felt all the blood rush out from her head. She stared at Aiden, who looked like a wolf ready to tear her into pieces.

Holding her head between her hands, she moaned. "You know."

"Damn straight I know," he growled.

"How, how long?"

"Long enough."

She lowered her hands and stared at him.

"I want the truth. The full truth."

"I suppose I should start at the beginning."

"A good place," he said dryly.

Stricken, her heart still racing, she licked her lips. "How do you know about my twin?"

"Met her, while you were at the graveyard. Now who are you? Are you Nikita?"

"No. I'm Nia, her twin."

Aiden rubbed a hand over his face. "Knew it. Knew that sly wizard wasn't only messing with me."

"What wizard?"

"Tristan. He was here the other night. Hinted that he knew what was going on, but didn't tell me."

Now she gripped the armrests of the chair in sheer panic. Her blood pressure plummeted. The wizard here on her property? He *knew*. He knew and he would take Niki away from her.

She struggled to breathe, to find her voice. Emotions in turmoil, her whole world in chaos, she reached deep inside for the control that had seen her through one tragedy after another.

And found nothing. Nia felt as if someone had turned her upside down and emptied her out. All her strength was gone.

I can't take anymore.

You must.

Rocking back and forth, her arms wrapped around her stomach, she stared at Aiden. "Is he here to take Niki away?"

The words were a bare whisper. Aiden shook his head. "I don't think so."

She began to pant, desperate for air. This was insane. Her people would see her, think she was falling apart. She had to hold it together. *Get a grip, get a grip.*

Aiden immediately left his seat and stood. In one swoop, he lifted her into his arms and headed inside to the kitchen. He set her down upon one of the chairs at a small table where her pack's children occasionally sat and watched the women bake cookies.

Nia felt almost childlike herself as she kept hyperventilating. Aiden sat beside her and gripped her hand. "Deep breaths. Control yourself."

Nia took long, calming breaths as he went and

fetched a glass of water. She took the glass and drank deeply. Finally she set it on the table and felt more composed.

He gave her a steady look. "Ready to level with me? Let's start with the reason why there are no males on your land. And why Rickie is terrified to die."

She nodded, struggling to rein in her emotions. "As you've seen, we don't have a single male over the age of 12. The boys who experience their first shift into wolf die shortly after. We've lost two and I can't bear to lose anymore. I don't want anything to happen to your men, or you."

"Shit." Blood suffused his face. He looked ready to tear her head off. "You don't want anything to happen to my men? Or me? What the hell's going to happen to us?"

Nia's temper rose. "Calm down, Mitchell. Don't go all alpha male on me."

"Oh yeah? I am a fucking alpha, damnit," he said, his voice growing quieter and more deadly. "Go on. What is it that kills the males?"

"Disease. The land is riddled with it and it's only on my pack's land."

Aiden went very still. He searched her face. "Why only your land?"

She struggled to find the right words. After years of being insular and protecting her pack, Nia didn't want to share their inside information. Her father had drilled it into her that no one must know. But Aiden and his men were at risk. And he deserved to know the truth.

She slumped against the chair, unable to meet his eyes. "My father took Pandora's Chest."

A low curse filled the air. Aiden sagged against his

chair. Now she did lift her gaze, saw the bleak despair on his face. "Fuck. That chest is cursed."

"You know of it?"

"Every sane werewolf from here to the east coast knows of the legend, and the dangers. Only a truly mad, or greedy alpha would allow his pack to acquire such cursed treasure."

The chest possessed the power to grant an OtherWorlder's dearest wish, but at a great price. Once the chest was opened, it released tendrils of magick to lure more victims into seizing the chest for themselves, igniting the hope that their wildest dreams were within reach.

"My father was neither. He was desperate." Nia pushed a hand through her long hair. "My mom died in childbirth after having us. Niki was older. I'm the youngest. I've kept my sister's existence secret since birth. There's a prophecy spoken in our family for three generations that the eldest girl twin in our family would be claimed by the Silver Wizard. He would come to get her and spirit her away to the afterworld, where she would perish. So when we were born, Dad hid Niki and pretended there was only one girl, the younger twin."

"I'm not truly your mate," she said, her voice quivering. "I've pretended to be something I'm not my whole life. Sometimes to give Niki a break, we'd switch places and I would hide in her basement apartment and she would be Niki, the alpha."

For a moment, silence draped between them. Aiden dragged a hand over his face then he gave her a level look. She began to quiver at the hardness of that look.

"You lied to me."

"I did it for my twin."

"You still lied to me. We're supposed to be mates for life. Partners. And you couldn't trust me with the truth?"

Nia fisted her hands. "Damnit Mitchell, I've spent my whole life living a lie. You forced me into hosting the Mating Challenge by waving the mortgage on my ranch over my head. You think a few vows and great sex are going to change that? My twin is in danger."

"And if you leveled with me, I could help protect her. Instead, you deceived me. You think I wouldn't find out? Your twin gets physically ill around me. She threw up after I kissed her."

Jaw unhinging, she stared. "You kissed my sister?"

Nia didn't know whether to be outraged, jealous or shocked. Or all three.

"Nothing like kissing you, sweetheart," he drawled. "I knew right there it wasn't you."

"I thought we'd have a little more time. I only wanted to buy a little time," she said, hating herself right now. "Niki has been so focused on finding a cure for the disease, and she's so close. She's spent the last five years dedicated to research."

He seemed a little calmer. "She seems frailer than you. Quieter."

"When..." Nia bit her lip, then continued. "When did you kiss her?"

"While you were still down at the graveyard. I thought you'd beaten me back to your cottage. She asked if I was happy with the mating. Seemed concerned."

Aiden narrowed his eyes. "I was happy, until now."

Nia blinked hard. "Technically, she should be your true mate, the one whose hand you won in the

Mating Challenge. You fought for the true alpha leader."

He grabbed her chin in a tight grip, forced her to meet his burning gaze. "You're my mate. Wolves mate for life. *I* mate for life. I'm not giving you up. As pissed off as you make me, I'm not giving you up."

Emotion closed her throat at his fierce devotion. "You got the bad end of the deal, Aiden. I lied to you."

"You'd better tell the truth now. Tell me about the chest."

"Dad took it about 10 years ago, when Niki fell ill. She was deathly sick, because of these berries she'd found in the forest. Dad didn't know what to do. He summoned the finest Lupine physician, but she was dying. And then he heard there was a nearby wizard looking for subjects for a breeding program. A couple volunteered to exchange themselves for the chest to save the alpha's beloved daughter."

Nia sighed. "They didn't realize what they were getting into. Dad got the chest and opened it, wishing for his eldest daughter to be returned to full health."

"It worked."

"Not only did it work, but suddenly everything on the ranch was prosperous. Our horse breeding program became wildly successful, and the couples who were newly mated became pregnant. And then, about five years ago, everything fell apart."

"Your father ignored the consequences. For all the good Pandora's Chest releases, it releases evil as well, a balance of good and bad. How could he be so fucking stupid?"

"He was desperate!" she burst out.

Aiden rubbed his cheek with one hand. "Was this when the disease started striking the males?"

Steeling her spine, she looked him straight in the eye. "It's worse than you can imagine. It affects only the male Lupines who have come of age and shifted. It's a magick bacteria, a plague, and there's no cure. My people have tried everything. It's airborne, in the trees, the dust, and the damn houses. We tried quarantining the males inside and filtering the air. But that didn't work.

"We call the disease parvolupus. It's a horrid, horrid way to die." Nia struggled to speak in a normal tone as horror clogged her throat. "First the victim feels only slightly feverish and his skin itches. That's where the scaly patches show up. That can last about a week. And then it progresses to the victim passing out. In the final stages, the victim can't breathe, they run such a high fever it feels like their body is on fire, and they're thirsty but nothing will quench their thirst."

She dragged in a deep breath. "My father was so dehydrated before he died. We had to shoot a syringe down his throat filled with water and he fought us. He was delirious, called us names and said he hated us. It was h-horrible."

And then the anger in him seemed to fade. He sighed. "It hurts like hell to lose someone you love. I can't imagine losing someone like that."

She blinked hard, focusing on the clinical, as her twin did. If she focused on how their father had died, she'd lose it. "Eventually the victim dies. The period from point of contact to death used to be five months to a year, but then it began to shorten."

This was insane. They should be celebrating a

mating, instead of untangling the complicated knots of disease that had held her pack in its grip for five long years.

"It starts as a black patch on the body. Symptoms include a pounding headache, neck ache, and weakness." She hugged herself, remembering the jerky movements her father made as he died. "It's a horrid, painful death."

He narrowed his gaze and withdrew his hand. "You knew of the curse, and you knew what consequences it has for all males. And yet you deliberately held this competition to draw a mate, and males, to your pack? To kill us all? Was that your fucking mating gift to me?"

"No! I knew I couldn't infect you because women are immune and we can't spread it. And the parvolupus only infects males who live here longer than two weeks. At least, it didn't, until now. That's why I've been trying to get all your men to leave. I didn't want anything to happen to them, or to you."

She hung her head in misery. "I wanted to tell you. But I made a blood oath to my dad on his deathbed. I've already lost so much." A vulnerability she hadn't felt in years seized her. "I don't want to lose you or anyone else."

"You're not losing me."

"You have to leave here." She stared into his dark eyes. "It's for your own good, Aiden."

"No." He leaned forward, his body tense. "You said the disease strikes after males live here for at least two weeks."

"I believe the incubation time is shortening, and it could be as little as a day or two. Look what happened to the male from Richard's pack."

Nia shuddered, thinking of how quickly the male had been stricken.

"Why didn't you tell me about the disease? When you knew every single male in my pack was at risk?"

A steeliness shone in those dark eyes. Aiden would not compromise easily. Neither would she.

"I made a deathbed promise to my dad never to tell outsiders. A sacred vow. And as alpha of my pack, it's my duty to safeguard my people."

Aiden nodded. "And now as your mate, it's my duty to safeguard you and everything important to you. That includes this ranch and your people."

He tipped up her chin with one calloused finger. "I'm still really pissed off at you, Nia. But at least you finally told me the truth."

She nodded. "And now that you know, you have to leave, Aiden. I'll deal with Carl, and this mess. Take your pack and mine and get out of here. The parvolupus is mutating. I don't know much longer you'll have."

He looked at her grimly. "I'm not leaving. I'll send the others away, but I'm staying until we find the chest and return it to Tristan."

"You can't risk it."

"It doesn't matter."

Aiden unbuttoned his shirt sleeve and rolled it up in silence. He held out his right arm.

Acid churned in her stomach as Nia stared.

On the underside of his strong forearm was a patch of black, scaly tissue about the size of a quarter. The disease.

"It's too late. I can't leave here because I have the disease, too."

CHAPTER 14

Aiden flexed his shoulders, feeling his muscles tense.

Congratulations. You've managed to win the woman of your deepest desires, get mated and contract a disease that will kill you, all in less than less than a month. The woman who didn't tell you that you risked your life by walking onto this ranch.

Fuck.

He touched his shirt sleeve over the black fungal mark, feeling it itch. He hadn't developed any of the symptoms she'd mentioned. Not yet.

But it was obvious he was ill.

And he didn't know how long he had until he started exhibiting other symptoms, and became like the others. And died. Or collapsed like Carl had.

"Oh gods, oh gods." Nia stuffed a fist into her mouth. "I can't believe this. You're infected. How long?"

Her panic threatened his already rattled composure. Aiden struggled to keep his voice even and not yell at her. "Noticed it this morning as I shaved."

"Any other symptoms?"

He thought hard. Nia fisted her hands. "Symptoms, Mitchell! Tell me."

"No." He gave her a level look. "Other than complete and total disbelief that you've lied to me all this time. Any other lies you care to own up to?"

His mind whirled with all the information Nia had told him. Nia. The younger twin. His mate.

Her lower lip wobbled. "I'm sorry, Mitchell. So sorry. I should have told you."

"Damn straight you should have!"

Aiden drew in a deep breath. Yelling at her wouldn't solve anything. Priorities. He scrubbed a hand over the bristles spiking on his chin and cheeks. "Have you tried to find a cure, other than looking for Pandora's Chest?"

Blood had drained from Nia's face. Moisture shimmered in her deep blue eyes and she stared at him with a woebegone look.

"I'm so sorry, gods, I'm so sorry. This is all my fault, Mitchell." She went and knelt before him. "I should have told you earlier, should have made you leave here. I never wanted this to happen. Never."

His chest tightened. He wanted to forgive her, wanted all this to go away, but he had to face the grim reality. He'd been too lax, too forgiving. His father was right. Never fall in love, because love is a bitch.

Or it will kill you.

"Is there a cure?"

"My sister has been working on one, while my aunt Mandy, Roxanne, and I search the ranch for the chest. Niki studied biology through online college courses. She's really smart, smarter than I am." Nia returned to her chair. "She's very good with research, and she's poured over the ancient Lupine texts to find clues. It's the reason why we went into foreclosure. Costs a lot to set up a private lab."

Nia sighed. "The ranch was falling apart, but the cure came first. We kept losing so many males. Niki sacrificed all her time to try to find a cure. I love my sister. I'd do anything for her. I'd protect her to the last drop of my blood. She's family."

Deep inside, he understood her pain, and her fierce devotion to protecting her sister. Hell, he'd done the same himself for his sister, taking Kara away from their mad father to live with him when he'd started the Mitchell Ranch. But he couldn't soften on her now. He had to remain strong, and find a way to eradicate this disease before it took down his whole pack. Aiden felt a chill race down his spine as he thought about young Rickie, and the fear in the boy's eyes.

"First, we're settling everyone down and checking every single adult and pre-pubescent male on this property. Are you certain the females aren't carriers?" he asked Nia.

Nia nodded. "Niki's research proved that."

"Good. We'll start with the children."

Two hours later, after everyone in both packs had checked for symptoms of the disease, most of their combined packs left for his ranch, including his beta. Darius began shuttling them in all available vehicles.

Only Roxanne and the devoted Garth remained, and Nia's aunt Mandy, who was nursing Carl.

And Rickie. Aiden's throat tightened. The boy had also shown signs of the disease.

Fortunately, everyone else seemed to be okay. He couldn't risk anyone else falling ill, not after what he'd learned.

Aiden watched the last truck filled with Nia's people depart for the ranch. He turned to Nia.

"We're going to visit your twin. Right now."

He did not take her hand as they walked down to the basement below Nia's cabin. Aiden felt like he had ground glass in his stomach. He'd trusted his mate, and she'd deceived him all this time. Needed to blow off steam.

"I'm not ready yet. I need a minute," he muttered.

He jogged over the wood pile near the basement. Nia followed.

"We have enough firewood," Nia said, sounding bewildered.

"Not for my purposes." Aiden took a log and the nearby ax and began splitting it. He chopped, wood chips flying, concentrating his anger on the wood. He cut and chopped until nothing remained of the log but kindling.

He slammed the ax into the log pile. "Now I'm ready."

She looked at the shards of wood with huge eyes. "Whoa."

Whoa is right. But he needed that physical release.

Nia knocked on the door, three brisk raps. When the door opened, Aiden stepped back, stunned.

Seeing was believing.

Her twin was a reflection of his mate; the same long, dark blond hair, and stunning blue eyes. But while his mate's eyes shone with passion, fire and tenderness, there was only fear in Nikita's.

The real Nikita, he amended. How could he have been fooled all this time?

And then he glanced from one sister to another, and knew they had spent their whole lives perfecting the deception.

They walked inside and Aiden closed the door, leaning against it.

"You told him," Nikita said to her twin, backing away from Aiden.

"I had to." Nia explained about Carl, and then pointed to Aiden's arm. "Show her."

He unrolled his shirt sleeve and Nikita's eyes widened. "Oh no! Not you!"

"I'll say," he said dryly, rolling back his sleeve. "In all these years this disease has plagued you, have you found a damn thing to stop it?"

Niki gave him a woebegone look. "I'm close, so close. I'm sorry, this is my fault. I should have known you'd be more susceptible than other males. You're a blooded alpha male, like our dad was. Your magick is stronger and that makes you more vulnerable to infection."

"It's not your fault, Niki. It's mine," Nia started.

His gaze whipped back and forth between the twins. It was like watching a tennis match. He held up a hand. "Enough," he roared.

Both sisters quieted.

"Focus on the immediate. What can I do to delay my symptoms while we search for the chest?"

Niki's gaze flicked to the side. Odd. As if she knew something... Aiden stepped forward. "Level with me. What do you know?"

"You have to shapeshift into a wolf and stay in your

wolf form. It's the only way to delay the advancement of the disease."

Nia's twin kept her distance, as if she were afraid of him. He almost laughed. How the hell could he ever have thought this sister was his Nia? They were as different as the sun and the moon.

"If he shifts into wolf, then how can we communicate?" Nia went to take his hand, but he sidestepped her.

He saw the hurt in her eyes before her expression shuttered.

"You'll have to learn," Niki said. "I need a little more time. I need to test it out my new formula. It works, but I have to be certain."

Aiden didn't dare hope. Nia's expression brightened. "You didn't tell me the vaccine worked!"

Niki smiled sadly. "I didn't have a chance. You've been too busy holding everything together, little sis."

"What are you testing it out on?" Aiden asked.

"I found two sick rabbits in the woods." Nikita looked defiant. "I didn't infect them, they were already sick. All my subjects in the past were Lupines already infected."

"And nothing worked on them." Nia sighed. "Come on. Let's leave her alone to work."

They went upstairs. Inside her cabin, Aiden paced. "I have to get back to my ranch and check over my men. I don't want this damn thing spreading to my people."

"And if you return there infected, you'll risk all of them." Nia shook her head. "You have to shift and delay the disease. It's the only way."

"I'm not staying as wolf when my pack, and yours, is endangered. I'm the alpha!"

"And right now you're a sick alpha," she snapped. "Do it."

Frustrated, he fisted his hands. "I wouldn't be in this predicament if it weren't for you, Nia."

Her face fell. "I know. I would apologize a thousand times if I thought it would help, but it won't. I'd take the disease into my own body to cure you, but I can't. I wish I could, Mitchell. Every time I was forced to watch another male I cherished, cared about, perish from this disease, I wanted to die myself."

Nia's mouth trembled. "And it kills me to know you're infected because of me. If you had never set foot on this property, you'd be healthy. I thought you had more time. And now look what I've done to you. I can't bear to watch you suffer and get ill like they did, Mitchell. Please, shift into wolf."

Aiden's stomach tightened. "Fine. But first, a few signals. If I give one warning growl, it means stay back. If I point to something, pay attention. And you're not leaving my side. I don't want you wandering around where I can't keep an eye on you."

"Deal," she said.

Taking a deep breath, he shifted into wolf. Nia blinked hard.

Sullen, he lay on the rug before the fireplace. She headed into the bedroom. "Aren't you coming to bed?"

Aiden put his head between his paws.

"Fine. I deserve that."

Damn straight you do.

She bent down and her scent flooded his nostrils, all warm, soft female.

Nia kissed the top of his head. "Good night."

Being a wolf usually made him feel more powerful, more in control.

Not now.

For the next two days, he sulked around the cabin, feeling helpless and angry as Nia and her aunt Mandy searched by the pond for the chest. Each afternoon, Nia returned, looking defeated. No luck.

Gods, he hated feeling this helpless. He needed to do something. But his strength had started to wane. Big, bad wolf, the alpha of the pack, now growing weaker by the day.

He needed to get out, search through the woods. He was an excellent hunter, even better than Kyle. He could find the damn chest.

Prowling through the forest, flushing out the scent, would be better than lying here like a domesticated dog.

Late that afternoon, Aiden got up from his usual spot before the fireplace, loped over to the door and scratched it. Nia set down her laptop and joined him.

"I can't risk taking you out in the woods as wolf." Nia rubbed behind his ears. "We've had threats from those Skin hunters. Montana doesn't ban wolf hunting and what the hell would I do if some greedy Skin shot you for your fur?"

She bent her head to his neck and rubbed her cheek against him. He closed his eyes, enjoying the contact. A wolf didn't care about lies, betrayal or anything. A wolf acted out of pure instinct, and needed his mate.

"You have such great fur, Mitchell. Wouldn't want to see you stuffed, or made into a rug before some stupid Skin's fireplace."

Aiden pulled away and butted her hand. Then he pointed a paw at the door again.

"No."

Okay then.

Aiden trotted over to the sofa and started to lift his leg.

"No, no!" She raced over to him. "Okay, okay. Fine. I guess you're not exactly house-broken in this form."

As soon as she opened the door, he bolted. Nia raced after him, shouting for him to stop.

He didn't slow until he reached the pond and then gained the forest. Then he stopped, glancing over his shoulder.

Slowpoke, what took you so long?

Panting, Nia joined him. "I know you're still furious with me, but you're not going in there without me. And now I'm angry at you, Mitchell. You didn't have to pee, did you?"

Aiden walked over to a tree and lifted his leg. He grinned at her exasperated look.

"I guess you've been cooped up long enough. But if we're going to walk, then we need a little protection."

Aiden opened his mouth, showing his fangs.

"Not good enough. Come on, back to the cabin. I'll get my sidearm and backpack."

A few minutes later, they returned to the pond and accessed the narrow pathway cutting through the thick forest. Aiden paced at her side, his paws padding silently over the dead leaves and twigs as he sniffed around the forest floor for where Pandora's Chest might be buried.

Every once in a while, he caught an intriguing smell of magick, like old, musty socks, and stopped to sniff. But each scent proved a dead end.

After about two miles, they stopped and Nia sat on a felled log. She removed a bottle of water from her pack and poured some into a dish she'd brought. He lapped it up, keeping an eye on her as she drank from the bottle.

He wandered over to a pine tree, sniffed at a toadstool. He glanced at her, pointing to the mushroom.

"The cure isn't in fungus, Mitchell." Nia sighed and capped the water, replacing it in her pack. "We have to find the chest. I thought it was near the old well by the pond, but Mandy and I searched. Dad must have dug it up and buried it someplace else. Let's walk a little ways more and then turn back."

They walked up the mountain, near a little creek gurgling as it threaded through the forest. They caught an unfamiliar scent. Aiden froze at the same time she did.

A twig cracked.

Nia ducked behind a thick oak tree, beckoning to him. He joined her, crouched down, his senses alert.

Clad in camouflage, his round face darkened by greasepaint, a Skin hunter stepped onto the path. In his hands was a rifle.

"Poacher," she whispered, her fingers gripping his fur tightly.

Aiden growled, and the hunter swung his rifle around.

Nia motioned for him to quiet. "Stay here."

Aiden looked at her. *Are you crazy? No fucking way.*

Then she withdrew the 9 mm pistol from her waistband holster. "This is my land. And I'll defend it, and you, to the death, Mitchell."

He shook his head. *No. It's my job to defend you.*

"Bullets out-do fangs," she whispered. "Stay back. I've got this. I'm a terrific shot."

Crouching behind the tree, she took aim and fired. Her shot hit the Skin in the hand and he dropped his rifle with a scream. Nia bolted toward the firearm, grabbed it, and flung it aside.

Aiden emerged from behind the tree and growled at the Skin hunter.

"Trespassing is a serious threat around these parts. I don't allow hunting of deer, rabbits, or any game." She glanced at Aiden. "Or wolves."

Face paling, the hunter clutched his bleeding hand. "Now wait a minute. I was just—"

"Trespassing. This is my land. There are signs posted all over."

As she pointed the pistol at the quivering Skin, the hunter held up his hands. "Please lady, don't shoot. I just wanted a wolf-skin."

Oh hell, the guy was going to pay now.

Then his gaze turned sly. "I'll give you good money to let me go…or I can do more for you. I heard you're alone out here, no one to run your ranch. You need a man to protect you. I'm very good. I can satisfy you in many ways."

Oh hell, now that guy was *really* going to pay. No one touched his Nia. Aiden growled.

The hunter glanced at Aiden. "Call off your wolf. I can report him, you know."

This was rich. *First you want to shoot and kill me, and now you're going to run to the authorities and complain about me? I'll give you something to really complain about, you bastard.*

"You're trespassing on my land. I have the right to protect myself with my weapons and my wolf."

She glared at the Skin who dared to invade her land

and try to hunt her people so he could kill them in cold blood and then stuff them. Then brag to all his he-man friends. *Hey, lookie what I killed, I'm such a manly man!*

"My wolf is very protective."

Yeah, I am. You dare to threaten my mate? You're toast. Okay let's do this. Sic balls.

Aiden charged, his mind a red haze of fury. He reached the Skin and his mouth opened as he met his destined target.

The Skin's screams echoed in his ears. Then Aiden released his death grip and the man screamed again, before he took off running, one hand clapped to his bleeding groin.

Aiden grinned a big wolfish smile.

The Skin would live, but he'd think about Aiden every time he went to take a piss. And he'd warn others off this land.

Aiden trotted over to the stream and drank deeply, eager to get the hot, metallic taste of the Skin's blood and the sour taste of his balls off his tongue. Blech.

Nia joined him at the stream, rubbing behind his ears as he sat up. "We have to find a cure for you, Aiden. We have to. Because I can't let you go."

His heart turned over as she buried her face into his thick fur and cried. He wanted to comfort her. His mate.

Aiden felt his strength suddenly diminish. Being a wolf was supposed to slow the disease, but what if it didn't work anymore? He lifted his head, and began loping back to the cabin. Sunshine dappled the undergrowth and the dead leaves as he walked.

He almost made it to the pond, when the nausea

overcame him. Aiden shifted back into Skin, dropped to his knees and retched.

His skin felt on fire. His guts churned like ground glass.

Nia caught up to him and put a hand on his naked back. "Sweetie, you shouldn't have changed back! You have to slow the progression of the disease."

Shaking off her hand, Aiden wiped his mouth with the back of one hand, knowing the grim truth. Fear and grief twined together inside him, knotting his guts. Betrayed by the one woman he wanted above all others. *Well dad, you were right, you bastard. Don't fall in love. Love makes you weak.*

In this case, it made him more than weak. It crippled him with a disease that killed.

Wolf or man, it was no use. He wasn't going to slow the progress of the disease spreading through his body like wildfire.

No matter what form he held, he was going to die.

CHAPTER 15

That night, Nikita Blakemore slipped out of her basement apartment and silently made her way down to the pond and the fire pit. This was her favorite time of night, when her twin slept soundly, exhausted by her heavy burdens of responsibility.

She'd made it a habit of coming here, not wishing to worry Nia. Gods knew Nia worried about her. Niki loved her sister, but lately she'd been so damn tired. She'd seen the joy in Nia's eyes amid the worry, and knew Aiden Mitchell was responsible for the joy. And the worry as well.

Some days Niki wished she could run so far away that the Silver Wizard would never find her.

But the wizard held power, and he would find her. Niki had resigned herself to that fact long ago, and knew no matter how hard her family fought to keep her safe, her fate was doomed.

She would die at the hands of the Silver Wizard.

Or die before he found her.

Reaching the fire pit, she rested upon one of the rocks ringing the pit. The few times she'd celebrated pack meetings had been here, in the night, the bonfire crackling, sparks spitting upward toward the sky.

Most nights she spent locked in her apartment, feeling so lonely she'd cry herself to sleep. But she had no right to complain. Everything Nia, Mandy, Roxanne and the elders did, they did to protect her.

She shifted into wolf and paced around the pond, sniffing the ground for intruders. Niki scented a powerful alpha scent and her wolf knew it was Aiden. The male had not wasted time marking his territory.

Shifting back into Skin, Niki returned to the fire pit and sat, hugging her knees and staring at the starlit sky.

This is my favorite place. And I had to come here one last time, one last visit.

Even now she grew weaker. She knew there was little time left. But only one vial existed. Who would be cured? Aiden, the powerful alpha and her sister's mate?

Rickie, the helpless, smiling teenager?

Or the hated Carl?

I can't decide who lives or dies. Gods, I wish Dad had let me die all those years ago and this never would have happened! He never would have opened that chest.

She started to stand to return to her apartment, when the hairs rose on her nape and a chill raced through her body.

A white wolf, large as a small pony, emerged from the forest. A stranger. Not a member of Aiden's pack or hers. This wolf carried the sharp scent of cold snow, and the tangy smell of cider and burning pine. Pleasing, like a cozy fire during an icy winter's night. But fear filled her, and her heart began to pound.

The wolf approached, his head lifted. He loped over

to the rock where she'd sat and lifted his leg. A male.

Arrogant, covering Aiden's scent with his own. Then the white wolf paced toward her and a beam of moonlight caressed his thick fur.

Not white.

Silver.

Legend said only one Lupine had that color fur. The Silver Wizard.

Niki's jaw dropped. Her pulse beat frantically and panic clogged her throat. She turned to run. But her legs weren't working as well as they had days ago, before she'd done the one thing she knew would weaken her.

She stumbled in the dark, fear a sharp razor in her mouth, and tripped over a rock. White-hot pain shot up her leg. She bit back a terrified scream.

Wolves hunted the weak and the sick…

Unable to stand because of her sprained ankle, she tried to crawl away. He might destroy her, as the prophecy foretold, but she wouldn't surrender without a fight. Adrenaline flooded her body, loaning her a burst of strength.

The wolf silently loped toward her. Lightning flashed, filling the glen with an eerie glow, and the wolf turned into a tall, dark-haired man clad in black.

Moonlight touched his face. He was handsome, with chiseled features and eyes dark as the night. He bent down next to her and she wanted to crawl away from him, from the smoldering sensuality whirling about him, but could not.

He placed a hand on her throbbing leg and she bit her lip from the pain. Suddenly the pain fled. Her heart resumed its normal rhythm.

Niki stared up at him wordlessly, her terror easing a

little now that her leg was healed. Perhaps he'd healed her to let her run, and then he'd give chase.

Wolves loved the chase.

She had no strength to crawl, let alone run. Exhaustion claimed her. The adrenaline rush left, leaving her cold and shivering.

Tristan, the Silver Wizard. Ruler of Lupines. Judge of Others. The grim reaper of her nightmares from the time her father told her that she must remain hidden to stay safe, to never let anyone know she was alive, Nikita the eldest twin, the one destined for the wizard. For Tristan would take her away to the afterworld, and she would perish.

He didn't look like the grim reaper her father had told her about, she thought in a drowsy haze of confusion. Niki rubbed her eyes. She could barely summon the strength to move.

"I'm not going to hurt you," he murmured. "Steady now."

Tristan picked her up into his arms. She had no strength to fight him. If he wanted to kill her now, he could easily snap her neck.

Didn't matter. She was dying anyhow, using her own body as a lab experiment to find a cure for the parvolupus disease. Nothing could save her.

He carried her easily, walking up the path. She felt as if she were floating, flying, and then managed the strength to look down.

They *were* flying. He floated through the air like a magick carpet from the fairy tales she'd adored as a child.

Tristan reached her basement apartment, nodded and the door opened. *More efficient than a key.*

He placed her on the bed, pulled off her shoes and jeans, and then tucked her beneath the covers. The Silver Wizard bent his head, his long, dark hair brushing her cheeks.

He kissed her forehead. "Rest now, Niki."

Compelled by the command in his voice, she shut her eyes. As she drifted off to sleep, she heard him say, "Later, I will return to make you my own."

Chapter 16

All his life, Aiden had struggled to be the perfect alpha. The perfect leader. Never letting anyone or anything get in his way. He'd fought to the death to protect his pack, waited patiently to mate with the woman he desired most, and most of all, never let the legacy of his old man ruin his future.

He would never grow weak like his father, and fall in love and allow love to ruin him.

Too late.

Now he was growing sicker by the hour, and there wasn't a damn thing he could do about it.

In the king-sized bed in Nia's cabin, he lay naked upon the sheets. Sweat coated the bed, and he tossed and turned.

The pain was pincer-like, gripping his muscles with squeezing agony. He'd never been sick, and now he could barely move.

Big tough alpha, he thought with dim humor. *Look at you now.*

He'd been too busy trying to take care of things, too busy with his people, and with getting Nikita/Nia into his bed and his life, to think about the impossible.

Dying. And there was nothing he could do about it.

Nia sat by his side, stroking his forehead with a cool, wet cloth. Aiden grabbed her hand.

"Promise me," he said in a thick voice. "Promise me...you and Darius...care for my pack."

"Our pack," she said softly, kissing his hand. "Don't wuss out on me, Mitchell. You're not escaping me. Nothing will take you away from me, get it?"

Her voice quivered. "Nothing. Let's get you well. You're going to come out of this. You will. Fight it, Mitchell. I thought you were a big, tough alpha."

"Not so tough." He drew in a breath and winced at the pressure in his chest.

She leaned over him, her expression fierce. His mate. His equal. He'd loved her, but resisted it. Couldn't tell her, give her power over him. But he had nothing to lose now. He was close to death.

"Go away," he told her.

He didn't want her to see him like this, didn't want her to witness his weakness. Nia, the Lupine who had caused him to fall ill.

She blinked furiously. "I'm not letting you die. Not you."

After flinging the damp washcloth onto the floor, she raced away. Aiden closed his eyes, his guts churning, feeling as if something ate him from the inside out.

He drifted into unconsciousness for a while, dreaming about his old man taunting him. "You're weak, Aiden. Too weak to rule!"

Never fall in love, his father had warned. *Love will make you weak.*

He had fallen for Nia, and now look at him. Dying.

Hearing a drawer open and close, he struggled to open his gluey eyelids. And then he saw Nia standing by the bed.

Tears shimmered in her blue eyes. "Promise me one thing, Mitchell. If something happens to me and you live, promise me you'll care for my sister, and my people, like I would. Protect them as I would."

She was not dying. It made no sense. "I promise," he said.

Then he saw what she held. The crystal containing the tears of the dragon.

"No," he managed to say.

Nia blinked furiously. "Yes. It's the only way."

Aiden roused every bit of his strength and struggled to sit up. "You'll strip...all your powers. You...can't live as Lupine. Have to leave the pack. You...could die."

"Then let me take the chance because I can't bear to live if you die. I brought you into this mess. I must get you out of it."

Her eyes wild, she held up the crystal. Nia ripped open her shirt, exposing her bare breast. She pressed the tip of the crystal's long end against her heart. The crystal began to glow an eerie white.

She screamed and staggered back. Her screams pierced his ears and he moaned, partly from the pain and partly from her agony.

Then she held up the glowing crystal. Skin pale, her shoulders slumped as if she were weary, Nia approached the bed.

"Cure, save...for Rickie. Protect the young."

"You're not dying on me, Mitchell. Not you."

With all his strength, he shook his head. "No."

Aiden labored to breathe past the elephant sitting on his chest. "Young…deserves to live. Protect pack…"

Nia's expression grew stubborn. "No. No more pack. Our whole lives have been consumed by pack. You're always putting your people first, my needs first as well. But not anymore. Today, you come first, you big, stubborn wolf."

He tried to move away, but she moved swiftly, his mate, and seized his jaw. Nia forced his mouth to open and popped the crystal inside. He felt it dissolve on his tongue. It tasted as bitter as vinegar and sweet as honey. No, no, no. Damnit, his life wasn't worth this.

Holding his mouth shut with one hand, Nia wiped away a tear.

"Please live," she begged. "This is all my fault that you're dying. Don't leave me like my father and brothers did, like all the males I loved did. I couldn't bear it. I love you, Mitchell. I was too proud and stubborn to admit it all these years."

Then she tickled his throat, forcing him to swallow. The tears of the dragon burned his throat like the bite of whiskey.

"Live, Mitchell. Please live," she whispered, crying. "I love you."

He lifted a hand to her cheek, touched her tears. "Love…you…mate."

Groaning, Aiden fell back among the pillows, feeling his strength leave him.

Damn stubborn female, stubborn as himself.

Closing his eyes, he surrendered to the grayish void.

Her wolf had to live. Even if she must die.

Utterly drained, Nia sat in the armchair near the bed. Xavier had not lied when he said the crystal would drain all a Lupine's magick.

She reached deep inside herself, tried to summon her wolf and met with silence. Her wolf, the beast who had given her strength, who had enabled her to lead the pack after her father died, was gone.

Tears trickled down her cheeks. She wiped them away with a shaky hand. And now what? She'd have to leave, forge a new life for herself. A Lupine without magick was doomed, like the Crystal Wizard had said. The pack would never allow her to live among them, either her pack or Aiden's.

And what about Niki and her people?

Aiden would care for them. He would protect her twin as fiercely as he'd protected his own. He promised.

All that mattered was for Aiden to live.

In all the years the disease had plagued them, she'd never seen it progress so quickly in a male. Aiden's superior strength and alpha traits had triggered it to overtake him.

Making the strong male weak.

Her man still breathed. He slept, his color still pale as milk.

On the nightstand, his cell kept going off. Summoning all her strength, she went to the nightstand, picked up the phone and marched into the bathroom, then dropped it into the toilet.

No one was disturbing them. All their time together had been for pack, all about pack. And now he hovered on that frail line between life and death.

If it was life, then she needed to be here for him.

If he died, she would be here as well.

Nia closed her eyes, willing Aiden to live. *Please*, she thought. *Don't leave me.*

An hour later, she sensed a change and stirred. Nia opened her eyes, cursing the fact that she'd fallen asleep. Gods, she was so damn weak now.

And saw Aiden sitting up in bed, the covers pulled to his waist. His thick hair was rumpled and matted with sweat, his eyes still glazed, but he breathed normally.

Joy filled her. She struggled to stand, then went to his side, touching his forehead. No fever.

Nia wrapped her arms around him. He stroked her hair as she sobbed in his arms. Finally she drew back, wiping her face with the corner of the sheet.

"Hey there," he said softly. "Don't cry, Blakemore."

"I'm no wuss, Mitchell. Cry over you? Those aren't tears. You're seeing things." She kissed him, hard.

"How do you feel?" she asked, as they parted.

"I feel fine. Need a shower." He frowned, looking at the covers. "Hard to remember what happened. I know I was sick, but how did I get better? All I remember is some nasty shit in my mouth and a burning taste down my throat."

Nia said nothing.

His nostrils flared and his dark eyes widened. "The tears of the dragon."

"It's okay," she soothed. "You're safe now. You will live."

Aiden seized her hands. He pressed his cheek against them. "Nia, Nia, why? Your magick, your powers…"

He gave her a hopeful look. She shook her head.

"Gone."

Emotion clogged her throat as he stared at her. Aiden framed her face with his big, rough hands. "My beautiful Nia, why did you do this for me?"

She stroked a finger over the thick stubble on his handsome face. "Because I love you, Mitchell. I've always loved you. And your life is worth more than my wolf. I can live without my wolf and my powers. I can't live with knowing you're gone forever."

He pulled her into his arms and hugged her tight. "We'll find a way to make it work," he said, his voice thick. "We will. After we get a cure for this godsdamn disease, you and I will make it work."

Pulling away, he said in a gruff voice, "I need out of this damn bed. I've been slacking long enough."

She slid off the bed and nearly collapsed. Aiden cursed and leapt off the mattress. He helped her to stand upright.

"Guess I'm really weak without my wolf." She gave a wan smile.

Picking her up into his arms, he carried her to the armchair. "Stay here and rest. I'm taking a shower and then we'll go see your twin. She's a biologist. Maybe she has some herbs that will restore your strength."

After he'd showered, Aiden emerged from the bathroom, clad in a towel. She stared at him, her joy turning into desire. "How do you feel, Mitchell?"

"Strong. Very strong." He enfolded her into his arms and stared down at her. "I don't remember a lot. But I do remember this. I told you how I feel about you."

"Uh huh. Maybe you should tell me again." She squeezed his taut ass and then let him go.

As she watched him dress, Nia sighed. "I know Niki. If anyone can help me, she can. She's always experimenting on herbs. That's why she got so sick when we were fifteen. She went into the forest and picked berries she thought were medicinal. They were to Skins, but toxic to Lupines. And that's how she almost died."

"She'll find a cure." Aiden's confidence in her twin fed her hope. "And when she does, Rickie will be saved."

"And Carl."

"And Carl," he agreed. "I want that son of a bitch to get better, so I can punch his face."

"Such a peaceful guy you are," she murmured.

They went down the back steps, to the basement apartment's back door.

Niki must know. They had a cure, and her twin had saved Aiden's life.

As she went to knock on the door, she noticed it was slightly ajar. Dread raced down her spine. Aiden looked at her and opened the door.

"Niki," he called out softly. "Niki?"

The room was dark, and smelled musty, of dampness and something else unpleasant.

She recognized the smell and fresh fear made her heart skid.

And then she noticed the figure lying prone on the carpet, so still.

So very still.

Chapter 17

Nia rushed over to her twin, praying she wasn't too late. She reached Niki and her senses screamed denial as Aiden snapped on a light.

Niki opened her eyes, bright with fever. "Thought I'd get this…over with…before you found me. Want to die…alone."

Oh gods, oh gods. Nia looked at Aiden. "Help her!"

As Aiden lifted Niki into his strong arms, Niki lifted an arm. "Found cure. In…lab."

Nia rushed into the lab as Aiden carried her twin into the bedroom.

Her heart pounded hard as she scanned the room, the counter, the vials of crimson fluid neatly labeled, and the syringes lined up in a row. Two rabbits in wire cages hopped around, frisky and healthy.

A red Biohazard box sat on the counter as well, along with a microscope.

Nia opened the refrigerator and scanned it. Dozens of vials of fluid, all labeled. None labeled "antidote." Maybe her sister had hidden it.

She picked up another vial and her blood ran cold.

Edmond Blakemore. She set it down, carefully,

noting there were several containers. And others, with their brother's' names. Several of them. A good portion of all the males who had died from the disease.

Nia slammed the door shut and sagged against it. "What have you done, Niki? What have you done?"

She had never bothered intruding into Niki's private lab, wanting her twin to have privacy for her work.

Now she wished she had. Dear goddess...

She raced into the bedroom. Niki lay upon her bed, her face pale. Aiden sat next to her, his expression taut with worry.

"She can't seem to breathe. What do we do?"

"Nothing," Niki gasped. "You can't do anything. Cure...Rickie and Carl...their blood will create more antibodies. Save...others."

Nia sat beside her twin. All this time she'd thought Niki was experimenting with animals, her twin had been doing far worse.

Taking the disease into herself in an attempt to find the cure. Because Niki was female, and only males caught the disease.

"I'll use the antidote on you," Nia cried out. "I can save you, Niki."

"No." Niki coughed. "Too late. Immune...system too compromised. Tried already. Won't work on me. Carl...Rickie...still in early stages."

"Why? Why? Why did you do this?"

"Found chest. By the cabin. Had to make amends... I opened it, wished for a cure. For knowledge." She gulped down a breath. "A Blakemore opened the chest and cursed us. It's only fitting a Blakemore lifts the curse. I...wished for a magick solution...my blood could create the vaccine."

Horror stole over Nia. That was the way the chest worked, the diabolical two-edged sword. Their father had wished for a cure for his beloved eldest daughter, but lost his sons, who were to lead the pack after him. And then the disease spread, from male to male until none were left.

And then Niki had found the chest. Her twin opened it and wished to cure the disease. She had. And now she was paying with her death.

"I won't lose you." Nia took her twin's cold hands into hers, willing them to be warm, to have the blood flow, to be filled with life once more. "No, Niki. I've already lost Dad and our brothers. I can't lose you."

Niki's gaze grew dimmer. "Afraid you have no choice, sis. I took the choice out of your hands. Be happy…with Aiden."

Closing her eyes, Niki wheezed, her breath thin and whispery. Nia bent close to hear her.

"Pandora's Chest…it's in my closet, hidden by my clothes."

Her eyes closed. "So thirsty…fridge…bottle of water. Please."

Aiden raced to the refrigerator and returned with the water. He held it to Niki's mouth. Her twin drank, and seemed to be a little stronger. She opened her eyes.

"Experimented with my blood. Injected the disease into my body. I'm female, immune, but have the same DNA strands as Dad, the original carrier."

Nia smoothed back her twin's hair. "When did you find the chest, Niki?"

Her sister's eyes closed. "Two weeks ago. Didn't want to tell you. Hid it. Had to wait for you to be settled, and happy. You loved Aiden...anyone could see it. Anyone but you."

"Stubborn wolf," she whispered.

Niki was gasping now, her face growing pale, patches of violent black spreading up her neck like wildfire.

Her twin was dying. She could almost feel the burning pain charge through her body, licking at it like fire. Two fat tears rolled down her cheeks. She'd spent her entire life shielding her sister from harm and now was helpless to prevent her death.

Please, someone help her. Please.

And then there was a brilliant flash of light in the room. Nia turned. Her heart slammed wildly against her chest.

Tristan. The Silver Wizard. The prophecy was being fulfilled at last.

"No," she screamed, throwing out her arms protectively to hide her twin. "Don't you dare touch her! Aiden, help!"

"You're not getting near her." In two strides, Aiden charged the wizard. Tristan flicked a finger and her mate sailed through the air, landing on the ground.

"Aiden!"

"Forget me. Save Nikita."

"Don't touch my sister." She sprang off the bed and rushed at the wizard, hammering at his chest with her fists. Not caring if Tristan could fry her with a single flick of his finger.

But instead, he caught her in his arms. "Hush, Nia. I won't hurt her. I'm going to save her. This is the only way."

He gently untangled himself from her grip and sat on

the bed. Tristan uncapped a glass vial he pulled from his pocket and held it to Nikita's mouth.

"Come on sweetheart," Tristan said softly. "Drink."

Nikita's lips remained blue, and closed.

"Drink," he said more firmly. He tipped the vial up to her lips and forced it past them. "I will not let you die."

She gasped and he poured it into her mouth, then she swallowed.

"Good," he told her, and there was something satisfactory, almost predatory, in the wizard's gaze. Nia could only stand by helplessly and watch.

Aiden joined her, rubbing the back of his head. He clasped her hand tightly, oh so tightly. She held onto him, feeling her world shatter as Nikita gasped for breath. She convulsed and Tristan held her, murmuring to her in soothing words she could not understand. His eyes glowed bright blue, then turned silver.

Niki seemed to recover, and he helped her to sit upright. Relief poured through Nia. Her twin would live. Oh gods, she was going to be okay, everything was going to be okay.

Nikita opened her eyes. They were silver, bright and shining as chrome. Silver like the wizard's.

Tristan placed a soft kiss against her forehead. Then he gathered her into his arms and his gaze glinted. "Mine."

His voice deepened, almost to a guttural growl. Instinctively, Nia stepped back. Aiden released her hand and partly blocked her view, standing before her in a protective stance. Her twin closed her eyes and appeared to sleep. Tristan laid her gently back on the bed.

"What are you doing, Tristan?" he asked, clenching his fists. "She's not yours. She's wolf."

"And so am I," Tristan said.

The wizard released Nikita and stood, straightening to his full height. His eyes glowed chrome, and then amber. And then he raised his arms skyward and growled.

The wizard vanished. In Tristan's place was a timber wolf the size of a small pony, with thick silver fur, his eyes glowing blue.

It growled at them, blocking their view of Nikita.

Nia gaped at the wolf, fear sliding down her spine. What was this? Tristan was Lupine, like them? Maybe not. Maybe his powers could enable him to shift into various forms.

The wizard changed back, his eyes now their normal dark color, his body clad in black leather pants, soft doeskin boots and a black tunic. But there was something different about him, a ruthless purpose that made Nia afraid for her sister.

Very afraid.

"Yes, Nia, I can shift into different forms. But I chose my original form for a small demonstration." Tristan folded his arms, and she saw a glimmer of amusement on his face.

"Stop reading my mind." This was downright spooky.

He appeared to ignore the remark and parked a hip on the bed, brushing her twin's hair back from her pale cheeks. "I was Lupine once, like you and Aiden. Like Nikita. Many centuries ago, when Nikita and I met and fell in love."

Sudden insight filled her. The dreams her twin had

of the handsome, dark-haired stranger who looked like Tristan, dreams in which she felt loved and cherished. "Niki was your lover."

"My wife." A shadow crossed his face.

Niki's dreams always turned into nightmares, because in the end, the dark-haired man screamed in pain and then vanished.

"Your wife?" Nia stared at him, and then her twin. "Your wife, reincarnated? You bastard, you loved her and you let this happen?"

As she rushed at him, Aiden caught her in his arms. "Easy, pixie," he murmured.

Tristan gave Nia a level look. "Had your father not insisted on hiding Niki from me, he would never have needed Pandora's Chest to cure her when she fell ill. I would have cured her when she ate the poisonous berries."

"Why didn't you?" she asked, calming a little.

He sighed and stroked Niki's forehead. "I tried. I appeared to your father one night as he roamed the forest, looking for an herbal cure. He told me he would never allow me to touch her while she was alive. He would fight me to the death to keep her from me. He had already lost his mate. He was not losing his daughter. I left, knowing his eventual fate."

Nia felt as if her world tipped on its axis. All these years she'd protected her twin, and Tristan knew she was alive. And their own father had deceived them, never telling them Tristan had actually been here, on the ranch.

"You could have interfered!" Nia burst out.

"No. I could not, not when he had not done anything evil to warrant it. I am forbidden to interfere in someone's destiny."

Tristan went to Niki's closet and pulled out the chest. He shook his head. "Such a waste of life. But it will harm no one else."

He waved a hand and the chest vanished. "Now that the chest has been returned, the curse on the land is lifted and the wildlife, and the earth will be restored to normal. There will be no more disease upon this land or in the people."

"Where did it go?" Aiden asked.

"Back to Tir Na-nog, land of the afterworld, where it will never again be opened. It is far too dangerous."

Nia sagged against Aiden, needing his strength. Emotion clogged her throat. Her beloved sister was going to leave her. Despite everything she'd done, she couldn't save Niki from her fate.

But the wizard didn't seem as if he would harm Niki. And the dreams her twin had…the man in them had loved her. If it was Niki's fate to be reunited with this powerful being, she could not prevent it.

Sudden desolation filled her. "If you take her, I have no one now. Nothing. I can't remain here, with Aiden. I'll never be his equal in power or status. How can an alpha leader have a mate who isn't even wolf?"

Aiden hugged her. "He can. I don't care what others say. If I have to stick to you like glue to keep other wolves from attacking you, Nia, I will. Or even…leave the pack and the ranch."

Stunned, she turned around. "You'd give up everything, your people, your ranch, your power, for me?"

"I love you, sweetheart. We'd find a way. Start another ranch of our own, forge a new life." He kissed her, his mouth warm and firm, and she felt her nerve endings flare with new life, as if he poured a little of his powers into her.

Tristan cleared his throat. "When you surface for air, I must tell you something."

Aiden broke the kiss, and Nia turned around to see the wizard. Kindness shone in Tristan's dark eyes.

"Xavier told you the tears of the dragon strip away all one's magick. It is one of life's greatest sacrifices, to surrender all your magick for the one you love. He failed to tell you that magick is not lost forever. It resides within Aiden now. Your mate."

Aiden blinked. "I can give it back to Nia?"

"You're a powerful alpha Lupine, Aiden Mitchell. And so is Nia."

"I'm not alpha," she protested. "I'm the younger twin. All my life I've pretended to be something I wasn't."

The wizard sat on the bed, stroking Niki's forehead with a gentle hand. "An alpha is a leader, someone who gives everything for his or her people, a Lupine willing to make tremendous sacrifices and do what is best for them. That, more than hereditary succession, is what makes an alpha."

Aiden wrapped his arms around Nia's waist and pulled her tight against him. It felt good to be surrounded by his strength. His love.

"What do I have to do?" Aiden asked. "Eat more of those damn crystals? Say a chant by the light of a full moon?"

Tristan grinned. "Do what comes naturally to you, Aiden. When you make love with your mate, without protection, your magick will flow into her and her wolf will return."

Blushing, she looked away. Aiden dropped a kiss on her head. "Sounds like a plan to me, sweetheart."

"But why didn't Xavier tell us this?" she asked.

"If he had, your sacrifice would not have meant as much. The tears work because the person willing to give up her magick knows she surrenders all." Tristan winked. "Besides, X was in a hurry to get to that car show. It is a very sweet cherry red Mustang."

Then Tristan slid his arms around Nikita, lifting her from the bed. Her twin opened her eyes and Nia was relieved to see they were once again blue.

"Don't worry about me, Nia. I'll be fine." Niki curled her arms around Tristan's neck. "I'm strong."

Nia blinked back tears. "You'd better come back to me."

"She will," Tristan promised. "You will see her again."

Then he gave Aiden a solemn look. "I already used Nikita's antidote on Rickie and Carl. They will recover and your niece, Beth, may use the antibodies in their blood to create more of an antidote just as a precaution. Take good care of Nia, alpha. She will need you."

Tristan waved a hand and vanished with Nikita.

Nia went to the bed and felt the indentation her sister had made. Felt the warmth where her body had lain. She climbed into the bed, hugged a pillow and cried into it. For 25 years, she and Niki had been together, had supported each other through joy and sorrow. And now her twin was gone. She was alone.

And then a big, warm male climbed into bed with her, holding her tight. "It's going to be okay, sweetheart. I'm here."

She wasn't alone, after all. She had the most important person in her world. Aiden.

"I love you, Blakemore." He stroked her hair, holding her tightly against him. "I know how much it hurts, losing someone you love. But I won't leave you."

"Even though you mated with the wrong twin?"

His gaze filled with fierceness, Aiden shook his head. "I mated the right twin. Like Tristan said, being alpha doesn't have to do with birth order. It has to do with giving everything for your people, and putting them first. You put me first, Nia. That's what true mates do for each other."

He stroked a finger down her wet cheek. "You're mine, Blakemore. No one, not our packs, a damn wizard or the goddess Danu herself, will separate us."

Nia turned and faced him, her cheeks wet. "Promise? Because I love you, Mitchell and I never want you to leave me. Ever."

"Not a chance. We're going to make love and restore your powers." Aiden gave a wicked grin. "And if it doesn't work the first time, we'll keep doing it."

She smiled. "Sounds like a plan."

For a long few minutes, they simply lay together, the sound of their breathing filling the room. Nia's heartbeat finally slowed and she could think straight. She buried her head against the crook of his shoulder, trembling deep inside.

Moisture blurred her vision as she lifted her head and studied him. Her male. Her mate for life.

"I just realized something. The biggest fear I've had all my life was losing my sister after I lost my family, so many of our pack. She was the center of my world. And then you came along and taught me how to be strong and let love push aside my fear. I fell in love with you, and you became my center."

She rubbed her cheek against his hand. "And then I saw you, so sick, and you were dying and everything else faded away. My biggest fear wasn't losing my sister. It was losing you. I knew then I'd have given anything to save you. Anything. Losing my magick was a small price to pay for your life."

Aiden thumbed away a stray tear, his expression filled with tenderness. "I never imagined growing weak would make me stronger. Until I met you, I thought being alpha was what my old man said it was. Having courage and being the strongest. It wasn't until you came into my life that I realized being alpha is much more. It's about having the courage to love, and love deeply."

He cradled her face in his hands and kissed her, his mouth warm and firm. Whatever they faced in the coming days, she knew they would face it together.

As equals.

Author's Note

Thank you for reading The Mating Challenge. I hope you enjoyed it!

Would you like to know when my next book is available? You can sign up for my newsletter at www.bonnievanak.com, follow me on twitter at http://twitter.com/bonnievanak, or like my Facebook page at http://facebook.com/bonnievanakauthor.

Reviews help other readers find books. I appreciate all reviews, whether positive or negative.

You've just read The Mating Challenge, the fifth book in my Werewolves of Montana series. The other books in the series are in order:

THE WEREWOLVES OF MONTANA

Werewolves of Montana boxed set
Prequel through Book 4.5

Prequel: The Mating Heat

Book 1: The Mating Chase

Book 2: The Mating Hunt

Book 3: The Mating Seduction

Book 4: The Mating Rite

Book 4.5: The Mating Intent

Book 5: The Mating Challenge

Lovestruck
a short story about Xavier, the Crystal Wizard

Book 6: The Mating Season
Tristan's story, coming soon

Book 7: The Mating Game
Gideon's story, coming soon

Book 8: The Mating Ritual
Xavier's story, coming soon

Book 9: The Mating Captive
Cadeyrn's story, coming soon

MATING MINIS
set within the Werewolves of Montana world

SEDUCTION

OBSESSION

PASSION

REDEMPTION

TEMPTATION

www.Bonnievanak.com

About the Author

Bonnie Vanak is a *New York Times* bestselling author of paranormal werewolf romances. A former newspaper reporter who became a writer for a major international charity, she travels to destitute countries to write about issues affecting the poor. Her books take readers from the mysterious, dark alleys of New Orleans to the sweeping plains of Montana. Visit her Web site at www.bonnievanak.com or email her at bonnievanak@aol.com.

Stay updated with previews of more Werewolves of Montana books by visiting my website, http://www.bonnievanak.com and signing up for my newsletter. Or visit my Facebook page at www.facebook.com/bonnievanakauthor

Made in the USA
Columbia, SC
13 November 2022